I0652794

A Song to Call Ours

Front Porch Promises
Book 5

by

Merrillee Whren

Copyright 2017 © Merrillee Whren

All rights reserved. This book may not be reproduced in any form or by any means, electronic or mechanical, in whole or in part, without permission from the author.

Merrillee Whren
http://www.merrilleewhren.com/

Publisher's Note: This is a work of fiction. All characters and events in this story are the author's invention. Locales and public names are sometimes used for atmospheric purposes. Any resemblance to actual events, locales, or persons, living or dead, or to businesses, companies, or institutions is completely coincidental.

A Song to Call Ours/ Merrillee Whren
ISBN: 978-1-944773-07-6

[Scripture quotations are from] THE HOLY BIBLE, NEW INTERNATIONAL VERSION®, NIV® Copyright © 1973, 1978, 1984, 2011 by Biblica, Inc.® Used by permission. All rights reserved worldwide.

"May he give you the desire of your heart and make all your plans succeed. May we shout for joy over your victory and lift up our banners in the name of our God. May the Lord grant all your requests."

Psalm 20:4-5 NIV

CHAPTER ONE

The car sputtered to a stop. Amanda Reynolds scowled at the check-engine light that had appeared like a flash of lightning on the horizon. She let out a heavy sigh and stared at the road sign. *Pineydale, Tennessee, Population 4,132*. She doubted a town this small would have a place that repaired foreign cars. She didn't want to think about being stranded in some out-of-the-way place in East Tennessee.

She had plenty of gas, unless the gauge was incorrect. What else could be wrong? She didn't have a clue. Setting the car in neutral, she hoped she could get this hunk of junk she called a car off the road. She got out, and with the door open, she pushed with all her might and managed to steer the car toward the shoulder.

Mission accomplished, she wiped the sweat from her brow with the back of her hand, then pulled her hair off the back of her neck. Her dreams of getting to Nashville waved goodbye right along with the heat waves rising above the pavement on the road ahead. She kicked at the tire. It didn't help. She should have opted for a reliable sedan rather than her father's discarded sports car.

The sound of an approaching vehicle made her look up. A faded-blue pickup truck rumbled toward her. She wasn't sure whether to be happy or cautious. A lone female on a deserted stretch of road might find an unsavory character behind the wheel. As the pickup drew closer, she could see the male driver. Would he stop or drive right by? Her heart thumped against her rib cage like the tires bumping along the uneven pavement.

As the vehicle slowed, Amanda prayed for safety.

The pickup stopped. The driver lowered the window. "Need some help here, or did kicking the tire solve your problem?"

Amanda didn't appreciate the joke coming from the man with the good-ole-boy accent. She couldn't see his face, obscured by the shadow of his ragged blue ball cap, sporting a big red A. She wished she could come up with some smart retort, but nothing came to mind. Did he intend to be helpful or just make fun of her situation? She wouldn't let him know he had annoyed her.

"I do need help. My car stopped running."

The man leaned toward the open window. "I can give you a ride into town."

That was an invitation she didn't want to accept. Would he get help for her? She had to take that chance. "I think I'd rather just wait here with my car. Could you get a tow truck for me?"

He took off his cap, revealing chestnut-colored hair cut in an almost military-style, twinkling blue-gray eyes, and a face she could only describe as movie-star handsome. He looked younger than she'd estimated at first glance. He probably wasn't much older than her twenty-five years. He grinned, revealing straight white teeth, not the missing teeth she'd expected.

"I sure can, little lady, but I got good air conditioning in here that's a lot cooler than standing out there in the heat."

She grinned back. "If it's all the same to you, I'll take my chances with the heat."

"Suit yourself." He put his cap on and shifted back behind the wheel. "Someone will be here to help you out shortly."

"Thanks." As Amanda watched the truck rumble down the road that carved its way through the deciduous forest, she hoped she wasn't making a mistake by sending him away. After the pickup disappeared over the hill, she kicked the tire again. The action wouldn't make her car start, but it relieved some of her frustration.

While she waited for the tow truck, she tried to start the car again. It made a terrible noise but didn't start. She should leave it alone, or she might do more damage. The heat was stifling inside the car, but it wasn't much better outside. The midmorning sun beat down on her. Was it supposed to be this hot in Tennessee in early June? Her pale skin was sure to sport a sunburn if she didn't get out of the sun. She slid back onto the driver's seat.

The minutes crawled. She drummed her fingers on the steering wheel. Maybe the guy never planned to send a tow truck, and the joke was on her. She got out again. Even her sunglasses did nothing to blunt the sun's rays. Shading her eyes with one hand, she peered down the road. Nothing.

The sign said she was in Pineydale, but no house or

buildings of any kind were in sight. Just trees, trees, and more trees of every description lined the road as far as she could see. She couldn't believe no other cars had come by. Was there another exit off the interstate leading to the little town? After her car had started making noise, she'd taken the first exit available, and it had led to an empty road in the middle of nowhere.

Could she walk into town?

Glancing down at her platform wedge sandals, Amanda wrinkled her nose. Her shoes weren't suitable for walking on uneven ground. She'd walked in these kind of shoes all over the city of Boston, but there sidewalks provided firm footing. She let out a heavy sigh. Was this a sign she should've stayed in Boston? Her father thought so, and he would not be sympathetic to her plight.

Amanda tried to dig out one of her suitcases from under all the paraphernalia in the trunk. Hopefully, she remembered which bag contained her tennis shoes. After she managed to get the suitcase out, she rooted through the clothes. Triumph rode in like a conquering knight as she pulled the red tennis shoes from underneath a pile of blue jeans.

As she held the shoes, she looked down at the mess she'd made. Could she get everything back into the suitcase and into the trunk? First things first. She had to change shoes. With the car door open, she sat on the seat while the steering wheel poked her in the ribs. She unbuckled her sandals and put on the tennis shoes.

She walked to the back of the car and repacked

everything, then slammed the trunk closed. She stared at the vehicle. Would it be safe if she left it by the side of the road? Not that anyone would want a car that didn't run, but she didn't want to lose her other belongings. She couldn't leave her guitar. It was too visible lying there on the passenger seat. It was the one possession she couldn't afford to lose.

With another sigh of resignation, she retrieved her purse and the guitar in its case.

She had fled from Pinecrest because she despised living in that little town. The joke was on her. Now she was stuck in a place called Pineydale—Pinecrest all over again with a southern accent.

***

"Hey, Boss, where ya goin'? Ya just got back."

Mitchell Cunningham leaned out the window of the tow truck as he looked at Bobby Crawford, the high school kid who worked for him on Saturdays. "Got a tow on the outskirts of town. Be back in a few."

"Okay." Bobby stepped back from the truck. "I'll keep an eye on everything while you're gone."

"I won't be long." Mitch motioned toward one side of the garage. "Have Johnny get that bay ready for a repair."

"Sure thing." Bobby hurried to obey orders.

As Mitch drove through town, he wondered about the young woman he'd encountered. What was her story? She was good looking with long auburn hair with a tint of red visible in the bright sunshine. Her white short shorts displayed a pair of long, shapely legs. He shouldn't have been ogling them, but he couldn't help noticing. And her sandals looked like they were impossible to walk in. Her foreign faded-red sports car and fashions told him she probably came from privilege, but she needed his help now.

He came around a curve and spied a lone figure walking alongside the road. As he drew closer, he recognized the young woman. She had replaced her ridiculous sandals with a pair of bright-red tennis shoes, and she carried what looked like a guitar case in one hand.

Slowing the truck, he rolled down the window. When he was beside her on the road, he stopped. "You fixin' to walk to town anyway? Couldn't wait for the tow?"

The woman tucked one side of her hair behind her ear. "I didn't know if you would send anyone for me, so I wasn't going to sit there and wait forever."

"I said I'd send someone for you."

"Yeah, but I don't know you. How could I trust that you were going to do what you'd said you'd do?"

"People around these parts can be trusted to do what they say." Mitch raised his eyebrows.

The young woman shrugged but didn't say a thing.

"You want to hop in, and we'll get that car of yours into town?" Mitch flicked back the brim of his cap and grinned as he read the hesitation in her expression.

After a few seconds, she hoisted her guitar case and stepped toward the truck. "Thanks. What should I do with my guitar?"

"I've got the perfect place for it." Mitch got out and walked around to where she was standing. "Give it to me."

"Okay." She handed over the case.

Mitch stowed it behind the front seat, then looked at her. "Go ahead and get into the truck."

She quickly hopped onto the passenger seat and buckled her seat belt. He didn't know what to make of her quiet demeanor. Was she wary about accepting help from a stranger? Probably.

She sat there stiff and tense. "Why didn't you say you'd be the one returning to tow my car?"

"What difference does it make?" Mitch put the truck in gear.

She didn't answer as she stared straight ahead.

Mitch started down the road toward her car. "I'm Mitchell Cunningham. My friends call me Mitch. Do you have a name you'd like to share?"

She still didn't look at him. "Amanda Reynolds."

"Hello, Amanda Reynolds. Headed to Nashville?"

She finally looked his way, her green eyes full of surprise. "How'd you know?"

"The guitar." Mitch nodded toward the back seat.

"Oh." She turned toward the front again and crossed her arms over her torso, tension still evident in her shoulders. "Good guess."

He could say something about her joining the hundreds of wannabes who flocked to Nashville each year in hopes of landing some kind of recording or songwriting contract, but he decided against it. She didn't need him to pile on after her car had broken down.

After he parked the truck in front of her car, he looked over at her. Her grim expression pricked at his heart. He hoped nothing major was wrong with her car. He'd fixed enough cars to know that some repairs ran in the thousands of dollars. He instructed her to stay in the truck while he made quick work of getting the car up on the back.

He slid behind the wheel and looked her way. "All set."

She turned to him, worry in her eyes. "Is there someone in your town who works on foreign cars?"

Mitch grinned. "You're lookin' at him."

"Oh, so you're the mechanic as well as the tow truck driver?"

"You got it."

She turned her gaze back toward the road, as if to dismiss him. She didn't seem too sure that he knew what he was doing. He would have to show her. They rode in silence for several minutes. He cast a surreptitious glance in her direction. She sat with her arms still crossed. Her expression made him think she was close to tears. What was her story besides her destination? Would she tell him if he asked?

"Where you from?"

She turned to look at him but remained silent, a shrug lifting her shoulders. "All over."

"Does that mean you've lived a lot of places or you

don't want to tell me?"

"Lots of places."

"And what constitutes a lot?"

"Well, maybe not a lot. California, Washington State, and Boston."

"No specific towns in California and Washington?"

"You wouldn't have heard of them anyway." She lifted one shoulder and let it fall. "I figured you've heard of Boston."

"And what were you doing in Boston?"

"Nosy, aren't you?"

"Just trying to make conversation and get to know you."

She let out a heavy sigh. "Going to music school."

"And now you plan to put all that knowledge to work in Nashville."

"Yeah, or that was the plan until this happened." She waved a hand toward the back.

"This is just a minor delay. You'll be back on the road in no time."

"I hope you're right."

Mitch slowed the truck as he came to the edge of town. He tried to gauge her reaction to the place where he'd grown up. He drove by a gas station that housed a Quick Shop with a bait and tackle section for locals and visitors who tried their luck at fishing and camping in the nearby lakes and hills. A steak house also greeted people on this end of town with its large wooden sign. A church, the post office, and town hall occupied the next block, the brick buildings a testament to better times in

Pineydale.

When Mitch stopped at the first of the town's three traffic lights, he looked over at her. She appeared to be surveying the place. What was she thinking after living in Boston?

Campers and fishermen in the spring, summer, and fall kept Pineydale alive, with the added bonus of leaf peepers in the fall. She'd probably find this place lacking, especially in shopping venues. One small clothing and shoe store had managed to hang on after the big box store had opened on the edge of town when he was in high school.

As the light turned green, he wanted to ask her what she thought, but he decided against it.

The combined elementary, middle, and high school building took up the next whole block. It had seen nearly a hundred years of graduates. He still liked to attend the high school sporting events and cheer on the local boys and girls.

"Did you go to school there?"

Mitch glanced over at her, surprised by her voluntary inquiry. "Yeah. If you live in Pineydale and the surrounding county, that's where you go to school."

"Kind of looks like where I went to high school."

"We have something in common."

"Maybe."

"Does your family live in Boston?"

"No." Her one-word answer, followed by silence, shut down the conversation.

Maybe she didn't get along with her family. He

wouldn't speculate. He should just forget the small talk. She obviously didn't want to reveal much about herself.

They rode the rest of the way to his repair shop without saying another word. He drove down Main Street, where he'd spent many an hour cruising with his friends on weekends. The barber shop and hair salon stood like bookends on a block that included the Pineydale Café, a bank, and a hardware store.

When they reached the other end of Main Street, Mitch turned left past a small lumberyard and stopped in front of the all-white block building with the large picture window emblazoned with big block blue letters that proclaimed *Wilbur's Garage*.

"Is Wilbur your boss?"

Mitch didn't know why it pleased him so much that she had asked the question, but her unexpected curiosity made him smile. "Not sure how to answer that question. Wilbur was my great-uncle. This was his garage, but he died several years ago. Now I run the place."

Amanda eyed him. "I'm sorry about your uncle."

"Thanks. He was a special man and taught me all I know about cars and engines. Cancer cut short his life." Mitch pushed away the sadness that inundated him still when he thought of his uncle. "He and his wife never had any children, so they kind of adopted me. I spent a lot of time with them through the years. So I miss him a lot."

"I'm sure you do. So now you're the boss?"

"Yeah. I'm the boss." Did that make a difference to her? He didn't know why he cared, but for some crazy reason he did. "So we're here. I'll get your car into the bay and check it out."

"Where should I wait while you do that?"

Mitch hopped out of the truck. "I'll show you. Follow me."

As Mitch made his way into the small reception area, he wished the chairs were better and the reading material newer. Why was he worried about impressing a woman who would get her car fixed and leave town without giving him a second thought? He didn't need another woman in his life who was all about appearances and little else. He let out a sigh. He shouldn't judge. Amanda was probably more than her impractical sandals.

After Mitch showed Amanda where she could wait, he got right to work. After listening to her explanation of what happened when her car stopped running, he had his suspicions about what was wrong. He quickly confirmed them. She wasn't going to like what he had to tell her, but there wasn't any point in delaying the bad news.

Mitch trudged toward the reception area and looked Amanda's way as he stood in the doorway. She was reading one of the ancient magazines from the pock-marked coffee table. What could possibly interest her in one of the fishing and sporting magazines? Maybe he had completely misjudged her. He cleared his throat, and she looked up.

"Is my car fixed already?"

Her optimism made his task even worse. He shook his head as he stepped into the room and handed her the estimate. "I'm afraid not. Here are the damages."

She took the paper and studied it for a moment. When she looked back at him, the expected incredulity painted every inch of her expression. "You've got to be kidding me. Thousands of dollars to fix that hunk of junk?"

"Yeah, the car probably isn't worth repairing, but it's up to you. The repairs cost more than the car is worth."

Placing a hand over her mouth as if to stifle a sob, she closed her eyes. Her shoulders slumped. The hum of the ceiling fan filled the silence. Finally, she looked up at him as she let out a loud sigh. "The car doesn't belong to me. It's my dad's."

"So you need to talk to him? I can send him the estimate by fax or email."

Amanda fished her cell phone from her tiny purse. "I don't know what I want you to do right now."

"Take your time. That car isn't going anywhere soon." Mitch walked back into the garage area, where he looked at the little red sports car. If he were Amanda, he wouldn't spend the money to fix it. The cost of replacing the engine was more than the car was worth, but he could fix this car and make it worth something. Maybe he could buy it from her. Then she'd have some cash to buy a used car or a bus ticket to Nashville, which was probably a ticket to disappointment. More disappointment than a broken-down car.

CHAPTER TWO

The marbled-gray tile on the floor of the reception area stared back at Amanda as she leaned her elbows on her knees. She wouldn't cry. She wouldn't let that big moose of a mechanic see her in tears. He'd stared down at her with that superior look, probably knowing she couldn't come close to paying for the repairs.

Was that really the cost? If so, she was in big trouble. How could she talk to her dad about ruining his car when he wasn't happy with her decision to drop out of school and head for Nashville? She would call Kelsey. At least talking to her sister might help. Maybe. She and her sister hadn't always gotten along while growing up. Amanda leaned back on the faux leather chair and punched in her sister's phone number.

Kelsey answered on the third ring. "Amanda, I'm surprised to hear from you. What's going on?"

Amanda didn't know how to start with her sister, who was five years her junior and a sophomore at Washington State University. Two sisters couldn't be more different. Kelsey had always been the parent pleaser, while Amanda had given her dad and stepmother more grief than they deserved.

"Kels, I'm in Tennessee."

"Oh, you made it to Nashville. How is it? Are you excited to be there?"

"Not quite."

"What do you mean *not quite*?"

Amanda sighed. "The car broke down."

"Oh no. Where are you?"

"In some little town in East Tennessee about three hundred miles east of Nashville." Amanda let out a halfhearted chuckle. "Get this. The name of the town is Pineydale."

"Pinecrest, southern-style?"

"That's exactly what I was thinking."

"Can you get the car fixed there?"

"There's a mechanic here who says he can fix it, but I know how Dad always had to take this car into Spokane to have it worked on. No one in Pinecrest worked on foreign cars." Amanda glanced toward the garage to make sure Mitch wasn't listening. "The cost is crazy, so I don't know whether to believe what he says."

"You have to talk to Dad."

Amanda cringed at the thought. "He'll blow his top."

"If you don't talk to him, you'll have to deal with it yourself. Which do you want?"

"I don't know." Amanda's voice came out in a strangled cry. "What would you do?"

"Talk to Dad."

"Of course that's what you'd do." An idea popped into Amanda's brain. "You talk to him. Maybe that will soften him up."

"I'll tell him you called and that you want to talk to

him."

Kelsey's statement told Amanda that she wasn't going to get much help from her little sister.

"At least tell him about the car."

"What about the car?"

Amanda grimaced. "It needs a new engine."

"Even I know that's bad." Kelsey's sigh sounded loud over the phone. "Okay. I'll talk to Dad, and he'll probably call you."

"Thanks, Kels. I really appreciate your help. Let's hope he's not too mad."

"Dad's not so hardhearted as you think."

"I wish I had your optimism." Amanda gripped the phone tighter. "Love you, Kels. Thanks again."

Amanda stared at the phone as she ended the call. How long would it take for her dad to call? What was she going to say to Mitch in the meantime?

"So have you made a decision?" Mitch's question made her jump.

"You shouldn't sneak up on a person like that. You sure walk quiet for a big guy."

A slow smile curved his mouth. "The better to surprise you, my dear."

"I'm not your dear." Amanda gave him an annoyed look.

"Not in a joking mood?" He raised his eyebrows. "Guess I wouldn't be either if my car was in the shape yours is in. What did you decide?"

"Nothing."

"So you're just going to sit here in my waiting

room?"

Amanda wouldn't let him know how helpless she felt. "I'm waiting for my dad to call back."

"I'll be glad to talk to him, if you'd like."

Would her dad want to do that? He might be so angry with her that he wouldn't be in the mood to talk to anyone. "I'll have to wait and see."

"I could make him a deal for the car."

"You mean you would buy it? Why would you want a car that doesn't run?" Amanda frowned.

"Because I know how to fix it."

Amanda narrowed her gaze. What was this guy's game? "So you're going to offer him money?"

"That's a possibility." He leaned against the counter as he raised his eyebrows.

Her dad was thousands of miles away, and he still had her in his grip. She couldn't do anything with this car without his approval. How had she gotten herself into this mess? Just when she thought she couldn't feel any lower, her phone rang. Her dad. She had to answer.

"Hi, Dad."

"Hello, Amanda. Kelsey tells me the car quit running."

"Yeah."

"So what's the exact problem?"

Amanda looked over at Mitch, who still leaned against the counter. "I'll let you talk to the mechanic."

"That's probably a good idea."

Standing, Amanda held out the phone. "My dad would like to talk to you."

"Be glad to explain everything." Mitch took the phone and introduced himself.

Amanda retreated to the couch and listened to the one-sided conversation. Mitch repeated everything he'd told her, then offered to buy the car for about half of what he had quoted her to fix it. She wasn't sure what to make of that or whether her dad would accept the offer. After a little back and forth, Mitch turned his back on Amanda, but she still heard him tell her dad to take the offer or leave it.

Either way, Mitch had the upper hand, and Amanda would lose no matter what her dad decided. He wasn't going to bail her out of this mess. She was on her own.

"Your dad wants to talk to you." Mitch turned back to her and gave her the phone.

His expression didn't give her one clue as to what had transpired or what he was thinking. He probably realized she didn't have a good relationship with her dad. What would he think about that? And why did she care?

Amanda took a deep breath and walked to the far side of the waiting area. "So what did you decide about the car?"

"I'm selling it to your mechanic friend there."

Amanda wanted to say that Mitch wasn't her friend. She had only met him an hour ago, but she let it go. "And that leaves me without a car."

"Yes, it does." Silence followed his statement.

Amanda refused to cry or beg or grovel. She jutted her chin out, as if her father were in the room. "Okay, then. I guess we don't have anything more to talk about."

"You made your choice to drop out of school, so now you have to deal with your decision."

"I will. Goodbye, Dad." Amanda didn't wait for his goodbye, just ended the call. She stood there for a moment and stared out the window toward the lumberyard on the corner.

"So I guess you know I'm buying the car."

Amanda forced herself to turn around. "Yeah, that's what my dad said."

"What are your plans now that you don't have a car?" He stepped away from the counter. "I can help you find an inexpensive used car."

"The little bit of savings I have won't buy even the cheapest car." Amanda stared back at Mitch. He had no idea how bad her finances were.

Her dad had told her she would be on her own if she went to Nashville. No credit card, no allowance, and no sympathy from him. Her cell phone was the only thing he still provided, only because it was on a family plan that lasted for another nine months. She could be thankful for that one thing.

"A bus ticket to Nashville? The bus comes through here daily. I can give you a ride to the café where the bus stops."

Amanda turned away to look out the window again. What did a bus ticket to Nashville cost? Is that what she wanted? To wind up in Nashville without a car, without a job, and without the security of her dad's money? On top of that, she was homeless. What a mess.

Tears threatened. No way was she going to let Mitch Cunningham see her cry. She pressed her lips together to fight back the tears. When she had her emotions under control, she turned to face him. "I'm not sure what to do."

"Would you like me to help you weigh your options?"

Amanda prayed that sympathy and not pity was what she read in his eyes. How much did she want to tell him? How could she consider telling a virtual stranger her problems? But right now she needed a friend and some advice more than she needed privacy. "My options are pretty limited. Stay here with no car, money, or place to stay, or go to Nashville and have the same problems. What would you do?"

Mitch removed his cap and put it on the counter. "Maybe it's none of my business, but why isn't your father helping you out here?"

Very intuitive question. Mitch liked to get right to the point. A straightforward question deserved a straightforward answer. "I made a decision he didn't like."

Mitch eyed her. "And I'm guessing that was your decision to go to Nashville?"

"Yeah."

"Is there more to the story you'd like to tell me?"

Would her story garner any sympathy, or would he be on her dad's side? She sighed, resentment sitting on her shoulder like one of those cartoon devils that urged the character to do the wrong thing. No matter whose side Mitch took, she needed a sounding board, and he was as good as anyone for that.

"You don't have to tell me a thing if you don't want to."

"Don't you have work to do? I don't want to keep you from your job."

He gave her an indulgent smile. "Yeah, I've got work to do. Since you can't go anywhere except on foot, you can stick around, and I'll take you to lunch."

Amanda glanced at her phone. Eleven o'clock. "What time do you go to lunch?"

"Noon." He raised his eyebrows as he stared at her. "Date?"

"Sure." Amanda gazed back at him. He didn't mean a real date, just an appointment. Now she had an hour to sit and stew about agreeing to talk to him. Was she a fool for trusting this stranger?

***

The wary expression on Amanda's face still hadn't disappeared when Mitch returned to the waiting room at five minutes before twelve. "You ready for lunch?"

She stood and glanced at the clock on the wall. "You're a little early."

"I finished what I was doing, so I'm fixin' to go to lunch now."

"Okay." Reluctance bubbled around that one word.

"What kind of food do you like?"

"There's a choice here?"

That question said so much about her attitude toward Pineydale compared to Boston. "Yeah. You can have possum gizzards or squirrel stew. And if you're lucky, today's special might be a roadkill sandwich."

She pressed her lips together in a grim line as she crossed her arms over her midsection. "I don't care. You choose."

When she didn't take the bait, his inhospitable response came across as childish. What was it about her that made him form judgments without enough evidence? "I'll take you to the Pineydale Café."

She followed him to his pickup. "Are the possum gizzards good there?"

Mitch laughed out loud as he opened the door for her. "I deserved that."

"Yes, you did."

When he parked in front of the café that was only three blocks away, she hopped out before he shut off the engine, and walked to the door. He rushed to catch up. "Hungry?"

"I am, but seems to me we could've walked here."

He glanced down at her feet. "I forgot for a minute that you changed shoes. I was thinkin' you were still wearin' those sandals."

"Those sandals are as good for walking as these shoes as long as there are sidewalks."

"At least they see you coming in the red ones." Mitch opened the door for her.

Yeah. They would see her coming all right. Why had

he brought her to the Pineydale Café where the local grapevine was greased and ready to spread the news that Mitch Cunningham had showed up today with an attractive woman in short shorts and red tennis shoes? He wasn't going to examine the answer to that question.

She looked at him, those green eyes full of questions. "The sign says seat yourself. Where should we sit?"

Mitch glanced around the restaurant. Curious looks came from every corner, even as he got greetings from several other customers. They were all speculating about Amanda and what she was doing with him. "The booth by the window."

Without a moment's hesitation, she headed that way and slid into the booth with her back to the rest of the patrons. He sat across from her with a full view of the inquisitive looks that followed them. He grabbed the menus from behind the condiments sitting next to the wall and handed one to Amanda.

"Thanks. Any recommendations?"

He grinned. "I already told you the squirrel stew is good."

She smiled back, and his heart tripped. This was the first time he'd seen her smile, and that smile made her even more attractive. This was much better than the disingenuous grin he'd seen when they'd first met. He forced himself to study the menu even though he already knew what he wanted. He couldn't let her good looks lure him in. A pretty face didn't always mean a good thing. He'd already seen enough of her sour side. Here he was judging again, but he couldn't deny the attraction.

"What about the Pineydale burger?"

"You don't look like a burger girl to me. I would've guessed you are more of a salad gal."

She shook her head. "You don't know me at all."

"True." He gave her a wry smile. "The burger's good, and this lunch is a way for me to get to know you."

"So you can tell me what to do just like my father?"

Mitch raised his eyebrows. "That says a lot right there, but I'll take some details."

Before Amanda could respond, her attention was drawn to the approaching waitress, a woman Mitch had known since he was a kid. Her son had been his best friend all through school. Now he lived in Atlanta.

"Hey, Mitch. What would you and your friend like to drink?"

"Hi, Julie, I'd like you to meet Amanda Reynolds."

Julie smiled, conjecture in her eyes. "Hi, Amanda, what brings you to Pineydale?"

Amanda glanced at him, then back at Julie. "My car broke down."

"Then you broke down in the right place. Mitch can fix anything." Julie's expression told Mitch that she intended to get more information. As he feared, word about his lunch companion would find its way to half the town's population before tomorrow. That included his parents.

"Good to know." Amanda smiled, but the set of her shoulders said she wasn't happy. "I'll have a cola."

Julie turned her attention to Mitch. "What about you?"

"The same." Mitch tapped the menu as he glanced at Amanda. "I think we're ready to order."

"Okay." Julie poised her pencil on the small tablet in her hand. "What can I get you?"

Mitch motioned for Amanda to go first. Even though she had asked about the burger, she still surprised him when she ordered one. He ordered the same. After Julie left, he stuck the menus back where he got them. "Now I'll take those details."

Amanda narrowed her eyes as she stared back at him. "And what if I don't want to give you details?"

"That's your choice." Mitch leaned forward and tapped the side of his head. "I can help if I know what's going on in your head."

"I doubt that." A halfhearted laugh accompanied her words. "My head's pretty cluttered."

"Let me help you unclutter it. Tell me what's going on with you and your dad."

Amanda pressed her lips together as if trying to keep words from coming out of her mouth. She sat silently until Julie returned with their drinks. Amanda unwrapped the straw and took a long sip of her cola.

Finally, she looked over at him. "My dad and I have been on opposite sides of almost everything since my mother died when I was nine."

Sympathy for Amanda flooded Mitch's thoughts. How was he supposed to respond to that? Everything he considered sounded lame. "That must've been tough losing your mom at such a young age."

"It was, especially when my dad buried his sorrow in work. He's always been a workaholic, but it got worse after my mom died. He pretty much ignored my sister and me. We were left to nannies and babysitters." With her gaze lowered, Amanda took another drink.

Now Mitch didn't have a clue about what he should say. He didn't always see eye to eye with his own father, but at least his dad showed an interest in his son's life. Sometimes too much. "Your dad doesn't seem to be ignoring you now."

Amanda made a sound that was half-laugh and half-groan. "Now that I'm not driving his car and heading to Nashville against his wishes, he'll definitely pay no attention to what I do."

Mitch had to dig deeper. "Let me get this straight. Your dad's been paying your way, but you decided to go against his wishes. Now he's cut you off. Do I have it right?"

"Mostly."

"If your dad paid for you to go to music school, why is he so opposed to your going to Nashville to try your luck with what you've learned?"

Amanda pressed her lips together in a grim line, then let out a long sigh. "That's just it. I quit school before I was finished."

"And why would you do that?"

Before Amanda could answer, Julie brought their orders. Amanda dived into her food without looking his way. What would she think if he gave thanks before he ate? Should he ask or just say a silent prayer that didn't include her? These days some people were offended by open displays of faith. He bowed his head and said a short prayer of thanks.

When he looked up, Amanda was staring at him. He waited for her to make a caustic remark.

A little frown creased her brow. "Were you praying?"

For an instant he considered telling her he was looking for something he had dropped. What kind of Christian was he? No doubt one who was tempted to hide his faith. "Yeah, I usually pray before I eat."

She tilted her head. "So you're a Christian?"

He nodded. "I didn't want to offend you."

"I'm not offended." She smiled. "I'm a Christian, too. I just don't always remember to give thanks before I eat."

"Me, too." Mitch squirted a big glob of catsup on his plate and dragged a french fry through it. Wow! He liked her smile. Not only did it light up the room, but it made his heart beat in double time. He didn't like what was happening. Why was he worried? She was on her way to Nashville. "So you never said why you quit school."

She took a bite of her burger and chewed slowly. Maybe she wasn't going to give him her reasons. She probably thought he was too nosy. She'd already said as much.

After she took another long drink, she gave a little shrug. "You see, I have this stepcousin Max. He was diagnosed with cancer. He's doing okay now, but it made me realize that we might not get tomorrow. I've written a lot of songs and performed at dozens and dozens of open mic events. I'm ready to try my luck. Max's situation made me think if I waited, I might not get the chance. So here I am stuck on my way to Nashville."

"Like I said, you can take a bus to Nashville. It stops here around two thirty." He could tell she was thinking about his suggestion. Something inside grabbed hold of him, and he wanted to tell her not to go. Why? He didn't have a clue. "So what do you say?"

"How much for a ticket?"

"The café doubles as a bus stop, so Julie probably has the prices. You want me to ask, or do you want to do it?"

"I'll do it." Amanda went to the counter. A minute later she slid back into the booth with a sheet of paper in her hand. "The cheapest fare isn't until Saturday."

"Are the tickets on the other days that much more expensive?"

Amanda shook her head. "But I don't have a lot of money to throw around."

Mitch shifted in his seat, still feeling that odd sensation that told him not to let her go. "It's your decision."

She glanced at her phone, then looked back at him. "So I have a couple of hours to decide? I often act without considering the consequences. So I'm a victim of my own bad decisions. I don't want to make one this time."

Now she decided to think about her decisions rather than before she took off for Nashville. Did he dare mention that it might be a little too late? "So you didn't get your degree?"

"Not the one in music. I have an MBA."

"Really?" Mitch frowned. "Then why are you pursuing music?"

"You sound like my dad." Amanda let out a halfhearted chuckle. "He's the one who insisted I get that MBA. After I did, I wanted more than ever to pursue my music. He begrudgingly said okay, but he doesn't really support my dream."

Mitch marveled at the resemblance between his relationship with his dad and Amanda's relationship with hers. Graham Cunningham had little respect for his son's desire to work on cars rather than a stock portfolio.

Mitch's phone rang. He picked it up and glanced at it. "Excuse me. I've got to take this."

"Sure." Amanda took a bite of her burger.

Wondering why Amanda's father was calling, Mitch strode out to the sidewalk in front of the café. Was he taking back his offer? "Hello, Mr. Reynolds. Have you changed your mind about the car?"

"No. I wanted to talk to you about Amanda. And please call me Grady."

"What about her?" Mitch remembered how she described her father as trying to run her life. Was he trying to do that now even after cutting off her support?

"I hope she hasn't left."

"Do you want to talk to her? She's still here but may

be heading to Nashville on the next bus through town." While Mitch talked, his cousin Jimmy and some of his crew nodded and waved as they sauntered into the café.

"I don't need to talk with her, but don't let her get on that bus."

Mitch didn't know how to respond. How could he keep Amanda from going to Nashville? "Sir, your daughter is a grown woman, and I don't see how I can keep her from leaving if that's what she decides to do."

"If you can keep her there, I won't charge you for the car."

The thought of getting that car for free gave Mitch second thoughts about Grady's request. But Amanda's decision should be her decision. Her father shouldn't try to manipulate her, and Mitch didn't want to be part of Grady's plan. "I'm sorry, sir, but I can't go along with that."

Grady's sigh sounded loud over the phone. "I don't want my daughter to ruin her life by chasing some pie-in-the-sky dream about making a music career in Nashville."

Mitch also had his doubts about Amanda's ability to make it in Nashville, no matter how much talent she had, but she should at least have the chance to try. He knew what it meant to chase a dream that a parent didn't share. "Sir, sometimes you need to let your kids fail. They learn something from it."

"You have kids?"

"No, sir."

"Then you don't have room to lecture me about my

daughter."

"Maybe not, but she should have the opportunity to pursue her dream." After listening to Grady, Mitch had sympathy for Amanda—something he hadn't had an hour ago. Making it in Nashville was a long shot, but she should have the chance to try. Convincing her father was a long shot, too. "I think we've said all there is to say, and I won't be a party to your plan. I'm sorry."

"You haven't heard the last from me. Keep that in mind."

The phone went dead, and Mitch looked at it with a sense of foreboding. What could the man do from thousands of miles away? Mitch hoped he didn't have to find out.

When Mitch stepped back into the café, Jimmy sat in the booth across from Amanda, while his crew sat in the booth on the other side of the room. Amanda and Jimmy were laughing and talking like old friends, or maybe more than friends. Mitch stopped short as a streak of jealousy as green as Jimmy's shirt flashed before his eyes. He didn't want to examine the reason for its presence, but he couldn't shake it either.

Mitch strode over to the booth. "Well, I see you two have met."

His gray eyes twinkling, Jimmy grinned up at Mitch. "Hey, cuz, how come you didn't tell me about the new gal in town?"

"I just met her myself." Mitch tried not to let his agitation show as he stared at Jimmy. "I'd like to finish my lunch."

"Oh sure." Jimmy hopped up and slid into the booth beside Amanda. "Amanda here was just tellin' me about her plans to go to Nashville, but I think I've convinced her to stay right here."

Had Jimmy unknowingly done Grady's bidding? That was almost funny. But Jimmy, voted most handsome in high school with his dark hair and ready smile, always thought he could sweet talk any girl, and he was trying his best with Amanda. Mitch gritted his teeth to keep from saying something he would regret as he sat down. He took a big bite of his burger and tried to gauge how Amanda was taking Jimmy's persuasive talk.

After taking a big gulp of his cola, Mitch set his burger on the plate. "So what do you think, Amanda?"

She gave Jimmy a sideways glance, then looked over at Mitch. "Jimmy says he can give me a job."

Mitch frowned at his cousin. "What are you going to have her do? Paint houses?"

"That's a good start." Jimmy shifted in his seat.

Mitch held out a hand toward Amanda. "She's got a master's degree in business. Should she be painting houses?"

"She needs the money, and she ain't gonna use no degree to sing songs in Nashville." Jimmy stared right back.

"Okay, you two. I'm sitting right here, and I don't appreciate you arguing about me. I can do what I want with my degree." Amanda motioned for Jimmy to move. "Please let me out."

Jimmy jumped out of the booth as if his pants were

on fire. "Sure thing, little lady."

Amanda stomped off toward the counter where Julie refilled someone's drink. Mitch couldn't hear what Amanda said to Julie, but when Amanda walked toward the back of the restaurant, Mitch guessed she was headed to the ladies' room.

Mitch glared at Jimmy. "Hope you're happy."

"You're just as much to blame as me." Jimmy plopped back down in the booth.

"Maybe you ought to get up and join your crew so Amanda can sit there and finish her lunch in peace."

"If she wants peace, then you should leave." Jimmy narrowed his gaze. "You've got her upset because she doesn't know what to do without a car."

Mitch had no response. Why had Amanda opened up to Jimmy, while Mitch had had to pry information out of her? He rubbed his thumb and fingers across his forehead, trying to ward off a headache. "Then you give her a car."

Jimmy gave him a sly grin. "I'm going to give her a job and a place to stay."

"And where's she going to stay?" Surely Jimmy wasn't talking about his place. Mitch couldn't fathom that. He looked up and saw Amanda approaching. "She's coming back. So I want you gone."

"Now that would be just rude not to give her my best wishes." Jimmy stood and turned to look at Amanda.

Mitch held his breath and hoped Jimmy wouldn't say something stupid to her.

"Nice meeting you, Amanda. Gotta get back to my

crew." Jimmy waved toward the booth across the way. "You let me know how I can help with a job or whatever."

"Sure." Amanda nodded as she slid back onto the seat.

Mitch watched Jimmy saunter away, not sure what to say to Amanda now. Did she want to stay and do menial work? She hardly seemed the type, but maybe he had misjudged her. He had a bad habit of doing that. "So what's the verdict?"

"About what?" Her expression was blank.

"Staying? Going? Jobs? Cars? Jimmy?"

CHAPTER THREE

The buzz of conversation, laughter, and the clanking of dishes and flatware sounded loud in Amanda's ears as she stared back at Mitch. She didn't have an answer to any of his questions. She wished she did, because she didn't want to appear helpless. She didn't need some man to rescue her. She'd been depending on her dad long enough. She had to fend for herself, but what kind of job could she find in a town like Pineydale besides painting houses?

She had to admit that she'd jumped into this Nashville thing without a plan. Big mistake. Now she was paying the price. She might have a graduate degree in business, but she'd never planned to use it. She'd only wanted to be a musician.

"Did you and Jimmy have a fun time talking about me?" Amanda raised her eyebrows as she looked across the table at Mitch.

"No."

Mitch's one-word answer surprised Amanda. "Then why are you asking me what I want to do?"

"Because I asked you that before Jimmy showed up."

True. Amanda glanced down at the bus schedule. She had to make a decision soon, at least about today. "What do you think I should do?"

Mitch hesitated as he drummed his fingers on the table and glanced down at his cell phone, which lay nearby. "I'm not here to give you advice. I'll be a sounding board. Nothing more."

Amanda couldn't believe she'd asked him what he thought. She was falling right back into the trap of depending on someone else to make decisions for her. But right at the moment, failure dogged all her decisions. How could she trust her own judgments? She had to get some clarity, but would Mitch be helpful or only skeptical of her ability to take care of herself? "Okay, then. Jimmy said something about a place where I could stay. Then you came in, and I never found out what that was. Do you know?"

Again Mitch didn't answer immediately, this time taking a big bite of his burger. Since she wasn't getting an answer anytime soon, Amanda ate her own burger. They sat there eating in silence for several minutes, neither of them making eye contact. The smell of fried foods and coffee swirled around them, and Amanda got a sick feeling in her stomach. Was she going to be stuck in this town or alone in Nashville without a car or a place to stay?

Finally, Mitch looked up from his meal. "I'm not sure what Jimmy had in mind, but I have a place where you might be able to stay as long as you're not allergic to cats."

"No problem with cats."

"Good. I'll have to make a phone call to check it out."

"Okay, thanks. That'll give me some time to really think about what I should do."

Mitch gave her a lopsided smile. "That's probably a good idea."

"At least you agree with that much."

Mitch picked up his phone. "I'll make that call."

"You can finish your meal. Your food's probably cold as it is."

"Thanks." He put the phone back on the table and resumed eating.

While Amanda finished her burger, she looked across the restaurant to where Jimmy and his friends sat. They were laughing and talking, not paying one bit of attention to Mitch or her. Could she trust these strangers, or would she be better off heading to Nashville, where she'd find herself among another bunch of strangers? Folly should be her middle name.

Mitch drained the last of his cola from the glass, then set it on the table with a final thud that almost made Amanda jump. She glanced at him as he grabbed his phone.

"Time to make that call."

"Okay." Amanda stared at him as her heart raced. She wasn't sure whether her accelerated heart rate had to do with him or with the prospect of being homeless if this didn't work out.

"Hey, Aunt Charlotte, how's everything?" Mitch grinned as he spoke.

Amanda hadn't realized until just a few minutes ago what a precarious situation she was in. She had no transportation, no place to live, and no good prospects to earn money. Stupid, stupid decisions had brought her to this low point, but she listened to the one-sided conversation with a bit of hope.

After Mitch ended the call, his gaze met hers. "That was my great-aunt Charlotte, and she has a spare room in her house that she's willing to let you have in exchange for help around her house."

"Does that mean I can't paint houses with Jimmy?"

Mitch glanced over at his cousin. "If you actually want to paint houses, you can do that, too."

"But how can I do both?" Amanda wasn't sure she wanted to do either. Confusion made her brain hurt.

"Do you want to paint houses?"

"Not really, but I have to earn some money somehow, and I won't be getting any money from your aunt—just a room."

Leaning forward, Mitch sighed. "Let's pay the bill and head over to Charlotte's place, and maybe a good night's sleep will help you see things more clearly in the morning."

As Mitch paid the bill at the cash register, Jimmy sauntered over. "Don't forget that job offer. It's still open if you want it."

Amanda tried to smile. "Thanks. I'll think about it."

"You're welcome." Jimmy tipped an imaginary hat. "See you around."

"Sure." Amanda followed Mitch outside, glad not to have to make a decision today.

Mitch opened the passenger door for Amanda, and

she climbed into the cab. When he was settled behind the wheel, he looked over at her. "Does your interest in the painting job mean you plan to stay in Pineydale?"

Amanda shrugged. "I don't know what I'm planning. Like you said, I'm going to sleep on it and see how I feel in the morning."

Mitch made no response as he put the pickup in gear. He drove down Main Street and turned on a side street lined with trees and modest clapboard houses. A few blocks later, he parked in front of a house with a big front porch. A swing occupied one end, and rockers sat on either side of the front door. The place beckoned Amanda to sit down and rock her troubles away, but that wasn't possible.

Mitch hurried to open the door for Amanda. Despite her bad first impression of him, he had turned out to be a perfect southern gentleman. But she didn't want to dwell on his likeability. Even if she spent a few weeks here, this place wasn't a permanent stop. She wasn't going to give up her dream of getting to Nashville.

Amanda hurried to keep up with Mitch's long strides as he went up the front walk and took the steps two at a time. He knocked but didn't wait for an answer before he opened the front door and went inside. "Aunt Charlotte. We're here."

"Be there in a few seconds," a female voiced called from another room.

With Mitch standing in front of her, Amanda peeked around his broad shoulders to the right as she took in the living room with the overstuffed sofa covered in a brownish material and accented with tan-and-brown striped pillows. Two brown tweed recliners sat at an angle to the sofa. Knickknacks and jar lamps decorated the end tables. Just like the porch, the room invited her to stay. Is that what she wanted? She pushed the question away. She didn't have to answer now.

Mitch stepped aside and ushered Amanda farther into the room. On the left was a dining room with a huge golden-oak table surrounded by ornately carved chairs. A matching sideboard and china cabinet completed the room. Everything about this house said *welcome— sit down and stay awhile.*

As Amanda stood there taking in the delicious aromas floating through the air, a tall white-haired woman wearing neatly pressed tan slacks and a black-and-tan knit top entered the room, a black-and-white cat following close behind her.

"Mitch, introduce me to your friend."

"Aunt Charlotte, this is Amanda Reynolds." Mitch turned. "Amanda, meet my favorite great-aunt and Minnie Pearl."

"Minnie Pearl?" Amanda raised her eyebrows.

"Yeah. The cat."

Her blue eyes twinkling with laughter, Charlotte extended her hand to Amanda. "Nice to meet you, and don't let Mitchell fool you. I'm the only great-aunt he has who's still living. And Minnie Pearl here is my mascot, my companion, and believe it or not, my guard cat. If she likes you, I know you're a good person. She has a real person sense."

Amanda managed to smile as she shook Charlotte's gnarled hand and wondered whether she would pass muster with Minnie Pearl. "I'm glad to meet you, too."

The older woman motioned toward the living room. "Let's sit in here."

Mitch didn't move. "Sorry I can't stay. I've got to get back to work."

"But all my stuff is still back at your garage." Amanda's stomach sank. She couldn't believe he was abandoning her. Even though his aunt appeared to be a nice woman, Amanda didn't appreciate being left alone with someone she had just met. Of course, how long had she known Mitch? A couple of hours longer? She might as well get used to being among strangers. That was her life going forward.

"After I close up, I'll bring it by." Mitch turned toward the door.

"Okay." Amanda hated the thought of being left here without any of her belongings. She should have insisted that they go back to the garage before coming here, but she hadn't known he planned to dump her here and leave. She forced herself to have a better attitude. At least she had a place to stay for the night.

As Mitch opened the door, Charlotte waved a bony finger at him. "You plan on having dinner here, young man."

Grinning, Mitch gave Charlotte a salute. "You don't have to twist my arm. You know I won't turn down one of your home-cooked meals. See you later."

Amanda stared after him and wondered how she

could feel an attachment to a man she had only met a couple of hours ago. But he felt like the only anchor in her sea of self-doubt.

"Let's go in the living room and have a talk."

Charlotte's voice made Amanda turn. "Sure."

"We need to get to know each other." Charlotte sat on the sofa and motioned for Amanda to sit. "I'm taking my nephew's word that you're a good risk to occupy my spare room. Can I count on that?"

Nodding, Amanda swallowed the lump that had risen in her throat. She had to look at this through the eyes of the older woman, who had agreed to take in a stranger. She appeared to be a no-nonsense kind of person who got right to the point. Amanda wanted to do the same. "Mitch said you needed help around the house in exchange for the room, right?"

Charlotte waved a dismissive hand. "That boy! He's always thinking I need help. I'm glad to give you a room. It's the hospitable thing to do. After all, the Good Book says, 'Do not forget to entertain strangers, for by so doing some have unwittingly entertained angels.'"

Amanda had heard that Scripture before, but she never thought it would pertain to her. "I can assure you that I'm no angel."

Charlotte chuckled. "The Lord brings people into our lives for all kinds of reasons. So let's find out why you're here in Pineydale."

"Didn't Mitch tell you my car broke down?"

"Oh yes." Smiling, Charlotte bobbed her head. "But there's a reason why your car broke down right here."

"I wouldn't know what it is." Amanda did wonder why she had wound up here. Did God really have anything to do with it?

"We'll eventually figure that out."

Amanda wasn't so sure that was true, but she wasn't going to argue. "I suppose."

"Now tell me a little about yourself." Charlotte patted the sofa. "Come sit with me."

Amanda moved to the sofa. As she did, the cat rubbed up against her legs. She bent over and ran her hand down the length of the cat's back. The feline circled Amanda's legs, and a rumble filled the room as the cat purred. She hoped that was a good sign.

"What do you want to know?"

"It appears Minnie Pearl has put her stamp of approval on you." Charlotte smiled. "And you can tell me whatever you'd like."

Nothing. The word popped into Amanda's head. She didn't know why. She didn't have anything to hide, so why was she reluctant to share with this woman? Amanda shrugged. "Not much to tell."

"I'm sure there is."

"Was Wilbur your husband? Mitch told me Wilbur died from cancer." *Cancer.* The *C* word had been on her mind more than she wanted to think about after her stepcousin had won his battle with the disease. She wanted to push those thoughts far, far away, but cancer and its uncertainty were everywhere she turned.

Sadness filled Charlotte's expression. "Yes, and I miss him every day. Sometimes I still can't believe he's gone."

"I'm so sorry." Amanda sighed. "Cancer is a hideous disease. It sent me on this trip."

Charlotte narrowed her gaze. "What do you mean?"

Amanda told Charlotte about her stepcousin's battle with cancer. "Life's too short to let any opportunity pass you by."

Charlotte nodded. "I understand, but what does the loss of your car mean to this trip?"

"Kind of makes me stuck here unless I want to hop on a bus and wind up in Nashville without any transportation."

"And what do you think about that?"

Amanda wondered whether Mitch had put Charlotte up to these questions. They made her realize what a misguided thing she had done. Was there any way to salvage the situation? "I think I'm like a person who set out in a boat without a life jacket. The boat has sunk, and I'm floundering."

"Let me throw you a lifesaver."

Amanda let out a halfhearted chuckle. "I wish you could."

"I can." Charlotte reached over and patted Amanda's arm. "Stay with me until you get your life back on track. I could use the company. This big old house is lonely without Wilbur."

Was Charlotte's loneliness the reason Mitch had brought Amanda here? Would she be a good companion for a lonely older lady? Amanda took a deep breath and let it out slowly. "I promised myself I wouldn't make any hasty decisions. Let me sleep on it and see how I feel about everything in the morning."

"Fair enough, but let's give you something to sleep on." Charlotte grabbed a piece of paper and a pen from the drawer in the end table. "Let's write down what you hope to accomplish and how you plan to do it."

"Okay." Amanda hoped things wouldn't look worse on paper than they did in her mind.

Charlotte raised her eyebrows as she looked at Amanda. "Is your ultimate goal to get to Nashville?"

"Yes." Amanda knew for certain that goal hadn't changed. It might be delayed, but she would get there one way or another.

After scribbling something on the paper, Charlotte looked up. "How do you plan to do that?"

The question made Amanda's mind a blank. She couldn't come up with an answer now that she didn't have a car. "Like I said before, I could take the bus to Nashville."

"What about money for a new car?" Waving the pen in the air, Charlotte eyed Amanda.

"Not in my budget. The money I had saved was to pay for a place to live until I could find a job."

"And what kind of job were you looking for?"

"Something that pays a decent salary. I have a business degree."

"Have you applied for any jobs there?"

Amanda knew that was one of her obvious mistakes—not securing a job before she started on this adventure. She hated to admit this major blunder. "No."

Charlotte tapped the pen on the paper. "That *is* a problem."

"I know." Amanda hung her head. What must Charlotte think of the rash decision to take off for Nashville without considering all these things?

Charlotte laid the pen and paper aside. "Here's what I think. You should stay here with me. Mitch has connections here in town and could probably help you find some kind of job here. You can save your money for a new car and apply for a job in Nashville."

"But what if I have an interview? I can't rely on the bus to get me there." Amanda wondered if she should mention Jimmy's offer to paint houses. What would Charlotte say about that? And what kind of a business job would be available in a town the size of Pineydale? Not many, if any.

"True." Charlotte nodded. "You can use my car."

Amanda couldn't believe this woman's generosity. "You're too kind."

Charlotte smiled. "Not kind at all. I'm really thinking of myself and how much I would enjoy your company for a while."

"How do you know that?" Amanda raised her eyebrows. "You don't know me."

Charlotte smiled again as she tapped the side of her head. "I have an intuition about people, and my intuition tells me you're a good and trustworthy person, and Minnie Pearl doesn't like just anyone."

Amanda had never thought of herself in those terms. She didn't consider herself a bad person, but she had a tendency to do things without really thinking them through. Could she live up to the good and trustworthy label? "Thanks for looking at me that way, but I still can't make a decision today."

"That's reasonable." Nodding, Charlotte stood. "Let me show you the rest of the house."

"Okay." Wondering about this whole scenario, Amanda followed Charlotte down a short hallway.

When they reached the first door on the left, Charlotte turned to Amanda. "I think you'll like this room."

As Charlotte opened the door, Amanda peered through the opening and caught her breath. "Oh wow! A baby grand piano."

"I thought you might like that, since you're an accomplished musician." Charlotte stepped aside and let Amanda enter the room first.

"Thank you, but you haven't heard any of my music."

Charlotte's eye's twinkled. "True, but you must have talent, or you wouldn't be headed to Nashville."

That whole statement served to make Amanda even more aware of the need to consider all her options. What if she wasn't talented enough to make it in Nashville? She pushed the doubts away. They would serve no purpose in her thinking.

She stood there for a moment and glanced around the room. A small desk sat between the lace-covered windows that looked out on the side yard where some kind of bushes displayed their purple blooms. The two walls on the opposite ends had floor-to-ceiling bookcases overflowing with books. In the two corners near the windows, wingback chairs guarded the volumes.

Amanda gently ran her hand over the gleaming ebony finish on the piano, then looked over at Charlotte. "Do you mind if I play it?"

"That's why I brought you in here." Smiling, Charlotte held up her gnarled hands. "These fingers used to fly over the keys, but arthritis has taken its toll on them. It's difficult for me to play these days, and I miss the sound of this piano."

Amanda pulled out the piano bench and sat down, her fingers poised above the shiny white keys. "Is there something you'd like me to play?"

"Play whatever you'd like." Charlotte ventured over to the chair in the corner and sat down with Minnie Pearl on her lap. "I just want to hear you play."

With a dozen tunes floating through her mind, Amanda wished Charlotte had picked out something. Did she want to hear a modern song or something classical? Maybe an old hymn? Amanda searched her memory. Could she play one without the music? A long time had passed since she'd done that.

For a moment Amanda closed her eyes and tried to picture the music of her paternal grandmother's favorite hymn, the one Amanda had played for Grandma Fran dozens of times. Charlotte kind of reminded Amanda of her grandma Fran, but Amanda couldn't begin to guess Charlotte's age. Amanda hoped the older woman shared a love of the beloved song "It Is Well with My Soul."

Amanda let her fingers glide over the keys as she played a few opening chords of a prelude before she started the hymn. Once she played the beginning notes of the tune, the hymn practically flowed from her fingers. She could almost hear her grandmother singing along. Then Amanda realized Charlotte was singing, her lovely soprano voice filling the room. Amanda joined in with the harmony when she remembered the words.

After Amanda finished, she smiled over at Charlotte. "You have a lovely voice."

"Thank you. So do you, and you play the piano very well, too." Charlotte stood. "How did you know that is one of my favorite hymns?"

Amanda shrugged. "I didn't. I'm just glad I remembered how to play it."

"Me too. It was a treat. Let's explore the rest of the house."

"Okay." Amanda hopped up from the piano and followed Charlotte into the hallway and wondered what other surprises she would find in this house.

Charlotte turned to the left, and Minnie Pearl padded after her owner. "This is my favorite room in the house. When Wilbur was still alive, he had the whole place remodeled like on those TV shows where they take an old house and make it modern. He put in this glorious kitchen that flows into the hearth room. I spend most of my time in here."

"I can see why." Amanda took in the huge farm sink in the massive island, where four barstools sat opposite the sink. "It's cozy but modern. You have all the latest appliances, and these granite countertops are gorgeous. They go so well with your dark wood cabinets. Is the flooring original to the house?"

"It is, and so is most of the trim work. We wanted to preserve as much of the original flavor of the house as we could. It was built in 1905."

"You did a wonderful job." Amanda wondered why a childless couple would have owned such a huge house, but it would be rude to ask. "My stepcousin introduced me to a couple who restored an old Victorian house in a small town near Boston. They run it as a bed-and-breakfast now. She has a restaurant there."

"This place might make a good B and B, but I'm too old to run one, and my arthritis even makes cooking difficult sometimes." Charlotte sighed and gestured to her right. "This was original to the house and was great when I used to do a lot of entertaining."

Amanda peeked around the corner. "Oh wow! A huge butler's pantry. My grandma Fran had one of those in her house. She was an amazing cook."

"I used to be, even if I do say so myself, but I don't cook much anymore. Not much fun to cook for one. That's why I invite Mitch and his friends over so I can cook for them." Charlotte chuckled. "They don't turn down my invitations very often."

Did friends include Jimmy? Amanda had no idea why she was thinking of Mitch's cousin. Maybe because he seemed too sure of himself, but so did Mitch. Maybe the confidence gene grew in the family. "Mitch did seem eager to come back for supper."

Charlotte chuckled. "Mitch spent a good deal of time in this house when he was younger. He and Wilbur shared a love of cars and so many other things. He's like the grandson we never had."

"Does Mitch have a lot of family in Pineydale?"

Charlotte let out a loud belly laugh. "Lots and lots of family. The Cunninghams founded this town. Sometimes I think if it weren't for the garage, Mitch would pick up and leave town in an instant. At times I think all this family smothers him."

Amanda took in that bit of information with interest. He seemed so settled, so much a part of this little southern town. Did he have the same feelings about a small town as she did? She wanted to know, but she wasn't going to ask a direct question. "What else can you tell me about Mitch?"

A little smile brightening her expression and her eyes full of curiosity, Charlotte motioned toward the hallway. "Let me show you where you'll be sleeping, and I'll tell you a little bit about him."

"Okay." Amanda followed Charlotte up the stairs that turned at a ninety-degree angle.

At the top of the stairs, Charlotte turned to the right. "This is your room here. You have your own bathroom."

Amanda stepped through the door. The hardwood floors gleamed in the light coming from the windows that looked out on the quiet street. A large oval rug in muted blue and brown tones lay on the floor next to the bed with its blue-and-white comforter. "This is a wonderful room. Thanks for letting me stay here."

"I'm glad to share my house with you, and you can stay as long as you'd like. Until you decide what you want to do." Charlotte opened the door to a walk-in closet. "You can put your things in here."

"This is wonderful, but I don't have much." Amanda turned back to Charlotte. "Now what were you going to tell me about Mitch?"

Speculation beamed in Charlotte's eyes. "So you want to know about Mitch. He's an interesting guy, and good looking, too, wouldn't you say so?"

Hoping Charlotte wasn't getting the wrong idea, Amanda gave a little shake of her head as she returned Charlotte's sly smile. "No comment. I just want to know who I'm dealing with."

"Okay." Charlotte placed her hands in a prayerlike pose in front of her. "Mitchell Cunningham is one of the best men I've ever known, and I'm not just saying that because he's my great-nephew. He's good and honest. He's sometimes a stickler for rules, but that's a good thing most of the time. He gets that from his dad, and they butt heads continually."

"And why is that?" Amanda found that bit of information interesting.

"Mitch's dad wanted him to take over one of the family businesses, but all Mitch wanted to do was work on cars." Charlotte let out a big sigh as she shook her head. "Graham Cunningham doesn't see much value in blue-collar work, at least for his son."

"That's Mitch's dad?" Amanda couldn't help

thinking Mitch might very well understand her argument with her dad.

"Yes." Charlotte placed her hands on her hips. "Maybe I shouldn't say anything, but I think you should understand how things are with Mitch and his father. The boy went to college and got a business degree to please his dad and even worked for his dad for a few years after he graduated from college. But he spent every Saturday working with Wilbur in the garage."

"So you're saying Mitch doesn't get along with his father?"

Narrowing her gaze, Charlotte shrugged. "It's not as simple as that. Mitch just wanted to do something that didn't please his father."

"Why did Mitch decide to go his own way?"

Sadness filled Charlotte's eyes. "When my Wilbur started his chemo treatments, there were days when he was too tired to think about going to work. Mitch started filling in, and pretty soon he took over. His dad couldn't argue with Mitch helping out his great-uncle. So when Wilbur passed away, Mitch took over running the garage. The situation didn't make his dad happy, but he learned to live with it."

Amanda considered confiding in Charlotte about the circumstances with her own dad, but she decided against it. She wasn't sure she wanted to draw comparisons between her plight and Mitch's. Although Charlotte's plea to stay was tempting, Amanda wanted to make a decision based on logic, not sentiment. Sentimental thoughts about Mitch or Charlotte wouldn't help

Amanda make a sound decision. She might be gone tomorrow. No Charlotte. No Mitch. No small town.

CHAPTER FOUR

Delicious aromas greeted Mitch as he walked through Charlotte's front door. He had looked forward to his aunt's cooking all day. And if he was completely honest with himself, he'd been eager to see Amanda as well. He tried to bury that thought, but collecting her things from the car that now belonged to him and toting them here did nothing to erase her from his mind. She was determined to leave, and he didn't need to think about stopping her.

That fact should keep him from thinking about her, but it didn't.

Mitch stepped into the foyer and wondered what Amanda had been doing all afternoon. His traitorous mind couldn't banish her from his thoughts. "Aunt Charlotte, I'm ready for some of that great cooking of yours."

In seconds Charlotte scurried into the hallway as she wiped her hands on a towel. "You're in for a treat. I've had help all afternoon, and we've cooked all your favorites."

"All of them?" Was Amanda that help? She didn't look like the type who enjoyed cooking. Not that it made any difference to him. He didn't know why he couldn't stop thinking about the auburn-haired beauty. Maybe that was it. He was attracted to her good looks. That was his weakness—good-looking women.

Charlotte chuckled as she tucked her arm into his. "Well, at least your favorite favorites."

"Then I'm in for a treat." Mitch patted Charlotte's hand as he guided her back into the kitchen. "Hi, Amanda."

Amanda looked up from where she was setting the plates and flatware on the rectangular dark-oak table, which sat in the breakfast nook beside the kitchen. "Hi. Did you bring my stuff?"

That question should put him in his place. She was more interested in her belongings than in him. "Yeah, they're in my pickup. Would you like me to bring your things in now?"

"That would be good." She gave him a little smile that made his heart zing.

"Okay." He turned on his heel and strode toward the front door and wished somehow he could put a shutter on his mind to keep out unwanted thoughts.

As he reached his pickup, the front screen door opened and closed. He turned. Amanda sprang across the porch and down the front steps. "I'll help. I'll take my guitar."

Nodding, Mitch reached over the side of the truck bed and picked up the guitar case. He handed it to her. Their fingers brushed, and his heart zinged again. He steeled himself against the reaction. She wasn't his kind of woman, and she didn't want to stay here. He had to shut down the attraction before it was his undoing.

"Here you go. Can you carry anything else?"

Amanda held the case in one and held out the other. "You can give me the small roller bag."

Loaded down with bags, Mitch followed Amanda upstairs to the room where she was staying. "I can't believe how much stuff you managed to get into that car."

Amanda ignored his statement as she put the luggage in the closet and leaned her guitar case against the wall near the dresser. "I'll take care of the rest of this later. I have to finish helping Charlotte."

"Does this mean you're planning to stay?" Mitch loped after her as she hurried down the stairs.

She stopped at the bottom and looked at him, her expression guarded. "I haven't made any decisions."

Why was he torturing himself by thinking of ways to get her to stay? Her presence would only serve to confuse him, tempt him, and keep him off balance. He didn't need any of those things. "I should've known that. You were going to sleep on it. I just couldn't help noticing that you had settled right in with Charlotte."

"She's a dear lady, and her offer to stay here is very tempting."

"She could certainly use your company around here. She just rattles around in this big old house now that Wilbur's gone."

A little smile curving her mouth, Amanda cocked her head as she raised her eyebrows and stared at him. "Wanting me to stay?"

If he jumped right in with a denial, would she guess

that it was a half-truth? "I'd like you to stay on Charlotte's account."

Amanda nodded. "If I decide to stay, Charlotte said you might be able to help with a job. Something besides painting houses for Jimmy."

So she didn't want to paint houses. That didn't surprise Mitch, but he had no idea what other kinds of jobs were available in Pineydale. If he were on better terms with his dad, Mitch might be able to find something with one of the Cunningham businesses. Those jobs were often in nearby towns and would require transportation. Something Amanda didn't have.

"I could check into it for you."

"If I plan to stay." Amanda didn't wait for his response but hurried off to the kitchen.

Mitch didn't follow right away but leaned on the bannister as he watched her race away. He reminded himself again not to let her good looks turn his head. Maybe it was already too late. He had let another woman with ambitions that would take her away pique his interest.

With a sense of uncertainty swirling through his mind like a tornado, Mitch went into the hearth room and stopped before he reached the kitchen. Amanda stood at the stove as she stirred something in a pan. The scene didn't fit the first impression he'd had of her. With her foreign sports car, designer purse, and fancy manicure, not to mention those wedge sandals, he had figured her for a spoiled rich kid. After talking with her father, Mitch was relatively sure his assessment was right. Now here she was punching a hole in his opinion.

"Fried chicken, green beans, and mashed potatoes. Can hardly wait to eat." Mitch sauntered over to the counter and plucked a chunk of the crispy coating from a piece of chicken.

Charlotte reached over and gave his hand a playful slap. "You can wait. No touching the food before we're ready."

Amanda stopped stirring and looked at him. "You'd better listen to her."

Mitch liked that Amanda felt comfortable enough to give him advice. He held up both hands as a sign of surrender as he stepped closer and peered into her pan. "Gravy."

"Yes. Gravy." She shot him an annoyed look just as the buzzer went off on the stove. She held up the wooden spoon. "You can stir while I get the cobbler out of the oven."

"Sure." Remembering the sparks that flew when he'd handed her the guitar case, he carefully reached for the spoon. He breathed a sigh of relief when there was no contact. His heart was safe for a moment.

But when he glanced at Charlotte, he recognized the matchmaker's gleam in her eyes. Ever since Whitney had broken up with him, Charlotte had been on the lookout to match him with someone. He was having enough trouble not thinking about Amanda without Charlotte's interference. He ducked his head and watched the gravy swirl in the pan. Was there any hope that Amanda wouldn't notice Charlotte's interest in pushing them together?

Charlotte appeared beside him, gravy boat in hand. "Let's get that gravy in here before you stir it to death."

"Be my guest." Mitch waved a hand in the direction of the stove as he backed away with a slight bow.

When he looked in the other direction, Amanda grinned at him as their gazes met. Steam rose from the cobbler as she set it on the trivet beside the stove. The delicious smell made his stomach rumble, and the domestic scene that Amanda created as she stood there with the oven mitts still on her hands made his heart thunder. If he hadn't been looking forward to this meal, he might be tempted to run the other way. A woman hadn't captured his attention in a long, long time. Why did the woman have to be one who didn't intend to stick around?

Surveying the kitchen, Mitch reminded himself that he had met Amanda less than eight hours ago. He barely knew anything about her, and he probably didn't need to. She was on her way out of town at the first opportunity. "Need me to do anything?"

"Grab that bowl of beans and sit at the table." Charlotte carried the bowl of mashed potatoes and the gravy boat.

Mitch set the beans down and wondered about the seating arrangements. Whenever he came over to eat with Charlotte, they usually sat on the barstools at the kitchen island. "Where do you want us to sit?"

Charlotte placed the mashed potatoes and gravy on the lace tablecloth. "I'm going to sit here on the end.

You two can sit near me on opposite sides of the table."

"That works for me." Amanda tiptoed up beside him and put the platter of chicken on the table.

Mitch tried to be a gentleman and pull out her chair, but Amanda sat down before he had the chance. He wasn't going to miss that opportunity with Charlotte. He raced to the end of the table and pulled out her chair.

Looking up at him, Charlotte settled in her seat. "Thank you. Since we have a special guest, this is a little more formal than our usual meals."

"You mean I'm not special?" Mitch chuckled as he slid into his chair.

Charlotte reached over and patted his hand, then grasped it as she held out her other hand to Amanda. "You know you're always special in this house. Let's give thanks for our food."

Amanda took Charlotte's hand, then glanced over at Mitch. Her expression told him that she wasn't all too sure about holding his hand, but she reached across the table. He took her small hand in his, his pulse racing faster than a hopped-up engine. Bowing his head, he hoped Charlotte didn't ask him to give thanks because he wasn't sure he could put together a coherent sentence. He breathed a sigh of relief when Charlotte voiced a short, simple prayer thanking the Lord for their guest and the food.

When the prayer ended, Amanda let go of his hand as if it were a hot potato. Did she feel the same electricity he did, or was this craziness all one sided? He shook the question away. He didn't need to know. He needed to put an end to this attraction the same way he disposed of toxic materials at the garage—never to be seen again.

With that thought firmly in place, he picked up the platter of chicken and handed it to Charlotte. "The cook gets first choice."

"Thanks." Charlotte took a piece of chicken and placed it on her plate. "Amanda gets to go next because she's been helping me. She picked the peaches for the cobbler. I've been meaning to get those peaches off the tree, but I just hadn't gotten around to it."

"You shouldn't be up on a ladder picking peaches. You should've told me they needed picking. I could've done that." Mitch took the chicken platter from Amanda after she helped herself.

Charlotte shook her head. "I know, but you're always so busy. I just hate to bother you."

"I'm never too busy to help you." Mitch loaded his plate with potatoes and smothered them in gravy.

"I didn't mind doing it. I've never picked fruit before. It was kinda fun." Amanda glanced between Mitch and Charlotte, then wrinkled her cute little nose. "But I wasn't a fan of peeling them for the cobbler."

Mitch looked down at his plate. Why did she have to be sitting right across from him where she was always in his line of vision? Maybe he shouldn't fight these feelings. He could enjoy her good looks because in days or maybe even hours she would be gone—out of his sight forever. The thought didn't bring him much comfort. Crazy.

Letting his gaze drift to Amanda, Mitch grinned.

"Charlotte makes the best peach cobbler around."

"But I didn't make the cobbler today. Amanda did." Charlotte raised her eyebrows as she stared at Mitch.

Amanda grimaced. "I hope it's good. I wouldn't want to disappoint you."

Mitch wondered if she really meant that. He couldn't help thinking about the conversation he'd had with her father. Temptation swirled around him like a pesky fly. Temptation to pursue Amanda and beat out Jimmy for her attention. Temptation to keep her here to get that car for free. Temptation to act on his attraction to her. None of them good.

While those thoughts troubled his mind, he forced a smile as he looked in her direction. "I'm sure it'll be good if you used Charlotte's recipe."

"I did, but I've never made cobbler before. In fact, I'm not much of a cook." A little smile curving her very kissable mouth, Amanda shrugged.

None of her confession surprised him, but he was in big trouble if he was thinking about kissing her. It was all Jimmy's fault. Mitch couldn't stand to see his braggadocios cousin get the girl. The stupid rivalry had been simmering for years. In fact, the whole disaster with Whitney probably wouldn't have happened without that rivalry. He had brought the heartache on himself because he'd had to beat his cousin at the game of love. Was he falling into the same trap again?

Mitch shouldn't blame his cousin. Mitch had made his own decisions and had pursued the wrong girl. No one had won.

"But she's a quick learner." Charlotte patted Amanda's arm. "I'm sure the cobbler will be delicious, especially with the homemade ice cream Amanda churned this afternoon."

Shaken from his musing, Mitch raised his eyebrows. "You made ice cream, too?"

"Yeah. That was also fun." She wrinkled her nose again as she hunched her shoulders. "And I know that it's good, because I licked the spatula."

"I do that, too." Mitch chuckled, pushing the image of her licking the spatula from his mind. What could they talk about that would keep his thinking on the straight and narrow? The way his mind was working today, maybe not much.

For a few minutes, the conversation lagged as they ate. Thankful for that, Mitch chowed down on the mashed potatoes. Nothing could beat Charlotte's cooking.

"So what are your plans for Amanda's car?" Charlotte asked, then daintily took a bite of her chicken.

Amanda turned to Charlotte. "Technically, it was never my car, and now my dad has sold it to Mitch. I don't have the first clue why he's buying it. It's old, and it doesn't run."

The thought of that car vexed Mitch. Guilt sat in his mind and robbed him of any joy at having that car. Even though he hadn't gone along with Grady's request, Mitch couldn't get the bribe out of his thoughts. "I like to restore cars. It's a challenge."

"Well, that hunk of junk will definitely give you a

challenge." Amanda cocked her head as she looked at him.

"What do you think about the idea of turning this place into a bed-and-breakfast?" Charlotte asked before Mitch could respond to Amanda's statement.

Mitch frowned as Charlotte's question took him by surprise. "You're not serious. It takes a lot of energy to run a B and B."

"Are you suggesting that I don't have any energy?" Charlotte grinned, then winked at Amanda. "Amanda mentioned that this house would make a good one."

Mitch turned to Amanda. "You did? Why would you do something like that?"

Amanda sat back in her chair, her eyebrows raised. "It was just a passing thought. Folks I know in Massachusetts run one, and the layout here is perfect with each bedroom having its own bathroom."

"All I can say is B and Bs require a lot of work."

Charlotte nodded. "But I was thinking if I could get Amanda to stay, she could work for me."

Looking at Amanda, Mitch couldn't visualize Amanda making beds and scrubbing toilets, but then he'd never dreamed she would bake a cobbler. "And what do you think about this?"

Wide-eyed, Amanda stared back at him, then glanced over at Charlotte. "Are you really considering this?"

A twinkle in her eye, Charlotte waved a hand at Amanda. "Mitch asked you a question first."

Amanda turned her attention back to Mitch. "I'm going to Nashville. That's my plan."

"Tomorrow?" Mitch asked.

"I don't know." Amanda let out a sigh that was nearly a cry. "I really need to sleep on this. Please don't pressure me."

Mitch read the angst on Amanda's face. He didn't want to contribute to her distress by asking her to make a decision. It had been less than twelve hours since her whole world had been turned upside down. She deserved some peace in which to decide her immediate future. Her long-range plans hadn't changed. She was headed to Nashville.

Charlotte reached over and patted Amanda's arm. "I'm sorry you feel like we're pressuring you to make a decision. Your idea about the B and B just sent my mind on a path to wishful thinking. When Wilbur was still alive, we considered making this place a B and B, but we decided against it because he was so tied up with the garage. We didn't know whether we could find the help we needed to run the place."

"How come you never mentioned this to me?" Mitch asked. "Dad might have helped. He was always interested in investing in local ventures."

Charlotte shrugged. "We did a business plan and decided we didn't want to take the risk, and there are lots of regulations that go along with opening one. Then Wilbur got sick, and the whole thing was shelved for good. When Amanda mentioned it today, the idea resurfaced. That's all."

Mitch glanced at Amanda to see her reaction. Her expression remained unchanged, and he wasn't about to make any waves. "I'm ready for some of that cobbler."

Charlotte frowned at him. "So soon? We need to let our meal settle first. Then we can have cobbler."

Mitch wasn't going to argue with Charlotte, but he didn't need to let his meal settle. "Can I help with the cleanup?"

"We'll all help." Charlotte placed her flatware on her plate.

Mitch did the same and grabbed his glass. He followed the two women to the sink, where they rinsed their dishes and put them in the dishwasher. When the task was finished, Charlotte looked at him while she motioned toward Amanda. "Have you heard this young lady sing?"

"No." Where was this headed?

"Then you're in for a treat." Charlotte turned to Amanda. "Do you mind playing and singing something for us?"

"I guess not." A look of uncertainty clouded Amanda's features.

"Wonderful." Charlotte clapped her hands "Let's go into the music room."

Charlotte led the way. Mitch brought up the rear as he tagged along behind Amanda. He tried not to notice her curvy figure as she sauntered ahead of him, but he wasn't doing a very good job. Charlotte immediately settled on one of the chairs in the corner and motioned for Mitch to sit on the other one.

Amanda slid onto the piano bench. She sat there with her hands in her lap and looked over at Charlotte. "Do

"Tomorrow?" Mitch asked.

"I don't know." Amanda let out a sigh that was nearly a cry. "I really need to sleep on this. Please don't pressure me."

Mitch read the angst on Amanda's face. He didn't want to contribute to her distress by asking her to make a decision. It had been less than twelve hours since her whole world had been turned upside down. She deserved some peace in which to decide her immediate future. Her long-range plans hadn't changed. She was headed to Nashville.

Charlotte reached over and patted Amanda's arm. "I'm sorry you feel like we're pressuring you to make a decision. Your idea about the B and B just sent my mind on a path to wishful thinking. When Wilbur was still alive, we considered making this place a B and B, but we decided against it because he was so tied up with the garage. We didn't know whether we could find the help we needed to run the place."

"How come you never mentioned this to me?" Mitch asked. "Dad might have helped. He was always interested in investing in local ventures."

Charlotte shrugged. "We did a business plan and decided we didn't want to take the risk, and there are lots of regulations that go along with opening one. Then Wilbur got sick, and the whole thing was shelved for good. When Amanda mentioned it today, the idea resurfaced. That's all."

Mitch glanced at Amanda to see her reaction. Her expression remained unchanged, and he wasn't about to make any waves. "I'm ready for some of that cobbler."

Charlotte frowned at him. "So soon? We need to let our meal settle first. Then we can have cobbler."

Mitch wasn't going to argue with Charlotte, but he didn't need to let his meal settle. "Can I help with the cleanup?"

"We'll all help." Charlotte placed her flatware on her plate.

Mitch did the same and grabbed his glass. He followed the two women to the sink, where they rinsed their dishes and put them in the dishwasher. When the task was finished, Charlotte looked at him while she motioned toward Amanda. "Have you heard this young lady sing?"

"No." Where was this headed?

"Then you're in for a treat." Charlotte turned to Amanda. "Do you mind playing and singing something for us?"

"I guess not." A look of uncertainty clouded Amanda's features.

"Wonderful." Charlotte clapped her hands "Let's go into the music room."

Charlotte led the way. Mitch brought up the rear as he tagged along behind Amanda. He tried not to notice her curvy figure as she sauntered ahead of him, but he wasn't doing a very good job. Charlotte immediately settled on one of the chairs in the corner and motioned for Mitch to sit on the other one.

Amanda slid onto the piano bench. She sat there with her hands in her lap and looked over at Charlotte. "Do you have a request?"

"Play something you plan to use when you go to Nashville." Charlotte sat forward on her chair in anticipation.

Mitch settled back in his chair and hoped he wouldn't have to pretend he liked this. Charlotte had said he was in for a treat, but was he? Saying he liked something when he didn't was something he tried to avoid. "Your audience is waiting."

"I like to use my guitar for my original songs."

Mitch jumped up. "I'll get it for you."

"You know where it is?"

"I watched you lay the case up against the wall." Mitch stopped in the doorway. "Unless you snuck upstairs and moved it."

Amanda chuckled. "Oh yeah. I forgot you helped me take things up to the room."

With that statement echoing in his ears, Mitch scrambled up the stairs and retrieved her guitar. As he walked back down, he reminded himself that she hadn't remembered his help. That should put him in his place. He was an afterthought. When he turned the corner to go back into the room, Amanda played a chord on the piano, then launched into a classical number that he had heard many times, but he didn't know the name of it.

He lounged against the doorjamb and listened. She was lost in the music as her fingers glided across the keys. She had the presence of a concert pianist, not a country singer. What were her compositions like? His earlier wariness abated. Now he could hardly wait.

After the final chord sounded, Mitch applauded and stepped into the room. "That was very good. I didn't know you were a classical pianist."

Amanda gazed at him as she got up and walked toward him. "You can thank my dad. He insisted that I learn to play the piano because that's what my mom would've wanted. I'm glad he pushed me in that direction, but then he didn't want me to pursue music. I still can't figure him out."

Mitch had the same thoughts about her father, but that was better left unsaid. "So here's your guitar."

"Thanks." She took the case, careful not to make contact with him.

As he returned to his chair, he wondered if that meant she had also felt the electricity between them.

After taking the guitar from its case, Amanda sat on one end of the piano bench with the guitar sitting in her lap as she strummed a few chords. She looked over at Charlotte, then back at him. "This is one of the songs I've composed. You might say it's my favorite."

Soft guitar chords filled the room as Amanda leaned over her instrument. Her fingers slid across the strings while she hummed a few bars. Just as she had done while playing the piano, she lost herself in the music. The humming grew a little louder until she started to sing.

"How do I know
When to let go?
How do I know
When to love again?

Why do I try?

Why do I cry

when someone says your name?"

The rich tones of the love song thrummed across Mitch's heartstrings. Her contralto voice enveloped the music room. Her talent shouldn't be left undiscovered, but too often talented singers and songwriters never made the big time. He hated to think of Amanda suffering that outcome.

When Amanda finished singing, Mitch joined Charlotte as they gave Amanda a standing ovation.

Charlotte padded over to Amanda and gave her a hug. "That was wonderful. I hope someone in Nashville realizes how talented you are."

Amanda blushed as she looked up at Charlotte. "Thanks. You're too kind. Would you like to be my PR person?"

"If it would do any good." Charlotte smiled.

Mitch stepped closer, but he wasn't going to give Amanda a hug. "Charlotte's right. You have a great voice."

Amanda gave him a shy smile. "Thanks. You don't happen to work secretly for a record company and want to sign me?"

Mitch chuckled. "Wish I could."

"Me too." Amanda returned her guitar to its case. "How about some of that cobbler?"

"Sounds good to me." Charlotte led the way to the kitchen.

While Mitch followed, the words of the song drifted

through his mind. Did they come from experience? Had she suffered a heartbreaking love? Mitch didn't cry over Whitney anymore, but he knew heartbreak, and he didn't want to go down that path again. That was why he shouldn't get involved in Amanda's life, but maybe it was already too late. Or maybe she would leave tomorrow and save him from himself.

CHAPTER FIVE

Streams of light filtered through the lacy curtains as Amanda rolled over in bed. She blinked her eyes and looked around, disoriented for a moment. Then she remembered. She was in Pineydale, Tennessee. Broken car. Broken dreams. Broken future.

Is that what her future held? Brokenness on every side?

Amanda lay there and stared at the ceiling. She snuggled down in the cozy bed. That definitely wasn't broken. Today was decision day. Had a night's sleep made any difference in her thinking? She sure would hate to trade this comfy bed for the unknown. That was exactly what she'd get in Nashville. Did that thought mean her decision was made?

Amanda glanced around the room until her gaze settled on her guitar as it leaned against the wall near the headboard. She remembered singing for Mitch and Charlotte last night. They both said Amanda had talent, lots of talent. If she stayed here for a while, was she trading her chance at stardom for comfort? She had raced away from Boston because she didn't want to waste time better spent pursuing her dream, but now she was considering postponing that dream. Or maybe she needed to make a wise decision for once and get her life together before she charged off again.

While she lay there, she laced her fingers behind her head and studied the room with light-blue walls and maple furniture. Could she make a difference here? Is that why God had brought her into Charlotte's life? Charlotte seemed to think there was a reason for Amanda's being stuck in this town. Did it have to do with Charlotte or Mitch? Or both?

Sighing, Amanda sat up and swung her legs over the side of the bed. She grabbed her guitar and strummed a few chords. The beginnings of a new song tiptoed through her mind. She picked a few more chords, then set the guitar on the bed and grabbed a pen and paper from the nightstand. She scribbled down the words that poured through her thoughts. Maybe the country air was good for composing.

For the next few minutes she strummed and sang and scribbled until she had a substantial amount of a new song. Amanda glanced at the clock on the bedside table. Nearly seven o'clock. She wondered how soon she could get to the piano and put this song in her music book. Maybe Charlotte was an early riser.

After Amanda washed her face and got dressed, she tiptoed down the stairs, guitar and notebook in hand. The smell of frying bacon drifted through the air. Charlotte was up. Amanda's stomach growled as she moseyed into the kitchen.

Charlotte looked up from the pan where she was cooking the bacon. "Good morning. Did you sleep well?"

maybe she needed to develop some new habits. She glanced over at Charlotte. "These pancakes are wonderful. Is it a special recipe?"

"The one my mother used."

"An old family recipe?"

Charlotte nodded. "I'll teach you how to make them."

"Thanks, but I think I've decided to head to Nashville today. I appreciate your letting me spend the night, but I did some research on open mic nights. Tomorrow night is one I really want to perform at."

"So you're taking the bus?"

"That's the plan."

"Will it get you there on time?"

"If I leave today." Amanda held her breath. She wondered what Charlotte would say.

"So you're packing up and leaving us." Charlotte's brow wrinkled. "Do you have a place to stay?"

"At a hotel."

"And you've booked a room?"

"Not yet. I don't have a valid credit card anymore." Amanda let out a halfhearted laugh. "My dad cut me off."

"I'm worried for you, taking off like this."

Amanda held up a hand. "Hear me out."

"Okay."

"This is my plan. Since you offered me a place to stay, I'm going to take you up on that."

A puzzled frown creased Charlotte's brow. "But I thought you said you're going to Nashville."

"I am, but just for a couple of nights." Amanda

glanced at the ceiling, then back at Charlotte. "That song came to me this morning, and I just knew I had to play it at an open mic event. I can't just stay here and wait who knows how long before I get financially straight. Do you understand?"

Charlotte leaned against the bar as she stared at Amanda. "You're only going to stay two nights to perform, then return here?"

"Yeah. I'm hoping that will at least give me a taste of what to expect."

"Have you bought your ticket?"

Amanda shook her head. "I have to pay cash for everything. I need to go to the bank and cash a check. I plan to walk to town, go to the bank, then purchase my ticket."

"And you're going to haul your guitar with you?"

"I'll have to." Amanda shrugged. "I've hauled it plenty of places. It's not that heavy."

"I just hate to think of you going to Nashville with a bunch of cash." Charlotte waved Amanda over to a small desk in the corner of the kitchen, where a laptop sat. "Let's book you a room online, and you can pay me."

"You'd do that?"

"Of course." Charlotte narrowed her gaze as she looked at Amanda. "And instead of you taking the bus, I think you should drive my car."

Stunned, Amanda stared at Charlotte. Why was this woman being so generous to a stranger? Yeah, she had quoted that verse in the Bible about entertaining strangers, but this was above and beyond assisting someone. "Are you sure you trust me with your car? That's so generous."

"Yes." Charlotte motioned toward the hallway. "When I heard you sing and play yesterday, I just knew you had to find your way to Nashville. I'm glad you decided to go, and I want to make sure you get there."

Tears welled in Amanda's eyes. Her dad had never encouraged her music even though he'd paid for music school. Her sister didn't care, and Maria, her stepmom, was neutral on the subject because she didn't want to go against her husband. Now this woman she had known less than twenty-four hours was giving her more support than she'd ever had from family and friends. "Thank you. You have no idea what this means to me."

Charlotte smiled. "Those tears tell me a little."

"May I give you a hug?" Amanda tried to blink back the tears, but one rolled down her cheek. She quickly wiped it away.

"I'd like that." Charlotte held her arms out, then folded Amanda in them.

Amanda hadn't had a hug like this since she'd finished grad school and her grandma Fran had hugged her hard and congratulated her. Amanda drank in the scent of Charlotte's floral perfume that mingled with the smells left from breakfast.

Amanda swallowed hard as she stepped out of Charlotte's embrace. "Guess I'd better pack up a few things to take with me."

"First, let's get that hotel room booked for you."

After they found a hotel a little over a mile from the open mic venue, Amanda wrote a check for the amount and gave it to Charlotte. "Thanks again. You are such a special person."

Charlotte waved a hand at Amanda. "Don't go giving me too much praise. It might go to my head."

"No one can give you too much praise." Amanda turned toward the stairway, then turned back for a moment. "This is so exciting. I can hardly wait to get on the road."

"You let me know that you've gotten there safely." Charlotte scribbled something on the pad on the desk. "Here's my number. You call as soon as you get there."

"I will." Amanda raced off to pack.

When she returned to the kitchen with her guitar in hand and her backpack slung over her shoulder, Charlotte gave Amanda another quick hug, then handed her the keys. "Drive carefully, and I'll see you in a couple of days."

As Amanda drove through Pineydale on her way to the interstate, she couldn't believe her dream was actually coming true. She drove by Wilbur's Garage and was tempted to stop and say hi to Mitch, but she went right on by. He would learn of her adventure when she returned. He probably didn't care anyway. He had seemed pretty skeptical of success for her in Nashville. And Amanda had to be honest with herself. The odds were against her, but she wanted to defy the odds in the worst way. She had to grab this chance and run with it.

***

The sun sat low in the sky just above the tree line, coloring the clouds with reds, oranges, and pinks. Mitch parked his pickup in front of Charlotte's house, where the windows reflected those colors. Was Amanda still here, or had she left for Nashville? When he hadn't heard from her all day, disappointment he hadn't expected nagged at his thoughts. Obviously, she wasn't concerned about his approval of her decision.

Mitch loped up the front steps and knocked as he opened the door. "Aunt Charlotte."

Charlotte came down the stairs and met him in the front hall. "Well, isn't this a surprise."

"Is your house guest still here?" Mitch looked toward the back of the house when he didn't see Amanda in either the living room or dining room.

"No. She's gone to Nashville."

A sinking sensation hit Mitch in the gut. Her choice to leave shouldn't affect him, but it did. "I thought she'd stay. Guess I was wrong. Did you take her to catch the bus?"

"She didn't take the bus. I gave her my car."

"You did what?" Mitch tried not to yell at his aunt, but his voice came out in a strangled roar.

"Just what I said. I let Amanda drive my car to Nashville." Charlotte put her hands on her hips and stared back at him.

"How could you let her go in your car?" Mitch let out a harsh breath and shook his head. "I don't believe it. You expect her to come back?"

"Yes. She's not a thief. She's not going to steal my car." Charlotte waved a finger at him. "Besides, she's a grown woman, and if I didn't lend her my car, she was going to take off on the bus. I just didn't like that."

Charlotte might not like that Amanda was going to take the bus, but Mitch didn't like that Amanda was halfway across the state in his aunt's car. The whole thing didn't set right with him, but he couldn't ignore the way his heart skipped a beat when Charlotte told him Amanda was coming back.

Mitch took a deep breath to calm himself, but it didn't work. "Yeah, of course she wouldn't steal the car because the police would come after her, but I still can't believe you trusted her with your car. I've had my share of bad experiences when I trusted someone I didn't know that well, or even someone I thought I knew."

Charlotte sighed and gave him an indulgent smile. "Yes, you've been burned a couple of times, but that doesn't mean you should distrust everyone."

"Yeah, but if you can't trust someone you've known forever, how can you trust someone you've just met?"

Charlotte poked her gnarled forefinger into his chest. "Listen here, mister. I've got a lot of years on you, and I'm a pretty good judge of character. That lovely young woman has a talent that shouldn't be overlooked. And I trust her to return just like she said."

Throwing his arms up in the air in surrender, Mitch backed away. "Okay, but I hope you're not sorry."

"I won't be." Charlotte gave him a speculative look. "So you came by today just to find out if Amanda was still here?"

After his tirade, did he want to admit that she'd guessed the reason for his visit, or should he play it cool and admit nothing? He wasn't hiding anything from Charlotte anyway, so he might as well be honest. He took a deep breath and let it out slowly. "Yes, I wanted to see if she was still here."

"I thought so. She'll be back. You can count on it." Charlotte gave him a knowing smile. "And when she returns, you should act on the attraction. She's a pretty girl, but there's more to her than good looks."

"I don't know enough about her to get involved."

"Well, get to know her." Charlotte grinned. "You know you'd like to, so don't be afraid."

"Once bitten, twice shy."

"I never knew you were a coward."

Mitch shook his head. "It's more than that. Amanda reminds me of Whitney in too many ways."

"Like I said, I didn't know you were a coward."

"You want me to pursue a woman who has no interest in staying in this town? Her heart is set on Nashville and a singing career." Mitch gritted his teeth. Arguing with Aunt Charlotte was like arguing with his father. She was never going to see things Mitch's way. "I'll consider your advice. Maybe. Now I'm off to see my folks. I'm meeting them at the country club. I hope Dad's in a good mood."

Charlotte laughed. "You can argue with him instead of me. Have a good time."

"Sure." Mitch turned toward the front door. "Did you

tell Amanda to let you know when she got there?"

"Can't get that woman off your mind, can you?" Charlotte raised her eyebrows.

"I'm concerned about your car."

"Sure you are." Charlotte gave him a wry smile. "She said she'd call, but I suspect she's scoping out the territory and getting things lined up before she takes time to call me. She had a whole list of places she planned to contact about finding a spot in their open mic events."

"So in other words, she should've called by now." Mitch motioned to the grandfather clock that ticked away in the foyer.

"She'll call."

"I hope you're right." Mitch opened the front door. "Talk to you later."

"Say hi to your folks."

"Will do." With a wave, Mitch sprinted to his pickup. As he started the engine, he said a little prayer that he could get through this dinner with his parents without any arguments. And he said a little prayer that Charlotte's trust in Amanda wasn't misplaced.

***

The hotel room invited Amanda in like a welcoming friend. The place was even better in person than the photos she had seen on Charlotte's computer. The price of the room was a little bit of a splurge, but she would make up the difference in not having to buy a bus ticket.

She set her guitar on the chair near the window, then opened the draperies and sheers to look out on the city. A colorful sunset of reds, golds, and oranges was a backdrop for the buildings near the hotel. Her heart thumped at the prospect of getting to play her music in Nashville. She had to pinch herself to make sure she wasn't dreaming. She was really in the Music City.

Giddiness captured her, and she sprinted across the room and flung herself onto the bed. She lay there for a few minutes and let the excitement take over her mind. She wished she had someone to share this with—someone who really cared. Of course, there was Charlotte, but Amanda longed for someone in her family to cheer her on. What would Kelsey say?

Amanda thought about calling her sister, but a call to Charlotte had to come first. Amanda grabbed her phone and punched in Charlotte's number. The phone rang three times.

Finally Charlotte answered. "Amanda, did you make it to Nashville okay?"

The sound of Charlotte's voice brought comfort to Amanda's heart. Maybe her family didn't care what she was doing, but someone did. "I did. I'm at the hotel."

"Did you get into the open mic event you were hoping for?"

Amanda sighed. "I put my name on the list. I won't know until I show up when I play. The open mic event starts at eight and goes until everyone has played. I get to play two songs. So I'm getting ready."

"Are you going to try the Bluebird Café? Wilbur took

me there when we visited Nashville a good number of years ago."

"That's a long shot. Besides, their open mic is on Mondays. So I've missed it. I'll try another time." Amanda walked back to the window and looked out. "I'm so glad you let me drive your car. The woman who checked me in asked about my music, since she saw my guitar. When I told her I played a mix of pop, country, and Christian music, she told me about a place that kind of caters to Christian music. I'm going there tomorrow night, and it's a bit of a drive from downtown."

"Wonderful. I'm so glad I could help by letting you use my car.

"So will there be talent scouts in the audience to hear the performers?"

Amanda could only wish that was the case. "Not usually. Tonight I already have a spot to play. I called as soon as I got here and reserved my place. According to the information I have, everyone who calls in and leaves a message gets to play. Tomorrow night there are contest judges. Either way, if you're good, people will notice and maybe refer you to someone in the industry. Anyway, I'm only here for two nights, so I can't expect much. I just want to get a feel for the music scene, since I've never experienced this before. I want to see what it's all about."

"Good for you." Happy encouragement sounded in Charlotte's voice. "I'll be praying for you."

"Thanks. I appreciate that." This was the first time someone had ever said a prayer for her music ambitions, and Charlotte's promise to pray reminded Amanda that she should put all of this in God's hands. That was hard to do. What if it wasn't in God's plan for her to be a success in this business? She didn't want to consider that possibility. Why would God give her this talent and then never give her the chance to share it?

"Is it appropriate to say 'break a leg,' or is that only for actors?"

Amanda laughed. "It's good for musicians, too."

"Good to know." Charlotte laughed in return. "I can hardly wait to hear all about your adventure when you get back."

Charlotte's comment made Amanda realize that she did have someplace to go. Knowing that gave her a sense of security. Although she debated with herself about staying in Nashville rather than returning to Pineydale, she knew the wise decision was to get a taste of the Nashville music scene for a couple of days, then go back. Charlotte and that little town were like a safety net. Amanda had someplace to land, even if it was nearly three hundred miles away.

"Thanks again for everything. I'll be in touch again to let you know what's happening."

"I look forward to it. Bye for now."

Amanda said goodbye and ended the phone call. As she stood there thinking about her future, Mitch's image drifted through her mind. Since she'd left Pineydale, she'd done a good job of not thinking about him. But when he came to mind, she couldn't help wishing he cared about what she was doing as much as Charlotte did.

That was just plain silly. Amanda didn't really know him. She tried to tell herself that he wasn't the kind of guy who should interest her. He might be all wrong, but the way he treated his aunt told Amanda that he could be just right.

Amanda tried to shove all thoughts of Mitch away. She needed to concentrate on her music, not some guy who looked at her with a jaundiced eye. Even though he had been more than kind, he had a barrier built around him that said, *Stay out of my life*. She didn't know if that was the way he looked at all women or just at her.

Time to stop thinking about Mitch Cunningham. She had music to think about instead.

Tuning her guitar was at the top of her to-do list. She went over her songs again, then tuned her guitar once more. She got ready with nervous energy roiling her insides. When she was dressed and ready to go, she punched the venue address in to her phone. She wasn't sure whether she was hungry or just nervous. Hopefully, she could find a place to grab a quick bite to eat on her way, but maybe she was too nervous to eat. She'd never had this feeling when she did open mic events in the Boston area, but more was riding on these Nashville events.

Spying a fast-food place, she turned the car into the drive-through lane. She let out a harsh breath as she waited in line to give her order. Once she was back on the road, she let the little bag of food sit on the passenger seat. She couldn't bring herself to eat it. After she found a parking place, she should try to eat something.

Minutes later, Amanda pulled into a parking lot near the venue. She grabbed the bag from the seat and opened it as her stomach rumbled. As much as she didn't feel like eating, she should. She certainly didn't want her stomach to growl while she sang. She ate about half the food and hoped that would get her through until she performed.

With her guitar in hand, she made her way to the venue less than a block away. She stepped inside, stopping to let her eyes adjust to the dim light before she ventured farther into the place. She had arrived well ahead of the open mic time, but the place was filled with patrons who listened to a duo, filling the venue with a country tune. She found a table and ordered a cola. Glancing around the room, she wondered how many other people were here for the open mic night. Too timid to strike up a conversation with anyone, she huddled at her table with her drink.

When the open mic time arrived, Amanda's heart raced. Surely she wasn't first on the list. The instructions said songwriters would perform in the order they had called in for a spot. She hadn't called until late in the afternoon. Although she didn't want to go first, she also didn't want to sit through dozens of other performances and get more nervous by the minute.

Amanda took a deep breath as a woman, carrying a guitar, went onto the stage. She settled behind the microphone and began to sing. Amanda eased back in her chair as she listened to the song. In all the open mic events she had done in the Boston area, she had never judged the other performances, but here she was thinking that her song could beat this one. Was she being too harsh or thinking more of herself than she should? Her own performance would answer that question.

The night dragged on, and surprisingly, Amanda's nerves disappeared. Some songs were excellent, and others weren't. The crowd grew antsy during the less-than-stellar singing. When her time finally came, she bounded up to the stage with new enthusiasm. She would treat this just like the open mic events in Massachusetts. She had always conquered the crowd.

When she started her song, the low hum of conversation continued throughout the place. Even though her voice was strong and steady over the sound system, the buzz of the crowd didn't dissipate. This was a tougher audience than she had expected. Throughout the evening they'd liked the music, but they'd also liked their conversation. Despite the applause after she finished, her heart sank. She hadn't made a conquest of this audience.

Discouragement dogged her all the way back to the hotel. What should she expect from her first performance? Accolades? Instant discovery? Miracles? None of those things should even be on her radar. This would take time and numerous visits to many venues. One night didn't make or break a career. Never give up. That had to be her motto.

***

Soft elevator music played from the speakers in the country club dining room. As Mitch stopped at the doorway, he spied his parents sitting on the far side of the room, along with his younger brother, Alec, and his wife, Shannon. They had made the trip from Johnson City for the weekly family meeting. His sister was blessed to live in another state and didn't have to attend the command performance every week."

As Mitch drew near the table, his father, a tall man with a full head of thick graying hair, stood and extended his hand. "Glad you could make it, Mitchell."

"Did you think I wasn't coming?" Mitch shook his father's hand, then leaned over and gave his mother, Donna, a kiss on the cheek. With her carefully coiffed and colored hair that didn't show a hint of gray, she still looked younger than her sixty years.

His father glanced at the expensive watch on his arm, then waved the server over to the table. "I was beginning to wonder. The rest of us have ordered."

"I stopped to see Charlotte before I came." Mitch pulled out the empty chair next to his mom and sat down, then quickly ordered the pulled pork sliders, his usual.

Graham knit his eyebrows, producing the beginnings of a frown. "Good thing you stopped by, since you foisted a stranger on her."

Mitch gritted his teeth. He hadn't foisted anything on

Charlotte. He'd asked, and she was glad to take in Amanda. Mitch wasn't going to set the record straight. He had learned long ago that arguing with his father was fruitless. "Charlotte's doing fine. Her guest is in Nashville for a couple of days."

"Another wannabe musician." Graham shook his head. "They're a dime a dozen."

His dad's statement made Mitch angry, but he recognized he'd had the same thoughts about Amanda when he'd met her. So he wasn't that different from his father. Then Mitch had heard her sing. His negative opinion of her ambitions washed away in the sound of her songs. "Charlotte's enjoying the company."

"I just hope she doesn't let her company take advantage." Graham stared at Mitch.

No matter what Mitch said, his father would find a negative slant. Better to change the subject. "So, Mom, how's the fundraiser going?"

"It's going well." His mom smiled and leaned closer. "But I'm still looking for more entertainment for our concert night. What about Charlotte's guest? Do you think she'd be willing to contribute?"

Mitch shrugged. He didn't know enough about Amanda to gauge whether she'd want to do something like that. "I could talk to her when she gets back, or you could go over to Charlotte's and ask."

Donna pointed her finger at Mitch. "I'll let you do the asking, since you know her and I don't."

That was just it. Mitch didn't know her. Would she be open to such a suggestion? She'd mentioned that her cousin or some relative was a cancer survivor, so maybe there was a good chance she'd be willing to support a cancer fundraising project. "Sure. I can do that."

"Then you're going to sign up for the golf part of the fundraiser?" Alec looked Mitch's way. "Dad wants us to form a team for the tournament. I got a guy from work who's a great player and can round out our team."

Mitch shook his head. "Are you sure you want me on your team? Golf isn't my sport."

Alec chuckled. "Yeah. We know that, but it's a best-ball tournament, and besides, you get sponsors who will donate a flat amount, or they can play the game by donating money for birdies, pars, etcetera."

"They better line up to donate for bogies, double or triple bogies for that matter, on my scorecard."

Graham clapped Mitch on the back. "It's all for fun and a good cause."

Smiling, Mitch nodded. His dad said that now, but when he got on the golf course, it wasn't all for fun. It was all about winning. "Okay. I'm in, but I'm still planning to go to Boston to ride in the Pan-Massachusetts Challenge."

Donna shook her head. "I don't understand why you have to go way up there to ride a bike to raise money for cancer."

"I want to ride in Wilbur's memory. I've been planning this ever since a buddy from college told me about it last year."

"Well, it just seems silly to travel so far."

Mitch wished he hadn't asked his mom about the

fundraiser. Was there any topic of conversation that wouldn't put him at odds with his parents? Maybe he should just keep his mouth shut and let everyone else do the talking. He hoped their food would come soon.

While Mitch sat there wishing he were someplace else, Alec tapped the side of his water glass with his spoon. "Shannon and I have some news. We're expecting."

"Congratulations!" Happiness for his brother and sister-in-law welled up inside Mitch. "Ya'll will make great parents. Any idea what you're having?"

Shannon shook her head. "Not yet. Next doctor's appointment will probably tell. We're so excited."

"I can hardly wait to be an uncle. Uncle Mitch. Sounds good." But that meant Mitch lacked one more thing in his father's eyes. Alec had the perfect job, the perfect wife, and now he would have the perfect grandchild. Mitch didn't have any of those. He had failed in all quarters.

Mitch watched his parents' joy as they exclaimed over the prospect of being grandparents. Despite the happiness he felt for his brother, Mitch couldn't stifle the jealousy that inched its way into his thoughts. He pushed it away. He wanted only the best for Alec and Shannon. Envy shouldn't have a place in his heart.

For the rest of the evening, the topic of babies, due dates, and baby showers filled the conversations. Mitch sat back and didn't say much. The good news had saved him from more awkward talk with his parents. Sometimes, he felt like a stranger in his own family, but he still loved them.

When dinner was over, Mitch made his excuses and bid everyone goodbye. As he moseyed to his pickup, he thought about Amanda. Had she called Charlotte? Should he stop and ask? Why was he interested anyway? He slid behind the wheel and stared out at the darkening landscape. Was Amanda on his mind because she was the first woman who had captured his attention since Whitney?

Mitch couldn't answer those questions. He started his pickup and drove toward home, the tiny house that used to belong to his mom's parents. Both of his parents had come from humble backgrounds. Most of the time, his father didn't remember that. He only remembered his success, the money he had made, and his standing in the community. He was a big fish in a little pond, and he enjoyed every minute of it and expected Mitch to feel the same way. He didn't, and that was a source of enmity between them.

Notoriety, fame, or riches didn't matter to Mitch. He liked being a little fish in a little pond. He enjoyed the quiet life he lived in Pineydale. The only thing he didn't like here was having everyone know his business. That was never truer than when Whitney and he ended their relationship. People felt sorry for him for months. All he felt was relief that he hadn't made the mistake of marrying her.

When Mitch drove by Charlotte's house, he didn't see any lights shining from the front rooms. He could only guess that she had already gone to bed or was reading in her bedroom at the back of the house. She loved to read. He had given her an e-reader for her birthday. She had complained at first about the newfangled gadget, but soon she was thanking him because she could adjust the font for easier reading.

He couldn't find out about Amanda tonight. He didn't know why she consumed his thoughts. Her car, her father, and her lack of resources troubled him. He had paid a fair price for her car, but the money had gone to her father, who seemed bent on keeping his daughter on a tight leash. Mitch didn't want to get caught up in that battle, but he had the bad feeling the chances of that happening were slim.

The picket fence around his front yard cast long shadows in the waning light. He drove his pickup into the detached garage and shut off the engine. As he walked to the house, a dog barked in the distance, and stars danced around the half-moon. Despite his mixed feeling about Pineydale, the peaceful little town was home.

Mitch settled on the couch and grabbed the TV remote. Maybe he could find a west-coast baseball game to finish off the evening. He had a feeling he wasn't going to sleep well tonight. He had too much on his mind. Mostly how he was going to deal with his interest in one pretty songwriter.

CHAPTER SIX

The following night, the buzz of soft conversation and occasional laughter swirled through the area filled with round tables and chairs. Amanda joined two other songwriters on the stage at the front of the large room. She plugged in her guitar and settled on the middle chair of the three that sat on the stage.

The competition consisted of several rounds of three contestants. The live audience and those watching online could vote for their favorite song at the end of the competition. That audience winner and the winner chosen by the professional judges from the music industry would move on to the semifinal round in a few weeks.

Amanda was contestant number eleven, performing between the two other contestants who joined her on the stage. So far a couple of the songs, in her opinion, were very good, but others were cringeworthy. She wasn't sure how she would stack up to the others who were yet to perform. Her chance would tell that tale, and she hoped it was a good one.

Trying to show her interest in the woman who sang before her, Amanda tapped her foot to the music even though the tune was lackluster. The competition was all about the song, not necessarily the singer, but surely a good singing voice would make the number sound better. Amanda had confidence in that. She didn't know about her song. The open mic events she'd been a part of in Massachusetts were all about the quality of the performance. This was something altogether different.

Was this something she should pray about? Was it selfish to ask God to help her win? What did God have planned for her life? Her earthly father didn't approve and didn't have these plans for her. She wished she knew what her heavenly Father had in mind. She could only do her best.

After the other woman finished and the applause died, Amanda took a deep breath and straightened her shoulders as she went to the microphone. The emcee introduced her, and she smiled at the audience. "Thanks. This is my song, 'I'm Not Afraid.'"

She strummed a couple of chords in the intro, then took another deep breath. Her voice sounded strong and confident.

"I'm not afraid when you are by my side.

I'm not afraid when you are my guide.

Let your light surround me.

Keep me close to you.

Be my partner in all I do."

After Amanda got through those first few lines, her nerves settled, and she was lost in the music. When she strummed the last chord, applause filled the room, but she couldn't tell what the judges were thinking. She had done her best. That was all she could do. Now she had to wait until the end of the night to find out the results. She hated the waiting. It was worse than the performing.

An hour later as the last contestants left the stage, anticipation filled the room. Now the voting would begin. Amanda's heart raced, and a lump rose in her throat. She glanced at the other performers and smiled as she tried to relieve the tension in her shoulders. When the emcee came back on stage, she held her breath. She was as afraid of hearing the results as she was afraid of not winning.

"Okay, folks, we have the audience's pick for the evening. That goes to contestant number fourteen, George Duncan. Come on up here." The emcee spent time congratulating the winner and giving him the prize from the event sponsor.

Amanda's stomach sank, and she let out her breath in a whoosh. She still had a possibility to be the judges' choice. Did she have a chance?

After the sponsors took several photos of the audience winner, the emcee stepped to the mic again. "Okay, folks, it's time to announce the judges' pick for tonight. Can I get a drumroll?"

Audience members tapped their fingers against the table in a mock drumroll as the emcee looked at the paper in his hand.

"Tonight's winner is contestant number three, Josie Adams."

Amanda applauded, but she couldn't help the deflated feeling in her chest. She wasn't used to losing when it came to her music. She had won numerous competitions over the years. But those were all about the performance, not about the song. She had to learn how to improve her songwriting. She'd taken courses on how to write song lyrics in college. Why didn't that translate into a winning song?

Fighting back the disappointment, she had to remember what she'd told herself after last night's event. One night didn't make or break a career, but two failures in a row didn't help her ego or her confidence. What had she expected? Overnight success? She should know better than that. This business wasn't easy. Persistence would win the day, not pessimism.

Amanda tried to keep her spirits up as the photographer took more photos of the winners. Then the emcee ended the event by inviting everyone to stay and network and even say hello to the judges. Amanda's first reaction was to go back to the hotel and hide out with her discouragement, but that wouldn't gain her anything. She had to put on a happy face and joined the crowd.

As Amanda stood there trying to think good thoughts, Josie, who petite with light brown hair and about Amanda's age, approached. "Amanda? Right?

"Yeah. You're Josie. Congratulations on winning the judges' award."

"Thanks." The other woman nodded and pointed to a nearby table where several other contestants sat. "Some of us are going to order a pizza to share. Would you like to join us?"

Amanda smiled, doing her best to push her jealousy aside. "I'd like that. Thanks for inviting me."

"I really liked your song." Josie led the way to the

table.

"Thanks. It's a brand-new one. I debated about doing it or one of my older ones tonight."

Josie nodded. "I know what you mean. Sometimes it's hard to know which one to perform when you only get to choose one."

"Are you from around here?" Amanda pulled out a chair and sat down next to Josie.

"About an hour away in Bowling Green, Kentucky. What about you?"

"Complicated story." Amanda went on to explain about driving from Boston and her car breaking down in Pineydale.

"You were fortunate to meet some nice people." Josie pulled her cell phone out of her pocket. "Would you like to exchange numbers?"

"Sure." Amanda fished her cell phone out of her purse. "Do you do many of these kinds of events?"

Josie shrugged. "I'm thinking about it. What about you?"

"I really can't make any plans since I don't have my own transportation. I need to figure out a lot of things, but being here tonight makes me think I need to be here or live closer than Pineydale. It's nice that you're only an hour away."

"That's true."

Amanda and Josie chatted as the group ordered drinks and a pizza to share. They talked shop, and Amanda exchanged phone numbers with several more people. Glad she had stayed, she wished there was some way she could move here. But she'd learned enough about rentals in Nashville to know she had a slim chance of renting an apartment unless she had a job. She couldn't rent a decent apartment unless she had a decent salary. Living on the money she would make from a minimum-wage job was out of the question. And she'd run through her savings too quickly if she had to pay for a hotel room, even one of those extended-stay places.

She had made one big mistake. She hadn't planned ahead for anything. No plans for a job. No plans for housing. No plans for any kind of emergency. How stupid she'd been. Now Pineydale was her only answer.

Amanda stayed until Josie said she had to leave. They walked out to the parking lot together. The lights beaming down from the top of tall poles illuminated the vehicles and cast long shadows across the pavement. With her key in one hand and her guitar case in the other, Amanda headed toward the spot where she had parked the car.

Stopping dead in her tracks, Amanda looked at the empty space. Was she confused? The parking lot wasn't like a mall parking lot where it was easy to lose your car, and she was sure this was the place where she had parked. She turned around in a circle as she surveyed the area. She had definitely pulled Charlotte's car into this parking space. She remembered the little sign advertising the pizza that sat at the curb. What had happened to her car?

"Josie. Josie." Amanda ran after her new friend.

Josie looked over from where she stood beside her

vehicle. "What's the matter?"

"I don't know what happened to my car." Amanda's voice came out in a strangled cry.

Josie walked toward Amanda. "You mean the lady's car you borrowed?"

Amanda nodded. "What am I going to do?"

"Are you sure you parked on this side of the lot?"

"I'm sure. I remember that little sign with the pizza on it." Amanda pointed toward the empty space. "I remember it because it seemed like a weird little sign that no one could see unless they parked right there."

"True. That is odd." Josie frowned. "Do you think someone stole the car?"

"That's the only explanation." Amanda wanted to cry. "I don't have a clue what to do."

Josie let out a long sigh. "I guess you'll have to call the police and report it."

"How can I do that when it isn't even my car? I'm not sure I even remember what model it is."

"That is a problem." Josie shrugged. "You still need to talk to the police and see what they say. You want me to stay with you?"

"That's asking a lot. It's late, and you still have to drive home."

Josie shook her head. "I don't mind. Really."

"I appreciate it." Amanda knit her eyebrows. "Should we go back inside?"

"Yeah, and I think you should tell the management. They'll want to know." Josie motioned toward her car. "I'd better go lock my car again. I don't want mine to get stolen."

After Josie returned, Amanda hurried into the building and stopped at the front counter to ask for the manager.

"Is there some kind of problem?" asked the young woman at the counter.

Amanda nodded. "I think my car was stolen out of the parking lot."

"Are you sure?" The woman narrowed her gaze. "Maybe you forgot where you parked."

"No. My car's missing. I'm going to call the police, but I wanted to let the manager know in case you have a security camera for the parking lot."

The woman gave Amanda a halfhearted smile. "I'll be right back."

Amanda turned to Josie. "What do you think they'll do?"

"I'm sure they don't want bad publicity with the police showing up, but it would be nice if they do have a security camera. Lots of places have them these days."

Amanda got out her phone. "While we're waiting, I'll put in the call to the police."

Amanda searched on her phone for a number to call. She located a nonemergency number and tapped it. When someone answered, she explained the situation. The person on the other end of the line informed Amanda that a police unit would arrive when one was available, probably within fifteen minutes unless they had an emergency.

After Amanda punched the little red button on her

phone, she told Josie what the dispatcher had said. "So I guess we wait."

"Should you contact the owner?" Josie gave Amanda a concerned look.

Amanda glanced back at her phone. "It's nearly midnight. She's an elderly woman and will surely be in bed by now."

"Yeah, but you need to get all the important information about the car from her." Josie raised her eyebrows until they disappeared beneath her bangs.

Amanda sighed. "I know, but this is so awful. I'm going to wake her up and give her bad news besides."

"It's got to be done. Better get the info before the police arrive."

Amanda nodded and scrolled through her contacts until she came to Charlotte's number. Her heart pounding, Amanda made the call.

Charlotte answered on the fourth ring, her voice groggy. "Hello."

"Charlotte, this is Amanda."

"Amanda? Why are you calling so late? Are you okay?"

"I'm really sorry to call at this time of night, but I have some bad news. I think someone stole your car."

"My car? Stolen?" Charlotte paused. "Oh my! Are you sure?"

"I parked it in the lot by the venue where I had my competition tonight. When I got ready to go back to the hotel, it wasn't there."

"Have you contacted the police?"

"Yes. They're on their way, and I need all the information about the car to give them. I need the make, model, year, and the VIN number. Can you get all that for me?"

"It'll take a few minutes to find the VIN number. Then I'll call you back."

"Okay." Amanda forced herself not to cry. "I'm so sorry this has happened. You don't deserve this after being so nice to me."

"Don't worry about me, dear. I'm safe here at home with plenty of friends to give me a lift if I need it." Charlotte's sigh sounded loud over the phone. "I'm worried about you. What will you do in a strange town without a car? How will you get back to the hotel?"

That was just like Charlotte to think about someone else rather than her own problems. "I can take a cab if I have to. Then I can take the bus back to Pineydale tomorrow."

"No bus. You need to save your money. We'll find someone to come get you." Something in Charlotte's voice made Amanda decide not to argue. "I'll call you back in a few minutes."

Amanda looked over at Josie. "You should head home. Who knows how long this will take."

"I hate to leave you here." Josie wrinkled her brow.

"I can always take a cab back to the hotel."

"If you're staying in downtown Nashville, that could be a little pricey."

Amanda's phone rang before she could reply. "Hi, Charlotte."

"Amanda, I have all the information you need," Charlotte said.

"Thanks. I'll write that down, then put it in my phone." Amanda searched through her purse and came up with a pen and paper. She scribbled on the details on the paper. After Amanda had all the information, she tried to talk Charlotte out of sending someone for her, but there was no convincing the older woman that it wasn't necessary. "Charlotte, I can't thank you enough. Would it be okay to call you again tonight if the police need to talk to you?"

"I'll do whatever I need to in order to get my car back. Don't you worry. I'll be praying."

Amanda took a deep breath. Yeah. Praying. That was what she needed to do. "Thanks, Charlotte. You're the best."

"No. God's the best. He'll be with you."

"Thanks for the reminder. Bye for now." Feeling less stressed, Amanda ended the call.

"Did you get what you needed?" Josie asked.

"Yeah." Amanda waved her phone in the air. "I'd better put all this info into the notes on my phone."

"I'm going to stay and give you a ride back to your hotel after you talk with the police." Josie motioned to some chairs near the door. "Let's sit down."

"You're too nice. You barely know me, and you're so willing to help." Amanda followed Josie and sat down

"It's nothing. Tomorrow's my day off, so I can sleep in." Josie shrugged. "It's my chance to help someone in need. Paying it forward."

"I've got a lot of paying forward to do. So many people have helped me in the last few days. Maybe that's why the song I sang tonight practically wrote itself the morning after my car broke down." Amanda thought about Charlotte and Mitch and Josie and the way God had used them in her life. Staying in Pineydale and helping Charlotte would only be a small part in paying back all the good things people had done.

"Yeah. Your song really has a great message, and I believe God puts people in our lives for a purpose." Josie smiled.

"You don't know how much I appreciate this. It's nice that we share a faith in God." Amanda tapped her fingers on the phone's screen. "Now I've got to get this about the car into my notes."

Josie nodded. "That's why I chose this venue, because they're friendly to Christian music. Would you like me to read it to you so all you have to do is type?"

"That'd be great."

Just as Amanda finished typing the last bit of information, two police officers strode through the doors. She jumped up and approached them. "Officers, I'm the one who wants to report a stolen car."

Worry nibbled at the corner of Amanda's mind. Would they think it was strange that she was reporting the theft of a car she didn't own? Would they find that suspicious? Saying a silent prayer, she explained the situation to them. They appeared to understand, but concern still clouded her thoughts when they asked if she was sure she had locked the car.

One officers gave Amanda a nod. "Did you use a key fob to lock the car?"

"Yes, why?"

"The car was most likely hacked."

"Hacked?" Amanda didn't understand.

The younger officer nodded. "These days car thieves have gotten quite sophisticated. They use a device, which works by picking up the signal from your key fob. When you locked the car using the key fob, the thieves were probably close by in the parking lot. Once they got the signal from your key fob, they transferred it to a relay box that was used to start your car. All of this can take place in less than two minutes."

"Why did they choose my friend's car?" Amanda shook her head.

"They like that model, and it's one they've probably stolen before."

When the manager came out, the officers asked about a security camera.

The manager nodded. "We have one. You're welcome to look at it."

The officers asked Amanda to wait while they viewed the security footage. She sat down by Josie and let out a loud sigh. "I suppose there's little chance they'll find the car. I guess I just shouldn't have a car. First mine broke down. Then the one I borrowed got stolen. What a mess. I made the wrong decision to come to Nashville."

"No you didn't. Otherwise, we wouldn't have met." Josie smiled. "And I think you're a good songwriter.

Don't give up."

"Thanks. I'm glad I met you, too." Amanda put her elbows on her knees and leaned into her hands.

Just then the officers reappeared, and Amanda hurried over to meet them. "Did the security footage show you anything?"

The older officer looked her in the eye. "The thief was waiting in another car in the lot. As soon as you were out of sight, he got out of his car. Within two minutes, he had unlocked your car and driven it away."

"Could you see who it was?"

The older officer shook his head. "He was wearing a cap, so you couldn't see his face. It was almost as if he knew where the security camera was located, because he kept his back to the camera."

Amanda sighed. "So now what do I do?"

"Here's a copy of our report. You'll need this when you contact the insurance company about the theft. They like you to wait a couple of weeks to see if the car is recovered, but after that be sure to file the report." A grim expression painted the officer's face. "Chances are we won't find the car. Sorry to give you that news."

"That's what I expected." Amanda sighed again.

After the officers left, she turned to Josie. "Guess it's finally time to leave."

"Let's get on the road." Josie headed for the door.

On the drive back to the hotel, neither of them said much. Amanda wasn't sure how much sleep she would get tonight. Her mind would have a hard time shutting down. Was there a little black cloud hanging over her head? How could she have a positive attitude when everything seemed to be going wrong? As she said goodbye and thanks to Josie, Amanda reminded herself that God was there in times of trouble. That was what she had sung about tonight. She had to put that into practice.

***

With Charlotte tagging along, Mitch punched the button for the fifth floor in the hotel elevator. Charlotte had said very little on the nearly five-hour drive from Pineydale to Nashville. She'd had her nose in a book the entire time, and that suited him just fine. His opinion about this fiasco with Amanda was something Charlotte didn't want to hear.

For whatever reason, Charlotte had practically adopted Amanda, or at the least made her the granddaughter she had never had. Mitch wasn't altogether sure this was good even though he'd been the one to set the whole thing into motion when he'd asked Charlotte to give Amanda a room. He'd never expected that she would decide to stay...or had he?

He didn't want to acknowledge his attraction to the pretty musician. He was nuts to even consider acting on it. A career in Nashville claimed her heart, and he wasn't going to get in the way of another woman who put him second.

As Mitch followed Charlotte out of the elevator, he looked at the sign indicating the direction of Amanda's room and motioned down the hallway. "To the right."

"You know you can say you told me so." Charlotte looked at him over the top of her glasses. "I won't be offended."

"I'd rather not talk about it. Besides, I'd be wrong to blame Amanda."

"I'm so glad you've cleared the air on that account." Charlotte stopped at the door to Amanda's room, then turned to look at him. "I know you said you're not going to blame Amanda, but don't you dare say one unkind word to her."

Mitch frowned at his aunt. "Do you think I'm a heartless bully?"

Charlotte patted his arm. "No, but I've had the feeling all day that you're unhappy with me."

Mitch leaned over and gave Charlotte a hug. "How could I be unhappy with my favorite great-aunt?"

"You don't want me to answer that question." Charlotte knocked on the door.

In seconds Amanda opened it, her face sporting a worried look that mirrored Charlotte's expression most of the morning. Before Amanda could get a word out, Charlotte enveloped the younger woman in a hug.

Amanda's eyes swam with tears. "You're too kind to come get me like this."

"Kindness has nothing to do with it. I want to talk to the police about my car." Charlotte turned to Mitch. "Get her suitcase, and we'll be on our way."

"I need to stop at the desk to turn in the key." Amanda picked up her purse and guitar case.

"You can do that while Mitch and I head out to his pickup." Charlotte sashayed out the door and down the hall.

"Charlotte is a woman on a mission. Don't get in her way." Chuckling, Mitch raised his eyebrows.

"I see." Amanda's tears had disappeared, but she didn't look any happier.

Mitch felt the strange urge to gather her in his arms and comfort her just as Charlotte had done. He shut down that thought before he took action on it. When he looked at her, his insides turned to jelly. Her presence jumbled his emotions. How was he going to survive the trip back to Pineydale with her just feet away in the cab of his pickup? Thankfully, Charlotte would be there to act as a buffer, or at least, that was what he hoped.

As Mitch and Amanda joined Charlotte in the elevator, they said nothing to each other. They rode to the lobby, their eyes trained on the numbers that lit up as they passed each floor. When the door slid open, he couldn't get out of there fast enough. Pulling Amanda's suitcase, he didn't look back as he headed to the parking lot as if something dangerous was chasing him.

He stowed the suitcase behind the backseat of the extended cab, then climbed into the driver's seat. He started the engine and the air conditioning. Charlotte and Amanda emerged through the glass doors at the front of the hotel. They laughed about something as they crossed the parking lot. The way Amanda made his aunt smile warmed Mitch's heart. Despite the mess about the car, Amanda was good for Charlotte.

But Amanda wasn't good for him. He put that thought front and center in his mind.

Charlotte opened the door to the backseat. "Amanda, you can put your guitar back here with me and sit up front with Mitch."

Mitch gripped the steering wheel and gritted his teeth. Charlotte was up to her old matchmaking tricks, but he didn't say anything. That would only make matters worse. He caught a glimpse of Amanda's expression. She didn't look happy either, but she had also learned there was no arguing with Charlotte.

Amanda stowed her guitar case in the back, then climbed into the front seat and buckled her seat belt. She gave him a sideways glance. "How do we know which police station to go to?"

"Call the number you used last night."

Amanda gave him a sheepish grin. "Yeah. That makes sense."

While she called, Mitch worked to get his thoughts under control. He was thinking how cute she looked as she grinned. She made his heart race. How could he stop that? Just not look in her direction. Keep his eyes trained on the road ahead, if he ever got out of the parking lot.

After she finished the call, she gave him the address. "Do you know how to get there?"

Mitch didn't want to look her way, but he did anyway. "No, but you can put that address into the maps app on your phone."

"Sure." She tapped the screen on the phone. "All set."

The voice from the phone's GPS told him to turn right out of the parking lot. He followed the instructions and fifteen minutes later stopped in front of the police station. "Here we are. You two can go in and do what you have to do."

Charlotte and Amanda made their way into the station as Mitch stayed behind with his troubled thoughts. Nothing had prepared him for his instant attraction to Amanda. Even his relationship with Whitney had started slowly until Jimmy decided to step in. Then Mitch had gone off the rails pursuing her only to have her break his heart. He'd be crazy to act on this sudden captivation with another woman.

While Mitch sat there with his thoughts spinning around and around, Amanda and Charlotte returned. "So what happened?"

"No news." Charlotte climbed into the backseat. "That's what I expected, but I just wanted to show my face and let them know I'm out here waiting for them to find my car."

"Did they give you any hope of that?" Mitch put the truck in gear.

"Not much, but then I expected that, too." Charlotte sighed. "Seems there may be a new car in my future."

"That's probably true." Mitch let out a halfhearted laugh.

Charlotte eyed him in the rearview mirror. "But I'm looking on the bright side. I should have one more new car before I leave this earth."

Amanda turned toward the backseat. "Charlotte,

you're the most optimistic person I know. You definitely know how to make lemonade out of lemons."

"You don't know me very well. There are plenty of times when I just let the lemons sit there and rot." Charlotte laughed. "Mitchell, before we leave Nashville, you have to take me to my favorite spot to eat."

"Anything for you, Aunt Charlotte. I'm on my way." Against his better judgment, Mitch ventured a glance in Amanda's direction. "Are you up for some good southern food?"

"I'm not sure." Amanda's gaze narrowed. "What is it?"

Mitch laughed. "Since you don't know, it'll be a surprise. Anyway, how do you expect to make it here in the South if you don't know anything about our food?"

"I just came here to sing, not eat."

Mitch laughed louder. "But you do have to eat."

"Didn't I get a taste of southern food at the Pineydale Café?" Amanda wrinkled her brow.

"Not really. That's just the local burger joint. You can get that kind of food anywhere." Mitch glanced at Charlotte, who caught his gaze in the rearview mirror again. "My mouth is watering already."

"Pay attention to your driving." Charlotte pointed toward the highway ahead.

Mitch gave her a salute. "Yes, ma'am."

"While we're on our way, Amanda can tell us all about her singing adventures." Charlotte tapped the side of the guitar case. "How did it go?"

"It didn't." Amanda frowned. "But it was good

practice."

"Of course it was." Charlotte reached toward the front and patted Amanda's arm. "You'll get more chances in the future."

Amanda shrugged. "I need to live in Nashville for that to happen, and right now I'm not in any position to do that. I mostly made a disaster of this trip. No headway on the music, and I got your car stolen."

"Now don't you worry about that. You just think about your music." Charlotte nodded. "You'll see. It'll all work out."

Amanda let out a sad little chuckle. "I wish I had your confidence. Mine is pretty low right now. In fact, I think a worm has a higher confidence level than I do. But I did make a friend."

"Well, see now. It wasn't all bad," Charlotte said.

Amanda sighed. "I suppose so."

Mitch turned off the main highway onto a side road and stopped at the four-way stop. "We're almost there."

Charlotte licked her lips. "I can taste it now."

Mitch loved how Charlotte tried to make Amanda feel better about her venture into Nashville that hadn't turned out like she had hoped. His aunt was good at that kind of thing. Her encouragement had kept him going after Whitney had shattered his world. Now Amanda had chosen a difficult path, one that few were able to negotiate with success, but Charlotte was saying the right things. He should, too. Did he dare ask about her future plans?

"So what's up next?" Mitch slowed his pickup as

they neared the restaurant.

Amanda shrugged. "Gotta get a job and make some money. That's all I know right now."

"At least you have a goal. That's better than some people." Mitch parked in front of the dark-brown cedar-sided building. "We're here."

Amanda put her hand on the door handle. "This place looks a little rundown. Are you sure the food is good here?"

Charlotte opened her door. "Haven't you ever heard that you shouldn't judge a book by its cover? Same goes for restaurants. Don't judge the food by the looks of the outside. This place has the best sweet tea around."

Amanda climbed out of the front and closed the door. "Not a fan of tea. Sweet or otherwise."

"That's criminal." Charlotte fell into step with Amanda.

Amanda shrugged. "Sorry."

"You have to give the sweet tea a try. It's not like the tea you just throw some sweetener in to." Charlotte raised her eyebrows as she looked at Amanda. "We shouldn't have to wait since the busy lunchtime is over."

Amanda grinned at Charlotte. "That suits me. I'm hungry."

Thinking he was in Amanda's camp, Mitch opened the door for the two women. He must not be a true southerner because he didn't like sweet tea either, and he was hungry. But he'd keep his mouth shut until Amanda tried some. He wanted to see her expression when she took her first sip.

Booths with wooden plank tables lined the walls, while square tables made of the same wooden planks were scattered around the interior. Several diners still occupied some of the booths and tables, but the place was relatively empty. Plaques with witty southern sayings hung on the walls over the booths. Mason jars filled with flowers adorned each table. A country tune played on the juke box in the corner.

As a waitress told them to seat themselves, Mitch couldn't help thinking Amanda would get her fill of southern life right here. He still thought Amanda and country music didn't go together, but maybe Nashville was the place for songwriters of any stripe. He didn't know much about the business other than it was hard to get a break.

From what he gathered, she'd had a taste of that these last couple of days. He didn't want her to hurt, and that thought scared him. He was already involved in her life more than he wanted to be, but there didn't seem to be a way to take it all back.

Charlotte slid into the nearest booth and proceeded to take up one whole side. That left Mitch with no choice except to sit next to Amanda. More of Charlotte's matchmaking.

Looking at Amanda, Mitch motioned to the bench seat on the other side. "After you."

"Thanks." Amanda slipped into the booth and picked up one of the menus from the holder that sat against the wall.

Charlotte tapped the menu lying on the table. "I know

what I want without even looking. A meat and three."

"A what?" Amanda wrinkled her brow.

Mitch opened a menu and pointed to the first page. "You pick out a meat from this list and then three sides from this list. So you have a meat and three sides."

Amanda shook her head. "I'm learning something new every day."

Mitch chuckled. "We'll make you a southerner yet."

Amanda let out a halfhearted laugh. "Doubtful. I'm really a California girl. I grew up there. I went to college there. My grandmother and a bunch of other relatives still live there."

"Then why didn't you go to LA to pitch your songs?" Mitch gave her a curious glance.

"LA is three times farther from Boston than Nashville is, and the cost of living in Nashville is much cheaper than it is in LA." Amanda let out a harsh breath. "I'd probably be stranded somewhere in Indiana if I'd planned to go to LA. At least this way, I'm hours from Nashville instead of days away from LA."

"That makes sense." Mitch studied Amanda as she turned back to the menu. She'd actually put more thought into this trip than she'd indicated. She wasn't just a fluff of female folly. She actually had a plan, and that plan didn't include staying in Pineydale. He'd better keep that in mind.

While Mitch contemplated Amanda's thoughts on Nashville versus LA, the waitress came over to take their orders. After the waitress left, Mitch cleared the menus from the table and put them in the holder.

Amanda frowned at him. "How come you didn't order the sweet tea?"

Mitch chuckled. "Can't stand the stuff."

"Really?" Amanda raised her eyebrows as she stared at him. "And here you were preaching to me about all things southern. What happened to you?"

"Must be my Scottish ancestry."

"And what does that have to do with not liking sweet tea?"

Mitch shook his head. "Nothing. I just don't like it."

Charlotte tapped the table with her index finger. "Speaking of Scottish ancestry, Mitch, you'll have to take Amanda to the Scottish games at Grandfather Mountain."

More of Charlotte's matchmaking. How was he going to get out of this one? "She's probably not interested in something like that."

"Oh, I think she'd love to see you in a kilt."

A grin painted Amanda's expression. "Really? A kilt? I have to see this. Tell me about it."

Mitch rubbed the back of his head, wishing he could do something to stop Charlotte from her meddlesome ways.

Charlotte waved a hand at Mitch and jumped into the conversation before he could say a thing. "In July they hold the Scottish games at Grandfather Mountain in North Carolina. We go every year, and Mitch wears the Cunningham tartan."

"Do you play bagpipes, too?" Amanda's grin broadened.

"I do not play bagpipes, but others do it very well."

"Sounds like something I'll have to see."

Charlotte clapped her hands. "Wonderful. You'll enjoy it."

"You're going too, right?" Amanda looked over at Charlotte.

Charlotte waved a hand. "We'll see how I'm feeling."

Mitch wasn't fooled by Charlotte's ploy. She'd probably tell them she didn't feel up to going but then show up with someone else, just to make sure he and Amanda would be alone. But what could he do about that? Absolutely nothing. When Charlotte got an idea in her head, no one could stop it.

A few minutes later their food arrived. Charlotte held out her hands. "Let's give thanks for our food."

Mitch held out his hand to Amanda and braced himself for his reaction to her touch. Her small hand fit perfectly in his, and a protective feeling toward her captured his emotions. His brain was telling him to run, run, run, but his heart was telling him to get to know her. Which one would he listen to?

After Charlotte's prayer, Mitch snatched a piece of fried chicken from his plate and took a big bite. Even the delicious food didn't erase the crazy thoughts he had about the woman sitting next to him. How could a woman he barely knew grab hold of his emotions and whirl them around like a race car speeding around a track?

"I see you haven't tried your tea." Charlotte held up

her glass as she looked expectantly at Amanda.

Amanda laughed. "I was waiting for just the right moment. I see Mitch has dived into his chicken with gusto. I can see why. It's delicious."

Mitch nodded as he set his piece of chicken on the plate. "It's delicious all right, but you should taste Aunt Charlotte's. Hers is even better."

Charlotte waved a hand at Mitch. "Now don't go braggin' on me."

"Not braggin'. You're the best cook I know."

"Don't you let your mother hear you say that."

"She knows it's true. The only thing she makes better than you is carrot cake." Mitch chuckled, then glanced at Amanda. "So are you going to try the tea?"

"I suppose I'll have to, or I won't hear the end of it." Amanda grimaced as she picked up her glass and took a sip. She made a face. "Wow! Too sweet for me. I don't like tea to begin with, and the sweetness just makes it worse."

Charlotte laughed. "Guess we didn't make a convert out of you. Oh well, there are worse things than not liking sweet tea. Like cheering against the Vols during football season."

"The Vols?" Amanda frowned.

Grinning, Mitch looked at her. "Yeah. You know, the University of Tennessee Volunteers. Gotta be a fan if you live in Tennessee."

"What if you aren't a football fan? Is that okay?"

"If we can't get you to like sweet tea, maybe we can make you a Vols fan." Mitch wondered whether she'd even be around by football season.

"I doubt that, too." Amanda shook her head. "I'm not a fan of any sports. Now I'm going to eat the rest of this meal. Everything's good except the tea."

"I'll agree with you there." Mitch resumed eating.

While they finished their meal, Mitch's mind whirled with his conflicting thoughts about Amanda. She tempted him to disregard every promise he'd made to himself after his breakup with Whitney. He had to be strong and resist.

After they were done, Mitch paid the bill and headed to his pickup while Amanda and Charlotte went to the ladies' room. As he got ready to climb into the cab, he noticed that his front tire on the driver's side was flat. How did that happen? He hunkered down to examine it and discovered a nail imbedded in the tire.

Standing up, he blew out a harsh breath. What else could go wrong? He stood there frowning as Charlotte and Amanda approached. "We have a problem."

"What?" Charlotte asked.

"Flat tire."

Charlotte pressed a hand to her chest. "How did that happen?"

"Looks like I picked up a nail along the way." Mitch pointed back toward the road they'd come on. "Maybe back there where that new housing development is going up. Construction areas are known for loose nails."

"Do you have a spare?" Amanda asked.

Mitch chuckled. "What kind of mechanic would I be without a spare?"

"A pretty bad one." Her gaze lowered, Amanda scuffed her shoe against the blacktop. "It's my fault."

"What do you mean it's your fault?" Charlotte asked.

"If Mitch hadn't driven to pick me up, then he wouldn't have gotten a flat tire." Amanda looked up, a pained expression in her eyes. "I'm just bringing you guys all kinds of trouble."

Charlotte immediately put an arm around Amanda's shoulders. "Now don't you go sayin' things like that. This is not your fault, and even if it was, they say trouble comes in threes. You've had three. So no more."

"Let's not waste time trying to figure out who's at fault." Mitch got into the bed of his pickup. "I've got a tire to change."

"Do you need help?" Amanda asked.

"I can handle it." Mitch wished he could handle his attraction to Amanda as well as he could change a tire.

In a matter of minutes, they were back on the road again. Charlotte was reading, and Amanda was doing something with her phone. He had nothing to occupy his mind except those same troubling notions. He might as well be a hamster on one of those little wheels. His mind went over and over the same territory without any change. Maybe when he got back home and settled into his daily routine, he could get a handle on his mixed-up feelings about Amanda. Then again, maybe not.

CHAPTER SEVEN

The following day, Amanda helped Charlotte with some cleaning in the morning. The whole time Amanda thought about job prospects. Charlotte had told her that Mitch might know of something, but chances were slim for any openings, especially in Pineydale. Sitting around thinking about a job wouldn't help. Amanda had to find her own job. That had to be her primary goal for now. Music would have to wait.

After lunch Charlotte lay down on the couch in the hearth room and took a nap. Amanda sat on the front porch swing and looked at job boards on her phone. This was a start.

Amanda found a couple of positions in Nashville that fit her qualifications. Now she had to get out her computer and polish her résumé. The thought didn't appeal, but she couldn't sponge off Charlotte forever.

Amanda had never planned to use her business degree, because she'd had her head in the clouds of a dream—a dream of a music career. She had never faced the reality of what that meant. She had to earn a living somehow while she pursued that dream.

Trying her best not to disturb Charlotte, Amanda retrieved her computer and set it up on the small desk in the music room. She gazed longingly at the piano and wished she could sit down and compose, but she wasn't in this room for that purpose. She had to find a job. Looking over her résumé only made her more depressed. Her internships had been over two years ago. Would those count now?

Prospective employers would wonder what she'd been doing for the last two years. If she told them she was in music school, would they count that against her? Few songwriters, like authors, made enough money to live on. They worked other jobs and did their writing on the side. Even though she was tempted to leave her recent schooling off, she decided she would have to explain eventually. She might as well do it up front.

After she added the new information, she saved it. She picked out the two most promising jobs and sent her résumé to the indicated email. How long would it take to get a response?

"What are you working on? Composing another song?"

Amanda looked up at the sound of Charlotte's voice. "No, I'm sending out résumés to a couple of places in Nashville."

Disappointment showed on Charlotte's face. "So you intend to leave us."

"Only if I get a job. In the meantime, do you have Jimmy's phone number?"

Charlotte raised her eyebrows. "I thought you didn't want to paint houses."

"I don't, but I have to do something." Amanda shrugged. "Did you have a good nap?"

"Yes. Makes me feel like a new person." Charlotte turned toward the door. "I'll get that number for you."

"I'll go with you." Amanda followed Charlotte to the kitchen, a sense of dread walking with her. She could do this. She didn't have a choice.

Charlotte grabbed a pencil and paper from a drawer in the kitchen. She wrote the number on the paper and handed it to Amanda. "Here it is. You make that call, and I'm going to start something for supper."

"Thanks. I'll call Jimmy, then call my sister. After that I'll help you with supper."

Charlotte waved her away. "You make your calls. Take as much time as you want."

"Thanks." With Jimmy's number in hand, Amanda meandered back out to the front porch.

Amanda sat on the porch swing and punched Jimmy's number into her phone. She listened to it ring with unease in her heart. After four rings the call went to voicemail. A sense of relief washed over her as she left a message. Although the respite would be short lived, she didn't have to beg for a job right now. She'd call Kelsey and enjoy the beautiful summer day here on the front porch.

Amanda hoped she wouldn't get another voicemail. She had no idea what her sister might be doing. The three-hour time difference always made the calling situation tricky.

"Hey, Amanda. How are things in Tennessee?"

Amanda could hear the smile in Kelsey's voice. "I wish I could say they're great, but I have to admit they're less than desirable."

"So what's wrong?"

Amanda regaled Kelsey with the tale of her trip to Nashville and the not-so-exciting progress of her job hunt but left out any mention of Mitch. Amanda couldn't explain her attraction to the man, so how could she explain it to her sister?

"There must be a black cat following you around."

"No, but Charlotte has a black-and-white one named after Minnie Pearl, an old Opry star."

"I think I remember Grandma Fran talking about her."

"Has Dad said anything about the car?"

"Nope. Other than it's out of his hair." Kelsey chuckled. "I think that's why he gave it to you in the first place."

"Has he said anything about me?"

"You mean about you being in Tennessee?"

"Yeah."

"I think it's a sore subject, so he doesn't talk about it." Kelsey paused for what seemed like a long time.

"Is there something wrong?" Amanda didn't want to alienate her father completely even though they didn't agree on a lot of things.

"There's big news."

"What kind of big news?"

Kelsey cleared her throat. "You're not going to believe this, but Maria's pregnant. We're going to have a half brother in a few months."

"Wow! I don't believe it. Dad will be on social

security before this kid's out of high school." Amanda let out a low whistle. "Are they excited?"

"Well, I think the appropriate word is surprised. After Maria had those two miscarriages, I think she'd just resigned herself to not having any children of her own."

"Even though she loves us like her own, she still deserves to have her own child. I'm really happy for her." Tears stung Amanda's eyes as she blinked them away.

"Yeah, and because of those miscarriages, they waited to tell everyone until last night. She's already into her fifth month. I just thought she'd put on a little weight."

Amanda chuckled. "Dad should be a grandpa, not having another kid of his own."

"At forty-two, Maria isn't exactly in the prime childbearing years either," Kelsey said.

"True, and I pray that nothing goes wrong this time."

"Me, too. That would be really hard on Maria." Kelsey cleared her throat, sounding as though she was as emotional as Amanda felt. "They're really happy. I've never seen Dad like this. I have a feeling this baby is going to make him a little more mellow."

"Does that help me?" Amanda could only hope.

"No telling, but in a few months he'll be occupied with sleepless nights, diapers, and all things baby." Kelsey laughed. "I can hardly wait to see it."

"You'll have to send me lots of photos."

"I will."

"I still can't imagine Dad with a baby. Maria, yes, but

Dad, no." Amanda laughed.

"So are you stuck in that town for a while?"

"Probably. I don't expect to hear anything from those places I just applied to anytime soon." Amanda sighed. "I think I'll wind up painting houses. That seems to be the only job around this town."

"Sounds like Pinecrest. Not many jobs here either. At least I have a part-time job at the nursing home."

"Let's not talk about jobs. How's your love life?"

Kelsey laughed. "How's yours?"

Mitch's image flashed through her mind. "I asked first, and besides, how could I have any kind of love life when I've been in this town for less than a week?"

"Oh, I thought you might have met a handsome country singer in Nashville." Kelsey's voice held a hint of curiosity.

"Didn't meet any handsome singers." Amanda wasn't going to mention any handsome mechanics. "All the good-looking men at the open mic events were married anyway."

"Too bad."

"Okay, spill. I have a feeling you're avoiding my question."

"No. Just trying to find out about you."

Amanda chuckled. "You aren't fooling me. You've met someone."

"Yeah. He delivers supplies to the nursing home, but he lives in Spokane, so it's not very convenient."

"Have you been dating long?" Amanda shifted the phone to her other ear.

"We've only had a couple of dates, but I really like him. Since he lives in Spokane, he just finishes his route on Fridays, then we go out somewhere here in Pinecrest."

Amanda couldn't help thinking about Mitch, but she wasn't, under any circumstances, saying anything about him. "I'm glad you've met someone, but don't get too serious. You want to finish school."

Kelsey laughed. "Look who's sounding like an old mother hen."

"I know. I know, but I've learned that getting serious with a guy just isn't the way to go when you're in school."

"Okay. I'll keep that in mind."

Before Amanda could respond, her phone buzzed, indicating another call. "Hey, Kels, I've got to let you go. My painting job is on the other line. Talk to you later."

"Sure."

Amanda quickly accepted the other call. "Hello."

"Hey, Amanda, this is Jimmy. So glad you called. You ready to start painting?"

Amanda hesitated. Was she? No, but earning some money was at the top of her list. "Sure. What do I have to do?"

"Great. We're starting a new job on Monday. So I'll need some information from you to put you on the payroll."

Amanda wondered how he could hire her without knowing whether she could paint. Was he desperate for help? She wasn't going to ask. "Sounds good, but I have to let you know I've applied for jobs in Nashville. If I get one, I'll be leaving."

"That's okay. I need one more person on my crew now. You can let me know if something else comes up for you."

"Super. What do you need to know for your payroll?"

"The usual stuff for tax withholding. I can stop by Charlotte's with the forms after I finish up here for the day."

"Sure." Amanda wondered whether Jimmy would flirt with her like that day in the café. She wasn't too keen on that. She hoped taking this job wasn't a mistake in that regard. She wanted a job, not some guy trying to make moves on her.

"We'll start at six o'clock on Monday morning. I'll come by and pick you up about quarter till. Wear something old."

Amanda tried to think if she had something old. "I'll be ready."

"See you tonight with those forms."

As Amanda ended the call and pocketed her phone, she thought about the start time. She hated getting up early, but she was suffering the consequences of her own actions. She'd better get used to going to bed earlier. And she'd better go help Charlotte.

Amanda hurried into the kitchen and found Charlotte peeling potatoes at the sink. "Are you planning to feed an army?"

"Mitch is coming over for supper again, and I can

always freeze whatever we don't eat tonight." Charlotte turned to Amanda with a smile.

Wondering about the conspiratorial look that accompanied that smile, Amanda stepped closer to the counter. "Well, it seems I have a job."

"Jimmy hired you?"

Amanda nodded. "And he's stopping by after work to have me fill out the stuff for withholding tax. He says I need old clothes. I don't have any. Do you have some that I could use?"

Charlotte stepped back from the sink and looked Amanda over from head to toe. "I do, but I fear they'll be way too big for you."

"Anything will do because I didn't come prepared to be a painter."

Charlotte chuckled. "I suppose you didn't. We'll look for something after supper."

"Great. Now what can I do to help?"

"You can take over these potatoes while I mix up a salad." Charlotte handed Amanda the potato peeler. "It's a good thing I planned a lot of potatoes, since Jimmy's stopping by."

"You're inviting him for dinner, too?"

"I am."

Amanda wasn't sure she liked that idea, but she might as well get to know her new boss. Maybe she'd find more to like about him than his first impression. "Does he come over to eat all the time like Mitch does?"

Charlotte shook her head. "Those two don't always get along."

"Then why are you inviting Jimmy?"

Charlotte wagged a finger in the air. "Because they need to let bygones be bygones."

Amanda had noticed how they bickered like two old ladies that day at the café.

Charlotte retrieved a bowl from the cupboard and set it on the counter, then looked over at Amanda. "I can see you're wondering why Mitch and Jimmy don't get along."

Amanda gave Charlotte a little smile. "A little."

"Well, let me tell you. It was like something out of a soap opera around here."

"That bad?" Amanda couldn't imagine what would set the cousins against each other.

Charlotte shook her head as she prepared the salad. "Those boys have been rivals since they were in grade school. They competed for the same spot on different sports teams—football, basketball, baseball."

"Who won?" Amanda liked to think it was Mitch.

"Both for different things at different times, so the rivalry stayed alive and well through their school years."

"Was that it?" Amanda thought the rivalry was silly until she thought about the jealousy that had plagued her thoughts after the open mic competition. But there was a difference. She had come to grips with her envy and had made friends with her rival. Still, she shouldn't judge.

"It wasn't just sports. It was girls, too." Charlotte sighed. "Jimmy was always the charmer and the better looking of the two. He always had the prettiest girl on his arm."

Amanda could debate that Jimmy was the better looking one. Mitch captured her interest, not Jimmy. "So why are they still rivals?"

Charlotte finished the salad prep and wiped her hands. "Not so much rivals now. They just had a really big falling out, and they've never quite let it go, even though the source of the rivalry is long gone."

Amanda had to wonder why Charlotte didn't just come out and say what the issue was between the two men. Was there a reason why she danced around the subject? Amanda had to know. "So what was the problem?"

"Whitney."

A woman. Amanda should have known. "Are you going to tell me about Whitney?"

Charlotte sighed again. "You might as well know."

"Know what?" Amanda wasn't sure she needed this information.

Charlotte clicked her tongue. "That girl was the toast of the town. Homecoming queen. Festival queen. Cheerleader. Valedictorian. Student council. Honor Society. If there was an award to be won, she won it. And besides all that, she's as pretty as they come. Blond hair, blue eyes, and a figure men would whistle at."

"And I'm guessing Mitch and Jimmy both wanted to date her."

"Not in high school. She was Jimmy's girl. He was homecoming king, star quarterback, and all-around nice guy."

Jimmy had beat out Mitch for the girl. Amanda

tucked that information away. "So how did they become rivals for her attention?"

"They all went away to college. Mitch went to the University of Tennessee in Knoxville. Whitney went to some women's college in Atlanta, and Jimmy went to East Tennessee State University right close in Johnson City."

"So they all went their separate ways. I don't see the problem." Amanda finished peeling the potatoes and put them in the big pot of water on the stove.

"Just wait. I'm not done with my story." Charlotte raised a hand. "Jimmy liked to party, and he did more partying than studying and eventually dropped out of school and joined the army. He spent a couple of years in the service, then came home and took over his dad's painting business."

"What happened with Whitney?"

"This is where the story gets interesting. Jimmy and Whitney broke up when he joined the army. She wanted a guy with greater ambitions than that. During that first summer, Whitney got a job working at the company Mitch's dad runs here in Pineydale. Mitch was working there, too. They started dating. The summer after they graduated from college, they got engaged."

Mitch was engaged. That piece of information hit Amanda like a boulder out of the blue. She didn't know why that surprised her. "Why didn't they get married?"

"Whitney had ambitions for herself and for Mitch. She thought he planned to take over the Cunningham business, and she would step into her role as the wife of one of the most important men in town." Charlotte's mouth formed a grim line as she set the temperature on the oven. "Although Mitch worked for his dad, he wasn't interested in taking over the family business. He wanted to work on cars."

"And that didn't suit Whitney?"

"She didn't mind that he worked on cars. She just didn't want that to be his primary purpose in life." Charlotte pulled a large casserole dish out of the refrigerator. "I hope you like meatloaf. It's another one of Mitch's favorites."

"I do." Amanda hoped Charlotte wasn't finished with her story.

Charlotte put the dish into the oven, then turned to look at Amanda. "I could see the wheels coming off Mitch and Whitney's relationship long before it happened."

"How so?"

"Wilbur used to love to go to car shows, and he would often take Mitch with him. In the beginning, Mitch would always invite Whitney to go along, but soon she was making excuses not to go. Then she would try to persuade him not to go, and the two would argue. Mitch would go anyway, and Whitney would pout like a spoiled child."

"Does Mitch still like to attend car shows?"

Charlotte nodded. "He goes to this big one down in Florida every spring. It's a pretty fancy affair. I could never understand why Whitney didn't gobble that one up, getting to hobnob with lots of celebrities and rich people. But it was a car show, so she didn't want to have anything to do with it."

"What does any of this have to do with Jimmy?"

Raising her eyebrows, Charlotte pointed a finger in the air. "Ah, that is yet to come in this story. About a month before their wedding, Mitch went to that car show in Florida with Wilbur. This was right after my poor Wilbur had been diagnosed with cancer, and Mitch wanted to make sure his uncle got to go before he had to start his chemo treatments."

Amanda hadn't known Mitch very long, but that sounded like something he would do. He had taken off a day of work to bring Charlotte to Nashville to see about her car. "Mitch told me how much he misses Wilbur."

Nodding, Charlotte wiped at her eyes, which filled with tears. "Wilbur loved that boy like he was his own. Anyway, while Mitch was away, Whitney didn't like being left alone and decided to look up her old boyfriend."

"Jimmy."

"You got it." Charlotte lifted the lid on the pot and checked the potatoes, then turned back to Amanda. "During the car show, Wilbur started feeling bad, so Mitch brought him home early."

"And Mitch caught Whitney with Jimmy."

"Oh yeah. Mitch punched Jimmy and gave him a black eye that lasted for weeks. Whitney cried and begged for forgiveness, but Mitch didn't want anything to do with her after that. Soon after that, she got a job in Atlanta and left town. The whole thing hurt Mitch really bad, and I'm afraid he still carries a grudge against Jimmy. But in my estimation, I think Jimmy did Mitch a favor and showed him Whitney's true colors."

Amanda nodded. "I'd have to agree."

"Now don't you dare tell Mitch I told you all this. He'd never forgive me."

"I'll never tell. You can count on me." Amanda put a finger to her lips and shook her head. She didn't know when she'd ever have reason to say anything to Mitch about his broken engagement. "Anything else you need me to do?"

"You can set the table." Charlotte went to the cupboard and brought out four plates.

"Sure." Amanda took the plates and headed to the breakfast nook.

"Just for fun, let's eat in the dining room." Charlotte pointed toward the front of the house.

"Okay." Amanda stopped and gathered flatware and napkins before making her way through the butler's pantry to the dining room.

As Amanda set the table, she thought about the upcoming meal. Would Mitch and Jimmy be polite to each other, surly and quiet, or outright antagonistic? This dinner could prove to be very interesting. Everything that Charlotte had told Amanda made Mitch more intriguing. Did she dare act on her attraction?

CHAPTER EIGHT

The white van decorated with paint brushes and emblazoned with the label ABC Painting churned Mitch's stomach. What was Jimmy doing here? Had he decided to stake his claim on Amanda? Well, he could have her.

Taking a deep breath, Mitch stepped out of his pickup. He could be civil to Jimmy. Charlotte didn't need their rancor in her house. Mitch had no claims on Amanda. He reminded himself that it was a good thing for so many reasons.

For Charlotte's sake, he would get through this dinner with a smile. Mitch rang the bell, then opened the door. He took a few steps and came face to face with Amanda, who appeared from the living room.

Jimmy followed close behind her. "Hey, Mitch. Good to see you."

Skepticism about Jimmy's statement clouded Mitch's thoughts, but he didn't want to appear churlish in front of Amanda. Mitch nodded. "Likewise. What brings you here?"

"This little lady." Jimmy grinned at Amanda.

Mitch couldn't help remembering the day he'd wiped that grin off Jimmy's face with a punch to the jaw. Not one of his finer moments, but it stuck in his mind like a rat in a trap.

"Yeah. I decided to take Jimmy up on his offer to paint houses." Amanda jumped in with the information before Mitch could say anything. "He's here for me to sign the paperwork. I start on Monday."

"I guess congratulations are in order. You've got a job." Mitch wished he'd tried harder to find her something else. He had mixed feelings about getting involved in her life, but he didn't want her involved with Jimmy either. When it came to Amanda, Mitch's emotions resembled a roller-coaster ride. He just wished for some equilibrium.

Charlotte sashayed down the hallway as she held out her hands. "Well, well. Looks like all my dinner guests have arrived."

Gritting his teeth, Mitch forced himself not to look at Jimmy. Charlotte had invited Jimmy for dinner any number of times when she had also invited Mitch, but this time was different. Amanda was here. Despite the warnings he'd given himself about not acting on his attraction to the cute singer, he had hoped to have a little alone time with her. Guess the presence of his rival would keep Mitch from doing something stupid like asking Amanda on a date. Charlotte had saved him from the temptation.

"You need me to help with serving?" Amanda stepped into the hallway.

Charlotte motioned to the kitchen. "Everything's ready. Let's all go back to the kitchen, and each of us can carry a dish to the table."

Like the Pied Piper, Charlotte led the group into the kitchen and handed each of them a dish. The foursome made their way through the butler's pantry into the dining room.

Jimmy set the bowl of potatoes on the table. "What's the occasion, Aunt Charlotte, that we get to eat in the dining room?"

"We're going to celebrate Amanda's new status as an employee and your status as her boss." Charlotte pointed a finger at Jimmy. "Be good to this girl. If you don't, I'll be on your case."

Jimmy saluted, then pulled out a chair for Amanda and gave her that signature grin. "Starting right now. Please have a seat."

Still trying to keep his cool, Mitch took his seat on the opposite side of the table next to Charlotte. Would he have to sit here during supper and watch Jimmy flirt with Amanda? Mitch balled a fist in his lap. He could imagine using his fist. No, he wouldn't go there. He would remain calm and civilized no matter how much effort it took.

"Mitch, will you ask a blessing for the food?" Charlotte held out her hands.

Mitch's outlook was anything but godly. He needed an attitude adjustment if he was going to pray. He took Charlotte's hand, then looked across the table at Amanda, who had stretched her hand out to him. Her touch would make his heart pump in double time and add one more difficulty to his attempt to pray, but he could do it. As he took her hand, he bowed his head and tried to ignore the way his pulse jumped.

He said a short prayer, then dropped Amanda's hand as if he'd touched a live wire. She gave him a curious look as she picked up the bread basket and offered it to him. He grabbed a roll and put it on his bread plate. Had she guessed that she had him completely captivated?

As they passed the food, Mitch's thoughts were consumed with how he could possibly reconcile his not wanting to get involved with her and yet not wanting Jimmy to either. Under no circumstances could he act on these crazy emotions that tempted him to best his cousin in a war over another woman. Or at least that was what he kept telling himself.

"I hope to see you three young people in church on Sunday." Charlotte's statement interrupted Mitch's meandering thoughts.

"Aunt Charlotte, you know I try to be there whenever I can, but sometimes work gets in the way." Jimmy looked as uncomfortable as a kid called into the principal's office.

"You aren't painting houses on Sunday, are you?" Charlotte eyed Jimmy.

"No, ma'am. I'm doing my books and payroll." Jimmy squirmed in his seat as he tried to defend himself.

Mitch didn't have any excuse for missing church unless he was out of town for a car show or training on his bike. He usually sat in the back anyway, so he could slip in and slip out without having to deal with his dad. But listening to Jimmy's excuse gave Mitch an idea. "You know, Jimmy, you could hire someone to do those books. In fact, that someone is sitting right here at the table."

Jimmy frowned. "You mean Amanda?"

"Yeah. She's got a business degree. Why not put that to use instead of having her paint?" Mitch stared at Jimmy, who looked even more uncomfortable.

"Okay, you guys, you're doing it again. Talking about me as if I'm not here." She waved her hands over her head. "I'm here, in case you can't see me."

Amanda nailed Mitch with her gaze. "Did you ever think to ask me before you decide what kind of job I should have?"

Shrugging, Mitch wished he'd kept his mouth shut. He'd wanted to best Jimmy so much that Mitch hadn't thought his suggestion might upset Amanda. "I just thought you'd rather not have to paint, but if that's what you want to do, don't let me stop you."

"I didn't say I wanted to paint houses or not paint houses. I just don't appreciate being talked about as if I'm not here." Amanda looked over at Charlotte. "You can count on me to be in church on Sunday, but I guess we'll have to walk."

"No, you won't. I'll pick you up." Mitch glanced at Jimmy to see his reaction.

"Thanks." Charlotte helped herself to the potatoes and passed them on. "Sorry I sent the conversation in an awkward direction, but I just think it's important to gather together, as the Good Book says."

Mitch took a slice of meatloaf. "I apologize for causing any problems."

"Apology accepted." Amanda took a bite of the meatloaf, then turned to Charlotte. "This is amazing. I've never had meatloaf this good."

Charlotte smiled. "Thanks."

"Can you give me the recipe?"

"No recipe. I just throw stuff together. I don't measure." Charlotte grimaced. "But you can watch me make it."

"I will." Amanda took another bite.

For the next few minutes, they ate in silence. What topic of conversation wouldn't cause a stir? Mitch definitely wasn't going to bring up the bookkeeping again, even though he thought that suited Amanda's skills better than painting houses.

He remembered the conversation he'd had with his mother about the fundraiser. Did he dare ask Amanda if she'd volunteer her musical talent, or would that make her feel put upon? He didn't want to alienate her further.

"Mitch, you still planning to ride in the bicycle thing up in Massachusetts?" Jimmy slathered butter on his roll.

"Yeah, why?"

Amanda set down her fork and stared at him in amazement. "Are you talking about the PMC?"

Mitch nodded. "You know about the PMC?"

"What's the PMC?" Charlotte asked.

"It's the Pan-Massachusetts Challenge. It raises money for cancer research. Folks come from all over the country to ride their bikes, and donors sponsor them." Amanda looked at Mitch, admiration in her eyes. "Have you been training?"

"Yeah. That's why I've missed church some this summer."

Charlotte wagged her finger. "Maybe it's a good cause, but that's no excuse to miss worship."

"I know." Mitch ventured a glance at Jimmy. Had he brought up the PMC because he knew Mitch had been riding his bike on Sunday mornings? Was it a way to deflect from his church absences? "I'll try to work in my training before church."

"My stepcousin and his wife and a bunch of their friends will be riding this year. My stepcousin will be celebrating his victory over Hodgkin lymphoma. He even had to have a bone marrow transplant. Are you riding from Wellesley to Wellesley or some other route?"

Mitch nodded. "Wellesley to Wellesley. That's why I'm training. One hundred and sixty miles is a long way to go."

"One hundred and sixty miles?" Charlotte's mouth hung open. "That's a lot of pedaling."

"Do you have all your donors?" Amanda asked.

"Yeah. I've raised all my money, but every time someone new learns about it, I gain more donations."

Charlotte raised a hand. "That would include me. Put me down for one hundred dollars."

Mitch smiled. "Thanks, Aunt Charlotte."

"My company will donate, too." Jimmy took a gulp of his drink.

"Thanks." Mitch hoped Amanda didn't feel like she

had to make a donation. He knew she was short on funds.

"I'll donate after I get my first paycheck." Amanda smiled.

"That's not necessary, but thanks." Mitch hated taking money from her, but he would embarrass her if he didn't accept it. Maybe this was a good time to mention his mother's fundraiser. "Since you're willing to donate to raise money for cancer research, would you be interested in donating your singing talent?"

"For what?" Amanda's brow knit.

"My mom does this fundraiser every year to benefit the cancer research at the university, and she always has this concert—"

"I'd love to do that," Amanda said before Mitch could finish his sentence. "We did one of those when I lived up in Boston."

"Great." Mitch smiled. "I'll tell my mom. She'll be thrilled."

"You can introduce me to your mom on Sunday at church." Amanda gave him a questioning look.

"Sure." Mitch hadn't considered that aspect of having Amanda play in his mother's fundraiser.

"I look forward to meeting your mom." Amanda picked up her fork. "I'll see what kind of song she'd like me to sing."

"I'm sure whatever you choose will be fine." Mitch resumed eating.

Would his mom start in on the matchmaking like Charlotte? Mitch shook the worry away. His dad would dampen anything his mother said with his caustic remarks about Nashville wannabes.

What did his cousin think about all this? Mitch glanced over at Jimmy to gauge his reaction. If he had a reaction, he wasn't showing it as he munched on his salad.

Jimmy glanced at Amanda. "So what do you think about Mitch's suggestion that you do books instead of painting?"

"Is doing your books a full-time position?"

Jimmy shook his head. "One day a week."

"That's not enough for me to make the money I need. I have to have full-time work."

"No problem. You could do books one day a week, and the rest of the time you can paint. How does that sound?"

"I could do your books this week, if you want to show me your setup."

Jimmy grinned. "Super. You can come over to my place tomorrow, and I'll get you started."

"Are you close by so I can walk?"

"No need to walk. I'll come get you around four o'clock, if that works for you."

Mitch listened to the conversation with growing irritation. He didn't have anyone to blame for the situation besides himself. He had made the suggestion, and Jimmy was eager to jump right in there and take advantage. Wasn't that the way he always worked? He'd moved in on Whitney while Mitch was gone. Now he had a choice to pursue Amanda or let Jimmy do it. Mitch had to quit waffling and decide what he wanted.

***

Without much effort Amanda had convinced Jimmy to buy some software to use for his accounting and payroll. With this addition, she would probably spend more time painting because the task of keeping his books would take less time.

After they finished inputting the information, Jimmy insisted that he treat her to supper at the local steak house. Amanda really didn't want to go, but she didn't have a good excuse not to. Her reluctance came from not wanting him to think of this as a date. She definitely didn't want to encourage his interest.

Amanda managed to get through the meal with a little small talk. The whole time she couldn't help thinking about how Jimmy had been the reason Mitch and his fiancée had split. What would Jimmy say about that now? Was the tension between the two men still about that, or did it include all the rivalries through the years? She wanted to know, but she wouldn't ask.

Jimmy paid the check, then looked her way. "Would you like to go for a drive? I can show you the highlights of Pineydale."

No way. She didn't know what he had in mind, but she wasn't going to find out. "Thanks for supper, but I think I'd like to walk back to Charlotte's and get a little fresh air. It's a nice evening, and there's still plenty of daylight left."

Jimmy stared at her, his blue eyes giving her no clue whether he was offended that she didn't want to spend more time with him. "I can give you a ride back to Charlotte's."

"I'd like the exercise. I used to walk every day in Boston, so I kind of miss my daily walks."

"Okay. If that's what you want to do." Jimmy shrugged. "Guess I'll see you tomorrow at church."

"Yeah. You better show up, or Charlotte might come knocking on your door."

Jimmy chuckled. "My great-aunt is quite a character. She used to teach school. Did you know that?"

"I didn't." Amanda smiled as she followed Jimmy out of the restaurant. "I definitely can see her in the classroom. Did you have her for a teacher?"

"No. She'd retired before I got to high school, but my parents both had her. She taught English."

"That must be why she has a room full of books."

"Yeah. Did you know she's written lots of poetry?" Jimmy stopped next to his van.

Amanda shook her head. "She never mentioned it."

"You should ask her about it." Jimmy gave Amanda a salute as he opened the door to his vehicle. "Enjoy your walk."

"Thanks. I will. And thanks again for supper." Amanda didn't look back. She almost felt guilty for turning down Jimmy's invitation, but not enough to change her mind. She was better off keeping everything low key with him.

The sun sat just above the buildings on the main

street as Amanda meandered down the sidewalk. She looked into the shop windows along the way. When she left the downtown area, the big oak and maple trees cast long shadows across the yards in front of stately old houses. There was something peaceful about the place. The thought surprised her. She'd loved Boston. She'd had the same feeling in Nashville. The crowds, the cars, the noise, the energy. She found none of that here, but strangely she didn't mind.

While she contemplated her surprising change in attitude, her phone played the country tune she had programmed as her ringtone. She pulled it from the pocket of her capris. Why was Heather calling? Amanda hoped something wasn't wrong with Max.

"Hi, Heather. Is everything okay there?" Amanda held her breath as she waited for an answer.

"Yeah. Everything's great." Heather's voice projected joy. "How are you doing? Did you make it to Nashville okay?"

"No." Amanda suddenly realized she'd been so wrapped up in her own disappointment that she'd forgotten to let people know about her circumstances.

"What happened?"

Amanda took a few minutes and told Heather about the broken-down car, her disappointing trip to Nashville, and how she'd met Charlotte. Amanda purposely only mentioned Mitch in passing. "And now I have a job painting houses."

"Wow. A lot has happened, and you've been gone less than two weeks."

"I know. It seems like I've been gone for ages. I miss everyone back there."

"And we miss you." Heather's voice held a bit of sadness. "We're all gearing up for the PMC."

"I figured you'd all be riding bikes to get ready." Amanda chuckled. "Funny thing. You know that guy Mitch I mentioned?"

"Yeah."

"He's coming up there to ride in the PMC. Someone he went to college with lives in Boston and urged him to ride with his team."

"Wow. It's a small world. You should come, too." Heather hesitated. "In fact, that's one of the reasons I was calling. You remember Tara Madsen, Hailey's mom?"

"I do."

"Well, she and Caleb Fitzpatrick are getting married."

"How wonderful. I imagine Hailey is really excited." Amanda remembered how the little girl who had suffered through cancer had been such an inspiration to Max.

"She is, and she's the reason I'm calling. She wants you to sing at her mom's wedding."

Puzzled, Amanda shook her head. "Me? She knows me?"

"Yes. Since Tara didn't have your number, she asked me to call you. Tara tells me that Hailey remembered all the times you sang and played your guitar at the fundraisers and our wedding. She wants to learn to play the guitar just like you."

Amanda stopped walking and took in all this information. "So when is the wedding?"

"The weekend of the PMC. They're going to combine the ride with their ceremony and get married on Sunday after the ride."

Amanda chuckled as she remembered how Max and Heather had surprised everyone and got married at Max's one-year anniversary celebration of his bone marrow transplant. "You guys sure like to have unusual wedding venues."

"It's perfect for them. They're raising money for cancer research and celebrating Hailey's second year of being cancer-free. Hailey's excited beyond excited."

Amanda wanted to say yes, but how could she afford to go back to Boston? Besides, she'd just taken this job with Jimmy. She couldn't ask to take off work before she'd even started. "Heather, I've got so much going on here right now. I'm going to have to think this over, okay?"

"Sure. I'd love it if you could come back for a few days." Heather sighed. "I understand that you might not be able to get off work, but maybe your boss will give you a couple of days if you ask. Tell him it's for a good cause."

"Maybe that'll work." What would Jimmy think? Amanda couldn't begin to guess. Maybe she could talk to Mitch and get an idea, or were the cousins so distant that he wouldn't be any help? And what would he think about the whole thing? "I'll call you back tomorrow."

"Okay. I hope you can work everything out."

Saying goodbye, Amanda didn't have a clue where she could come up with the money for this trip. And Heather had no clue that Amanda was living on next to nothing since her dad had cut her off.

Amanda squinted her eyes as she drew near to Charlotte's house. Was that Charlotte sitting on the front porch with someone? Was that someone Mitch? Amanda's heart skipped a beat. Had Charlotte waylaid Mitch so he'd be here when Amanda got home, or had it just turned out that way? Probably the latter, because Charlotte wouldn't have any idea when Amanda would return.

Mitch's presence made Amanda quicken her steps, but she slowed her pace just as she hit the edge of Charlotte's yard. She didn't want Mitch to think she was in a hurry to see him. She moseyed up the walk. Neither Charlotte nor Mitch saw Amanda approach.

"Hey, you two out here enjoying the nice evening?" Amanda climbed the steps.

"Oh!" Charlotte put a hand to her chest. "Amanda, you startled me. I didn't hear you come up the walk."

"Sorry. I didn't mean to scare you." Looking over at Mitch, Amanda tried to gauge his reaction, but she couldn't read his expression.

"Hi, Amanda, how was your supper?" Mitch stood and motioned to the chair where he'd been sitting. "Would you like to sit here?"

Amanda waved at him. "No, you sit there. I can get my own chair."

Mitch hurried over to help her with the rocker she dragged from the other end of the porch. "You walked home?"

"Yeah. It was a wonderful evening, and I've missed walking like I did in Boston."

"You mean you didn't drive your car up there?" Mitch asked.

"Not unless I was going a good distance." Amanda settled in the rocker and looked over at Mitch, who had returned to his seat. "You don't know how hard it is to get a parking spot there. Once you have one, you don't want to move your car unless you absolutely have to. I once spent nearly an hour driving around looking for a place to park. When I finally found one, it was about six blocks from my apartment."

Mitch shook his head. "I don't see why anyone likes to live in a big city."

"There's lots to do there."

"I've got plenty to keep me busy right here in a small town." Mitch raised his eyebrows, curiosity radiating from his blue-gray eyes. "You never did tell me how supper was."

"Good. The steak house has excellent food." Amanda had the feeling Mitch didn't care about her dinner, but he wanted to know how things were between her and Jimmy. Was he a little jealous? She shook the silly question away. "How did you know I went out to eat with Jimmy?"

"I told him." Charlotte grinned. "He was disappointed to find out you wouldn't be with us tonight."

Amanda wondered whether Mitch would agree with Charlotte's statement, ignore it, or deny it. Would she be disappointed if he wasn't jealous? He made her heart trip whenever she looked at him. She'd known him for such a short time. She was crazy to entertain even the first thoughts of a relationship with him. But there they were—plaguing her, making her uncomfortable like an out-of-tune guitar.

"Yeah, I was hoping to see your red tennis shoes. But when you show up, you're not wearing them. But second best are those sandals. I'm surprised you don't just topple over on your face. I still don't know how you walk in those things." Mitch gave her a lopsided grin.

"Maybe you should get a pair and find out."

Mitch laughed out loud. "They don't make those for men, or at least I'm reasonably sure they don't."

"I wouldn't be surprised if there aren't some for men out there somewhere." Amanda chuckled.

Mitch shuddered. "I have to shut that image out of my mind."

"Me, too." Charlotte held her hands over her eyes. "I do not want to see any men I know in those kinds of sandals."

Mitch chuckled some more. "So you got Jimmy's books in order and had time for supper, too?"

"The books are easy when you have the appropriate software."

Mitch shook his head. "Yeah, I been tellin' Jimmy for years that he needed to make life easier with some accounting software, but he didn't want to take the time to learn it or input the information. Glad to see you persuaded him to get into the twenty-first century."

"He was ready. He just needed a little nudge." Amanda wondered if Mitch was trying to one-up his cousin.

"And you gave him that nudge?"

Amanda nodded. "That probably means more painting and less bookkeeping for me."

"Have you ever painted houses before?" Mitch narrowed his gaze.

"Yeah, if you count the volunteer work I did at the House for Families project my friend Heather spearheaded."

"What's House for Families?" Mitch leaned forward in his chair.

"Heather's an oncology nurse and works at a cancer clinic near Boston. She saw the need for a place for families to stay while a family member was getting treatment for cancer. She found a house and raised funds to buy it with the help of a whole lot of people. The house had to be renovated to suit its new purpose, so a lot of us helped with that. I painted."

Surprise registered on Mitch's face. "Then you do know how to paint."

"You mean you thought I took this job without any experience?"

"Well, I know Jimmy doesn't care whether you have experience painting or not."

Amanda suspected the same thing about Jimmy, but

Mitch's saying it didn't make her happy. She jutted out her chin as she stared at him. "What makes you say that?"

Mitch smirked. "I just know Jimmy. He likes good-looking women."

"Am I supposed to take that as a compliment?"

"You can take it however you'd like, but what I said is true."

"So you're saying Jimmy hired me because of my looks, not my skills?"

Charlotte rapped her knuckles on the arm of her rocker. "Mitch, you should stop while you're behind. Just because your cousin enjoys the company of a lovely young woman like Amanda is no reason to bad-mouth him."

Amanda pressed her lips together to keep from laughing at the expression on Mitch's face after his aunt's reprimand. Amanda hid her smile behind her hand as she let out a slow breath. She glanced at Mitch, who looked contrite. She almost felt sorry for him. Almost.

"All right, Aunt Charlotte. I won't mention Jimmy again tonight."

"That's not the point." Charlotte eyed Mitch as she motioned toward Amanda. "Do you think you should put this sweet young lady in the middle of the feud you have with your cousin? It's time to end this craziness. You're both grown men."

Mitch looked over at Amanda, his brow wrinkled. "I'm sure you don't want to hear this, and Aunt

Charlotte is right, but I'd like for you to understand why Jimmy isn't on my list of best friends."

Amanda gave Charlotte a questioning glance.

Before Amanda could ask the question, Charlotte nodded in Amanda's direction. "It's okay to tell him that you know."

"She knows about Whitney?" Mitch frowned.

"Yes. I told her the whole story before Jimmy had dinner with us the other night." Charlotte gave Mitch a pointed look. "I didn't know how things would go with you and Jimmy at the same table, and I thought if you two were feuding, Amanda ought to know why."

Mitch's expression resembled a rainstorm on the horizon, but it softened as he looked Amanda's way. "Aunt Charlotte's right. I should get over the past, but every time he's around, I'm reminded of the whole sorry affair."

"I've said my piece, and now I'm going to call it a night. You two are welcome to sit out here and chat as long as you'd like." Charlotte got up and headed for the front door. Before she stepped inside, she turned. "Mitch, you'd better make plans to take Amanda to the Grandfather Mountain Highland Games. If you don't, you know what will happen."

Mitch let out a halfhearted laugh but didn't say anything as Charlotte left. After she closed the door behind her, Mitch turned toward Amanda. "You don't have to go if you don't want to."

Smiling, Amanda remembered the previous conversation about this event. "I wouldn't miss seeing you in a kilt for anything. Maybe we can get you some of those platform shoes to go with your kilt."

Mitch laughed. "I already have my footwear. I have my Ghillie Brogues."

"I have no idea what those are, but I intend to see you wear them."

"I'll be doing that on Saturday. On Friday I'm participating in the Grizzly Bike ride. That should help get me ready for the PMC in August."

Amanda wondered whether she should mention the conversation she'd had with Heather. What was the point? There was no extra money for such a trip. "Yeah, you have to train in order to do that race."

"Have you done it?"

Amanda couldn't shake her head fast enough. "No, I'll do my fundraising with my music, not my legs."

"That reminds me. My mom wants to meet you, and they won't be at church tomorrow because they've gone over to Johnson City to spend the weekend with my brother and his wife. She suggested that you join the family for our weekly dinner at the country club on Tuesday night."

"Sure. I'd love to." Amanda couldn't tell whether Mitch was good with this invitation or whether he issued it at his mother's request. She shouldn't care, but she did.

"I'll pick you up."

Amanda suddenly remembered her new job. "What time? I hope I'll be done with work."

"Just tell Jimmy you have an appointment with my

mom about the fundraiser."

"I hope it's as easy as that."

"And why shouldn't it be?" Mitch frowned.

"Because you two seem to butt heads all the time."

"Jimmy's feud is with me, not my mother." Mitch's mouth formed a grim line.

"So you're telling me it should be okay?"

Mitch nodded. "Jimmy has no quarrel with his aunt Donna."

"Good to know."

Amanda wondered what other family dynamics might exist in this small town. People in small towns often had nothing better to do than keeps tabs on all their acquaintances. Was this town that way? Amanda kind of gathered that from what Charlotte had said about Mitch and Jimmy. Amanda didn't want to get caught up in that kind of situation. So she should steer clear of both Jimmy and Mitch, but that seemed impossible when she worked for one and had someone constantly finding ways to put Mitch and her together.

CHAPTER NINE

Sunlight brought out the reddish highlights in Amanda's auburn hair as Mitch opened the door of his pickup for her to get in. His heart skipped a beat as she smiled at him. Her white sundress trimmed with some kind of fancy dark-blue stitching was just the thing for a country club dinner. She knew just what to wear to such an occasion. That would put Amanda in good stead with his mother, but how would his father react to this woman he had called a "Nashville wannabe"?

"I hope this is appropriate attire for the evening." Amanda buckled her seat belt and looked at him as he slid behind the wheel.

Mitch hoped he hadn't been staring at her. Was that why she'd asked the question? He contemplated the wisdom of complimenting her on the dress. She looked terrific, and he should say so. "It's fine. You clean up well."

"Thanks. I think that was a compliment." Amanda laughed.

Her laughter gave Mitch the confidence to actually give her a compliment. "It was. You look great. The dress is perfect."

"Thanks." She patted the skirt. "This is definitely better than my painting clothes."

"I don't know. I haven't seen you in those clothes. You might look great in those, too." Wow! He was blathering on now. She had him a little discombobulated. Better talk about something else. "How is work?"

"It's work. That's about all I can say about it." She ran a hand through her hair and let it fall to her shoulder. "At least I was able to get the paint out of my hair. I have to learn to be a little more careful."

"So what does Jimmy have you doing?"

"Scraping, scraping, and more scraping."

"I thought you said you got paint in your hair. How can you do that if you're scraping?"

"We eventually got to the painting, but the first day was all scraping." Amanda sighed. "Tomorrow I'm wearing a cap. I should've done that to start."

"You have ball caps to wear?"

"Yeah, but I kind of hate to ruin my Red Sox cap."

"Hey, I've got some old caps you can have. I'll bring a couple by on my way to work tomorrow."

"That would be great." Amanda gazed at him, her eyebrows raised. "Jimmy picks me up at five forty-five. Would you be over by then?"

Mitch didn't usually get up that early, but he'd make the effort for Amanda. He wanted to beat out Jimmy for Amanda's attention. Tonight's outing was a good start. He hoped.

Jimmy had found his way to church on Sunday and had settled himself in the pew next to Amanda. Mitch had forced himself to remain at the back where he usually sat, but Amanda and Jimmy were in full view during the entire service.

Mitch spent most of the time praying that he could learn to get along with his cousin, but like an unwanted guest, the temptation to do just the opposite sat next to Mitch the whole time. This Sunday had taught him one thing. He needed to move up front. No more lurking in the back.

Despite his initial first impression of Amanda, he was finding more and more to like about her. He'd told himself over and over again to no avail that it was lunacy to entertain any kind of relationship with her. His brain got that message, but his stubborn heart refused to listen. "Sure. You can count on it."

"Thanks." Amanda spread out her arms. "I'm going to be the best-dressed painter in town with Charlotte's hand-me-downs and your caps."

Mitch wanted to tell her she'd look good in anything, but he stifled those words as he drove into the parking lot. He'd already said too much. What would she think of the brick-and-frame building that served as the clubhouse for the eighteen-hole golf course, four tennis courts, and a swimming pool? "Here's the local country club, such as it is. Nothing fancy. A little golf course with cow-pasture fairways, and a tiny clubhouse that does serve decent food. I have to give it that."

Amanda unbuckled her seat belt and glanced around. "Looks pretty nice to me. Pinecrest didn't even have a country club."

Mitch nodded, not actually sure she wasn't just being

polite. "Maybe it's okay for a small town."

"It definitely is." She motioned toward the tennis courts and pool. "Do you play tennis or golf?"

Mitch shrugged. "I've tried both, but I've pursued neither in earnest. My dad and mother play both, but my dad prefers golf."

"I'm looking forward to meeting your parents." She smoothed her dress as she stepped out of the pickup.

Mitch wasn't sure she should be so eager to meet his parents. He was pretty sure his mother would be charming and amazing, but he never knew how his dad would react. The man was a mystery to Mitch most of the time. He'd like to say they were eager to meet her, too, but he couldn't count on that. "I hope this is a productive meeting."

"Me, too." Amanda smiled up at him. "If your mom needs a singer, I can fill that role."

Mitch's heart tripped over that smile. He took a deep breath to calm his nerves as he opened the door for Amanda. He looked at his phone as they stepped inside. "We're a little early. That's good because my dad loves punctuality."

Amanda gave him a curious glance as they walked toward the dining room. "Do you think I'm going to embarrass you?"

Mitch stopped in his tracks. "That never crossed my mind. Why would you ask such a question?"

Amanda licked her lips. "Because you seem really nervous."

Mitch wondered what else Amanda had noticed about

him. Did she have a clue that every time she smiled at him that his pulse rate skyrocketed? Should he admit that a meeting with his parents wasn't his favorite thing? "This has nothing to do with you. You might as well know that my dad and I are not always on the best of terms. He thinks I'm wasting my time with the garage."

"Yeah. I think Charlotte mentioned something about that."

Mitch shook his head, a crooked smile curving his mouth. "That Charlotte is giving away all my secrets. Or maybe it's the curse of living in a small town."

"That's another thing. She said she thought if it weren't for the garage, you'd pick up and leave Pineydale. Is that true?"

The question took Mitch by surprise. Was that true? Sure, sometimes family bugged him to no end, but Pineydale, for all its drawbacks, was still the only place he wanted to live. "This is one time Charlotte's wrong. It's true I complain about the local grapevine and everyone knowing everyone else's business, but I love Pineydale. I can't imagine living anywhere else."

"So you love the small-town life?"

"I do."

Amanda smiled. "That makes one of us."

"That must mean you're eager to leave our lovely little town." Mitch's heart twisted at the thought, but he'd known that from the beginning. She was determined to leave.

"You're correct." Amanda sighed. "In fact, how much money do you think I'll need to buy a used car?"

"Depends on the car."

"I just want something reliable that I can drive to Nashville."

"If you'd like me to look around for something, I can. Then I can give you a price. I get people who come into the garage who are looking to sell their cars. So I'll let you know when something comes up." Mitch had to get it in his head that she wanted to leave. He was crazy for entertaining any other thoughts about her, especially when he'd known her for barely over a week. But in that time, he'd seen her talent, her willingness to work no matter what the job, and her kindness to Charlotte. All those things said something good about Amanda. She was more than just a pretty face.

"Thanks. Maybe by then I'll have enough money saved to buy one."

While they stood there talking, Graham Cunningham ushered his wife through the door. He approached Mitch. "Good. You're here on time for once."

Mitch gave Amanda a sideways glance, and she sent him a knowing smile as he shook his dad's hand and hugged his mom. "Mom, Dad, I'd like you to meet Amanda Reynolds."

Amanda stepped forward as Mitch's mom extended her hand. "I'm pleased to meet you, Mrs. Cunningham."

"Please call me Donna." The older woman nodded. "I hear you've been to Nashville to try out your songs."

"Yes. There's lots of talent trying to break in there, so it's not easy to get discovered. But I intend to keep trying." Amanda looked over at Mitch. "Unfortunately,

I've had a little setback with my car."

"And Charlotte's." Graham frowned as he stared at Amanda.

Mitch wanted to step in and protect Amanda. Did he dare stand up to his father, or would that get the evening off to a bad start? Mitch couldn't let his dad intimidate Amanda. "That could've happened to you, Dad."

"True. Thankfully, I don't have to go to Nashville very often." Graham smiled at Amanda.

Mitch wanted to wipe the insincere smile from his father's face, but that would accomplish nothing. He wished he'd never agreed to this dinner. He should have suggested that Amanda meet his mom at another time.

Donna slipped her arm through her husband's and propelled him toward the dining room. "Now, dear, Charlotte will get her car back or get a new one. She isn't upset, so you shouldn't be either."

"Yes, sweetheart." Graham fell into step beside his wife.

Leaning closer, Mitch offered his arm to Amanda. "Don't pay any attention to my dad. He'll probably grumble all evening about something."

"I'm used to it." Amanda smiled up at Mitch. "Your dad and my dad might be brothers separated at birth."

Mitch chuckled as he remembered the follow-up phone call he'd had with Grady Reynolds. Amanda wasn't far off the mark. "Could be. But my mom is cool most of the time. Since my brother and his wife won't be here, it's just the four of us."

"Is that good?"

Mitch shrugged as he lowered his voice a little more. "It could be. I won't have to listen to my dad praise my brother all night."

Amanda raised her eyebrows as she gazed up at him. "Are you in competition with all your male relatives?"

Mitch let that question sink in. Is that how Amanda saw him? Competitive? He'd never seen himself that way, but maybe she had nailed his behavior. Did she see it as a negative? He hoped not. "Never thought of it that way. Guys are competitive in general. Do you get along with your sister?"

Amanda stopped short. "Okay. You got me there. My little sister and I were always in competition for my dad's attention. She usually won because she's a people pleaser, and I'm not."

"So there you have it. Sibling rivalry. You can't avoid it unless you're an only child." Mitch gave her a lopsided smile as they approached the table where his dad was pulling out a chair for his mom.

When Mitch reached the table, he did the same for Amanda. As soon as they were seated, a waiter appeared with menus and took their drink orders. While they studied the menus, he hoped this evening would go smoothly.

Graham laid his menu aside. "Amanda, I understand you've gone to work for my nephew."

Amanda nodded. "Yeah. I never dreamed when I started this trip that I'd wind up painting houses."

"You're from Boston?" Graham stared across the table. "That's a long way from here."

"That's where I studied music and composition. I'm really from Washington State by way of California. That's where I was born."

"Tennessee must seem like a different world to you."

Amanda shrugged. "A few things are different, but people tend to be the same wherever you go."

Mitch was thankful when the waiter returned to take their orders. Mitch wanted to tell his dad to quit peppering Amanda with questions, especially questions that seemed to put her on the defensive. Did she feel uncomfortable under the barrage of inquiries? Mitch wished he could think of something to stop his dad from the inquisition.

As soon as the waiter left, Graham lifted his glass of sweet tea. "Let's have a little toast to the success of the fundraiser."

"Thank you, dear." Donna raised her glass. "Here's to success."

They clinked glasses, and before the glasses were back on the table, Graham started in again.

"Tell us about your family."

Mitch cringed. Couldn't his dad leave Amanda alone?

Amanda smiled. "My dad and stepmom live in eastern Washington State in a little town near Spokane. I have a sister who attends Washington State University, and I just learned I'm going to soon have a half brother."

Mitch looked Amanda's way. That was new information, but he wasn't going to ask about it. He didn't want to join in his dad's game of twenty questions.

"How wonderful," Donna said. "You must be excited."

"Excited, surprised, not believing my dad is going to be a father again after all these years." Amanda let out a little laugh.

Donna leaned forward in her chair. "Tell me about your music."

"A lot of the songs I sing are songs I've written."

"She's got a great voice." Mitch jumped into the conversation.

"What kind of music?" Graham asked.

Mitch gritted his teeth. At least this time the question was about Amanda's music and not about her family. She managed to answer his dad's inquiries without blinking an eye. She didn't seem to mind, even though Mitch found them annoying.

"I have a variety of music I've composed. Some of it's pop, some country, some Christian. I like to perform different styles of music."

"That's wonderful to have such a talent. I'm sure you're enjoying Charlotte's grand piano."

Amanda nodded. "I guess if my car had to break down somewhere, it's good that your son knew a good place for me to stay."

"What instruments do you play besides the piano?" Graham couldn't stop the questioning.

"Guitar, of course, and I can play several woodwinds, flute, piccolo, and oboe. I've tried some brass instruments, but I like woodwinds better. I bang around on the drums a little, but mostly I stick to piano and guitar."

"You are a very talented young woman." Donna nodded. "I'm so glad Mitch led you to Charlotte's place."

Amanda nodded. "Charlotte's an amazing woman. Jimmy told me she's written a lot of poetry."

Donna placed a hand over her heart. "She has. I had forgotten about that. She used to read her poetry at church from time to time, especially at ladies' meetings. Her poems are always inspirational."

"Do you suppose she'd be interested in having me set some of them to music?" Wide-eyed, Amanda looked over at Donna.

"I think she'd be thrilled. You should ask her."

Amanda smiled. "Thanks. I will."

"I hope you don't think you can take advantage of my aunt by using her poems as lyrics for your songs." Graham frowned as he stared at Amanda.

"No, sir. She would get full credit for the lyrics if anything should come of the songs I compose. I would never dream of stealing someone else's work." Amanda sat up and straightened her shoulders. "I came here because I wanted to help a good cause, and all you've done is try your best to make me uncomfortable. If this meeting weren't about a fundraiser, I'd be out of here in a second. You are very rude."

Mitch wanted to stand up and cheer, but he held his breath instead.

Graham leaned back in his chair and let out a belly

laugh. Then he bent forward as he slapped the table. "Amanda, you've got gumption. I like that. I like a woman who can't be intimidated. My Donna's like that. She's always putting me in my place."

Donna nodded. "And it's a good thing, or you'd run roughshod over everyone."

Turning to Mitch, Graham motioned toward Amanda. "She's a good one. I'd keep her around, if I were you."

Mitch didn't have a clue what to say. He wished his dad wasn't so confrontational. Mitch wouldn't blame Amanda in the least if she got up and walked out. How could he possibly explain his father? Maybe there was a lesson in here somewhere.

Mitch forced a smile as he looked at his dad. "She might consider staying around if she didn't have to put up with your questions."

"She was fielding them like a pro." Graham laughed, then wagged a finger at Amanda. "You have to be tough to make it in the music business."

"Yes, sir. That's true." Amanda gave Graham a big cheesy grin. "You have to have a tough exterior to survive."

Before Graham could respond, the waiter appeared with a huge tray filled with their orders. As the waiter served them, Mitch prayed that the rest of the evening would be more congenial. Amanda had survived his father's combative style. Mitch had to give her credit for her brave front.

Amanda was made of tougher stuff than Mitch had originally thought. His first impression of her had been all wrong. The realization made him admire her even more. Could he persuade her to stay? While they ate, that question plagued him over and over, because the answer was always no.

***

Shadows covered Charlotte's front porch as moonlight beamed through the trees. Darkness lurked in the corners around the house, but Mitch's presence chased away the gloom as Amanda emerged from his pickup. She hadn't waited for him to open the door for her, even though she knew he had hurried around to do so.

She didn't want to get caught up in his world. He loved Pineydale and the life he lived here. She needed to keep that in mind every time he looked at her and made her heart race. They were two ships passing in the night, and nothing more. But she liked him way too much. Could he persuade her to stay, as his dad had suggested? She banished the thought.

He'd made the short drive from the country club to Charlotte's house without saying a word to her. The evening had ended on a good note, but Amanda completely understood why Mitch and his father often butted heads.

As Amanda hurried up the walk to the steps, Mitch strode beside her. "Hey, I hope you're not angry with me."

Amanda stopped on the bottom step and turned to

look at him. "Should I be?"

"I wouldn't blame you. My dad was way out of line."

"He was, but your mom's plans for the fundraiser made the evening worthwhile." Amanda turned to go up the steps to the porch but looked back, sensing she should let Mitch know she understood. "And I can't blame you for your father's behavior."

"You could, but thanks for not doing that." Mitch sighed. "I honestly don't understand how my mom puts up with him."

"They love each other."

Mitch let out a halfhearted laugh. "Yeah. I guess like that verse in the Bible that talks about love covering a multitude of sins. Although it's talking about how Jesus's love covers our sins."

"True, but when two people love each other, they can overlook at lot of stuff." Amanda's heart thumped as she looked at Mitch in the dim light. She couldn't begin to describe the way he made her feel, like something she'd never experienced before. When he wasn't around, there was this hollow space in her chest.

"Is that how we have to deal with our fathers?" Mitch gave her a questioning look.

"Maybe that's how we have to deal with everyone. Love them no matter what." Amanda swallowed hard as she stood eye to eye with Mitch. He was standing so close that she could hardly catch her breath. She wanted to kiss him in the worst way, but that would only complicate everything. Besides, if she kissed him, what would he think about her forward ways?

Amanda stepped back to avoid the temptation to lean in and kiss him. She moved too quickly, forgetting she was already on the first step. Her mind consumed with kissing Mitch, she lost her footing. Mitch grabbed her as her arms flailed in the air.

In a second they were in each other's arms, their lips meeting in a kiss that made Amanda's mind spin and every nerve zing. Nothing existed except this man—this wonderful man who made her want to forget why she had started this journey.

No. She couldn't let that happen.

Pulling away, she stared at him, her mind still whirling from that kiss. All she wanted to say was *wow, oh wow*, but she managed to keep the words from rushing out of her mouth.

He gave her a lazy grin. "That was some kiss."

"And it shouldn't have happened."

He touched her arm. "I'm sorry you feel that way. I didn't get that impression while we were kissing."

Amanda couldn't deny the truth of Mitch's observation, but she wasn't going to admit that to him. No doubt she had kissed him with abandon. That was the problem. She had abandoned the promise she'd made to herself to let nothing distract her from her goal. Making it in Nashville. Not a broken-down car, lack of funds, or a handsome, charming man whose kiss was delicious.

Amanda hung her head and bit her lower lip. Finally, she looked up. The grin had become a wry smile. He probably guessed she was having a hard time disagreeing with his assessment of that kiss. She closed her eyes and prayed she wouldn't make a mess of this. When she opened them, he was still staring at her.

"Mitch…" Her voice trailed off as she grasped for something, anything, to say.

"Yeah. That's my name." He joined her on the steps. "Would you like to sit down and discuss this?"

Did she? That just might make things worse, but she couldn't ignore it either. "Okay. What do you want to discuss about it? A kiss is a kiss."

"Not that kiss." Mitch ushered her to the porch swing and motioned for her to sit down. "You can't deny it."

She could, but it would be a lie. Her heart still pumped furiously, making her pulse race as if she'd just run a mile. "Okay. There was chemistry at work, but that still doesn't mean it's a good thing. I'm not staying in Pineydale, and it would be a mistake to act on the attraction when there's no future in it. I can't ignore that fact."

Mitch didn't say anything for a few moments as he put his arm along the back of the swing and stretched his legs out in front of him. "Yeah."

Amanda tried to figure out what she heard in his voice. Resignation, disappointment, or some kind of resolve? "Can we still be friends?"

"You're serious?" Mitch let out a sound that was half-laugh and half-snort.

Amanda licked her lips, the lips that were so thoroughly kissed. "I am. I don't want you to be my enemy. You and Charlotte are the people I know best here. I don't want to lose you as a friend just because we shared an ill-conceived kiss."

Mitch let out a long sigh as he shook his head. "I don't know. Every time I look at you, I'm going to remember that kiss."

His statement held more truth than Amanda wanted to admit. "You still have to take me to the Highland Games. I want to see you in that kilt."

"Okay. We can still be friends, but you'd better be prepared to resist my charms, especially when I'm wearing my kilt." Mitch's wry smile brightened his features. "Now that I've kissed you, I intend to kiss you again."

Amanda's stomach somersaulted. Was she a challenge he couldn't resist, or did he have genuine feelings for her? Either way, nothing good would materialize. "If you're going to be my friend, you can't be thinking in those terms."

"In what terms?"

"Kissing me."

"Oh. I'm not the one who's going to be kissing you. You're the one who's going to beg to kiss me."

Amanda got up from the swing and put her hands on her hips. "Really? Your ego has gotten a little out of hand. Just because I kissed you once doesn't mean I'll kiss you again. And you definitely won't find me begging you to do it."

Grinning, Mitch stood and looked down at her. "We'll see who wins this standoff."

"I will. You can count on it."

Mitch smirked. "I am counting on you kissing me again."

Amanda huffed as she stomped to the door. "You're impossible. Good night."

"Don't forget. I'll be by early in the morning with your caps." He followed her across the porch and saluted as he turned toward the steps. "Good night to you, too. Sweet dreams."

Amanda opened the door. The light from the front hall beamed out, illuminating the smug look on Mitch's face. She took a deep breath. "I'll be dreaming about besting you in this little contest."

"I knew you'd be dreaming about me."

Amanda wanted to give him a smart retort in the worst way, but she wasn't going to win this battle tonight. "See you in the morning."

"Bright and early." He waved as he jogged to his pickup.

She slipped inside without another word and closed the door behind her. Although Mitch was out of sight, he was front and center in her thoughts. She couldn't get that kiss out of her mind, and he knew it.

Standing in the front hall, Amanda glanced around. Darkness enveloped the rooms on either side of the entrance hall. A little light beamed from the kitchen. The quiet house meant Charlotte had retired for the night. Amanda made her way up the stairs, thankful that she didn't have to face Charlotte. The older woman's intuition would probably give her a clue that something had happened between Amanda and Mitch.

Amanda got ready for bed. She lay on her right side, then her left side. She punched her pillow and switched sides again. Nothing she did helped. Finally, she sat on the edge of the bed and stared out the window at the streetlight. Mitch might as well be sitting right there in the room. His image was sitting in her mind—his grin, his good looks, and his kiss. She couldn't shake them from her thoughts. Not only those things appealed to her, but he was kind and helpful.

Amanda let out a helpless cry. Why did she have to like him so much? Why did he have to be so nice? And why did he have to be such a good kisser? Was she doomed? No. With a capital *N* and a capital *O*. She would not let him win. She had songs to write and places to sing them. She wasn't going to let a good-looking guy, no matter how wonderful, keep her from those things.

With a huge sigh, she flung herself back on the bed and stared at the ceiling. But she lay there reliving that kiss. It clung in her mind like the stubborn paint she'd scraped from the side of that house on Monday. She'd managed to scrape the paint away. She could do the same thing with Mitch and his kiss.

CHAPTER TEN

Whistling a tune, Mitch took the steps two at a time as he raced onto Charlotte's front porch. He rang the bell but waited rather than barge in as he usually did. His heart thumped at the prospect of seeing Amanda. Ever since the night of their kiss, he'd seen her several times a week, but only because Charlotte had invited him over for supper or his mother had insisted that he give Amanda a ride out to his parents' house so they could discuss the music for the fundraiser.

Mitch had also spent time with Amanda at the big family Fourth of July celebration at his parents' house. If he could call spending time with her, sharing that time with dozens of his relatives, including Jimmy. Mitch had kept a close eye on his cousin to see whether he intended to put any moves on Amanda. Jimmy had surprised Mitch and paid Amanda little attention. Maybe having Amanda as an employee had kept Jimmy at a distance. Whatever the reason, Mitch was happy.

He didn't mind the way his mother and great-aunt orchestrated their little matchmaking plan, but he couldn't believe he welcomed it. What had happened to the guy who had sworn off women after the debacle with Whitney? He had kissed Amanda, and she had turned a frog into a prince. A prince who was falling in love. He should be scared spitless, but he wasn't.

He was determined to get her to change her mind and stay right here in Pineydale with him.

The door opened, and Amanda stood in the front hallway, her auburn hair gleaming in the sunlight. "Where's your kilt?"

Mitch laughed. "In the pickup. You don't think I'm going to drive all the way to Grandfather Mountain in it, do you?"

"Why not?"

Shaking his head, Mitch laughed again. "Because the thing is made of wool, and it's almost ninety degrees."

"You'll still have to wear it when you get to the games."

"Yeah, but it's a little cooler up in the highlands."

"I see."

Mitch took in her red tank top and tan shorts that showed off her long, shapely legs. He shouldn't go there, but he couldn't help himself. "And I see you're dressed for the warm weather, and your footwear is appropriate for roaming around the meadow."

Amanda stuck out a foot. "I wore these especially for you because I know how much you like these red shoes."

"I do. I can keep track of you in those." Mitch stepped into the hall. "Are you and Charlotte ready to go?"

Charlotte appeared from the kitchen before Amanda could answer. "I'm not going."

"Why not?" Mitch had his suspicions.

"I'm not feeling so well." Charlotte rubbed her head. "I've got one of those awful headaches. I just wouldn't enjoy myself, but you two run along and have a good time."

"But you haven't missed the games in years." Mitch frowned.

Charlotte sighed. "I know. I hate to miss it, but I don't want to drag my headache all the way to North Carolina and back. There'll always be next year."

Mitch didn't know why he was arguing with his aunt. She had just handed him the perfect opportunity to be alone with Amanda, something he'd been hoping for. He didn't know how she felt about this, but he wasn't going to complain.

He looked at Amanda. "Let's go."

Amanda grabbed her blue backpack and slung it over her shoulder. "Ready."

"Bye, Aunt Charlotte. Take care of that headache." Mitch opened the door for Amanda.

"Don't worry about me. I'll be fine." Charlotte waved. "Take some pictures for me."

"We will." Amanda gave Charlotte a hug before going out.

Mitch followed Amanda to his vehicle. Would she say anything about being alone with him for the hour-and-a-half drive? They hadn't been alone together since the night of that kiss. Every time he thought about it, his stomach did flip-flops and his heart beat in double time.

Mitch opened the door for Amanda, and she hopped into the cab. He hurried around to the driver's side and got in. Suddenly nervous, he hoped this day would provide him ample opportunity to win her over to his way of thinking. She needed to stay in Pineydale.

Amanda buckled her seat belt and put her backpack on the floor at her feet. "Don't your parents go to this thing?"

"They used to go when we kids were younger. My dad would rather play golf now, and my mom was never excited about going." Mitch put the pickup in gear and headed out of town.

"So your dad's not into the Scottish kilt thing?"

Mitch laughed. "He never did wear a kilt. He just went to hobnob with people. Those were the days when he was still building his business, and he needed the contacts. After my folks quit going, I always went with Wilbur and Charlotte. Then after Wilbur died, I always took Charlotte, until this year."

"I hope she'll be feeling better before we get back. I hate that she's missing all the fun."

"How do you know it's fun?"

"Charlotte's been telling me all week about the festivities. I'm really looking forward to it, especially seeing you in a kilt." Amanda waggled her eyebrows as she looked at him.

"You're in for a treat."

Amanda laughed. "How did your bike ride go yesterday?"

Mitch let out a long breath. "I finished. That's about it."

"So you didn't win any prizes?"

Mitch shook his head. "That wasn't the point. I was just training for the PMC."

"You should look up my friends while you're there."

"Why don't you go and introduce me?" He gave her a sideways glance.

"I'd love to, but I have work. Besides, I'm saving my money for a car. I can't spend it on a trip to Boston, no matter how tempting."

"So you're tempted to go because you want to be with me?" Grinning, Mitch could see Amanda's frown out of the corner of his eye.

"No. That's your inflated ego's interpretation of what I said."

Mitch laughed. "My inflated ego would love to have you along. Why didn't you tell me your friends asked you to come up to sing in their wedding?"

"How did you know about that?"

"Charlotte's a wealth of information."

Amanda crossed her arms and let out a heavy sigh. "I can't believe she told you."

"Amanda, haven't you figured out she's doing her best to push us together? That's why she didn't come today."

"You mean she was faking a headache?"

"I believe so." Mitch gripped the steering wheel as he negotiated a turn on the highway. "You should go. That way it'll take you longer to get the money for that car, and you'll have time to realize you don't want to leave. You want to stay here with me."

Amanda placed her hands on either side of her head.

"Wow! Are you trying to make my head explode with your self-important chatter? Why would I want to stay in Pineydale when there's a music community waiting for me in Nashville?"

"Because you know you like me."

"You wish."

"See. You can't deny it."

Amanda let out a helpless laugh. "Okay. I do like you, but that doesn't mean anything beyond friendship."

"Sure it does." Mitch tapped his fingers on the steering wheel. "You just have to give it time. Who will give you caps and make sure you've got all the paint out of your hair and off your face?"

Amanda sighed. "How can I argue with that logic?"

"Face it. You can't." Mitch shook his head.

Amanda crossed her hands over her heart. "Mitch, you can't keep teasing like this."

"Who's teasing? I'm very serious."

"I don't want you to be serious."

"Why?"

"Because serious is for people who are ready to settle down, and I'm not. I want to write songs and sing them for the world."

"And you can do that, but that doesn't mean you have to ignore a relationship that could be very good for both of us."

"What happens when we find out it's not going to work?"

Mitch didn't have an answer for that question. He'd been through that with Whitney, and yet, here he was ready to jump into the romance game again. Thoughts of Amanda consumed his mind from the moment he got up in the morning until he went to bed at night. She was like a disease with no cure.

"That's what I thought. You can't tell me." Amanda turned in her seat. "Let's talk about something else or not talk at all."

Mitch's stomach sank. He'd pushed her too hard. He had to back off. His instincts told him she had feelings for him, but she didn't want to admit it. Patience might work wonders if he could muster enough of it in the weeks to come. "Okay, we'll do it your way. How's the painting business?"

"Thanks." Amanda settled back in her seat with what sounded like a contented sigh. "Actually, it's kind of fun, except these freckles. I thought the caps would help keep the sun off my face, but I guess not."

"I hope you're using sunscreen."

Amanda motioned toward the floor. "I am. I've got a tube in my backpack for today."

Mitch wanted to tell her he thought her freckles were cute, but she probably didn't want to hear that. He also wanted to ask how closely she worked with Jimmy, but Mitch was certain that he should steer clear of that topic, too. He didn't want to come across as jealous that his cousin got to work day in and day out with the woman who occupied more and more of his thoughts.

Mitch had to do his best not to say anything that could be construed as promoting a romance between them. Failure to do so could spell doom for any future with the pretty little songstress. How could he convince her not to go to Nashville when her dreams lay there?

No answers populated Mitch's mind, only frustration. Prayers might be in order, but he feared praying that prayer. God might have other plans for him. Charlotte often reminded Mitch of that fact by quoting a verse from Proverbs. *Many are the plans in a person's heart, but it is the Lord's purpose that prevails.* What was the Lord's purpose for Amanda? What was the Lord's purpose for him? Mitch wished he knew.

For the rest of the trip, they talked about the fundraiser, the PMC, and the bounty from Charlotte's garden. Even though they avoided any mention of their previous conversation, the specter of that topic swirled around in Mitch's mind and threatened to come out of his mouth unbidden. Somehow he managed to contain his thoughts.

When they arrived in Linville, Mitch parked his pickup and donned his red-and-black tartan kilt over his shorts.

"So now I know what a Scotsman wears under his kilt." Amanda chuckled as she watched him dress.

"At least this Scotsman. I can't vouch for the others." He held up a finger. "But wait. There's more."

"I'm waiting."

"A kilt isn't complete without all the traditional accessories." Mitch proceeded to put on a leather belt with a decorative buckle and attached a small leather pouch to the belt.

"Is that your man purse?" Amanda put a hand to her

mouth to cover a grin.

Mitch gave her an annoyed look as he patted the pouch. "If you want to call it that, but it's called the sporran. No pockets in a kilt, so I need one. And here's my kilt pin."

"And where does that go?" Amanda cocked her head as she looked him over.

"Right here on the front of the kilt." He pinned it on, then motioned to the front of the pickup as he sat on the end of the truck bed and took off his sandals. "Grab that bag in the backseat for me."

Smiling, Amanda retrieved the bag and handed it to Mitch. "What's in the bag?"

"The rest of my stuff. You'll see in a minute." Mitch opened the bag and pulled out a pair of hose and put them on, then took a small knife from the pouch. "I tuck this right inside the top of my hose."

"You're beginning to look very Scottish, laddie," Amanda said in a fake Scottish brogue. "I can see why you didn't want to wear all this stuff on the ride up here."

Mitch nodded. "Glad you can see that. One last thing. The shoes, my Ghillie Brogues."

Amanda knit her eyebrows together. "Um, do I dare say those are very odd-looking shoes?"

"Say what you like, lassie. This laddie is ready for some fun." Mitch imitated Amanda's Scottish brogue as he hopped down, grabbed her hand, and gave her a twirl. "Are you ready?"

"I am. Let the games begin." Amanda fell into step

beside him. "You look very handsome in your kilt, even if you are wearing a purse."

"Thank you, lassie." His heart lighter, Mitch breathed a sigh of relief that she didn't take offense when he had twirled her around. It took all his willpower not to twirl her right into his embrace. Today would be a test of his willpower all day long. He could do this.

They took a shuttle bus up to the meadow where the games were held. Booths of the different clans lined the area. Mitch took Amanda to the Cunningham booth and showed her the map of Scotland and areas the Cunninghams had occupied through the years.

Amanda turned to him. "Have you ever been to Scotland?"

Mitch shook his head. "But I hope to go some day. Have you traveled there?"

"I have. I spent a semester in London when I was in college, and we made a couple of weekend trips to Scotland. We went to both Edinburgh and Glasgow. We visited the William Wallace Monument. The view from the top is amazing. You can see all across the countryside."

"When I go, I should hire you as my guide." Mitch raised his eyebrows in a question.

"I hardly think I qualify as a guide."

"But it would be fun to have you along."

"Maybe."

As they wandered through the meadow, Amanda fell silent. Mitch feared that his talk of taking her to Scotland had crossed the boundary she had set in their friendship. If there was some way to change her thinking, he wanted to know what it was.

Mitch forced himself not to think about it. Instead he vowed to enjoy the day and Amanda's company. They took in the turning of the caber, the sheaf toss, and some highland dancing, along with dozens of other competitions. They ate a Scottish meat pie while they listened to fiddlers and watched the pipers and drummers play Scottish songs as they marched around the track surrounding the infield. Mitch even paid for Amanda to have a lesson on the bagpipes.

As they walked away from the bagpipe lesson, Mitch pointed toward the area where the wrestling competition was being held. "Now you can say you play the bagpipes, as well as all those other instruments."

Amanda laughed. "I think it takes more than one lesson to say I can play them."

"No one will ever know you've only played them once."

"I'm still not going to make that claim. I've tried, and that's enough." Amanda frowned at him. "You're Scottish. You're the one who should've taken the lesson."

"But you're the musician." Mitch pointed across the meadow. "You want to watch the wrestling?"

Shaking her head, Amanda motioned toward another area. "I'd rather go over there and listen to the singing."

"Sure." Mitch was willing to do whatever made Amanda happy. That was his main goal today.

They made their way over to one of the tents where

folks were gathered to listen to the singing competition. Mitch ushered Amanda into the tent, and they found a seat. One by one the competitors sang Gaelic lullabies, rowing songs, or laments. He didn't understand the Scottish Gaelic, but there was a beauty to the language of his ancestors. He glanced over at Amanda, who appeared transfixed by the allure of the songs.

As the applause ended for one of the singers, the emcee for the event came forward to announce the name of the next contestant. When Mitch heard Amanda's name, he jerked his head in her direction. "You're competing?"

She smiled. "I am."

Mitch had a dozen questions. When had she decided to do this? How did she know the song she was singing? How did she even know about this particular competition? He sat on the edge of his seat as she grabbed a guitar on the way to the platform. And where had she gotten the guitar? Was it hers?

Amanda strummed a few chords. When she started to sing, the sound of her voice played across the strings of Mitch's heart. He'd never heard something so soothing and peaceful. Did he dare hope she'd done this for him, or was it just another music competition to her? He didn't want to hope too much that it was the former.

When she finished singing, the small audience applauded with gusto. Mitch applauded the loudest. She was making it very hard to keep his thoughts on nothing but friendship. That had been hard enough before. Now it was nearly impossible.

When she came back to her seat, he didn't know which question to ask first. "How? Why?"

She put a finger to his lips. "Sh. There are other performers. I'll explain later."

The touch of her finger on his lips was nearly his undoing. He just wanted to gather her in his arms and kiss her. Even though she had touched him, there was this invisible barrier she had put between them, and he didn't know how to get rid of it.

After all the competitors had sung, the judges announced the winner. Mitch didn't understand why Amanda hadn't won. Her voice outshone all the others.

He leaned closer as she picked up the guitar and stowed it near the stage. "You should've won."

She gazed up at him with a smile. "Thanks, but I think there's more to this competition than the singing. I probably didn't pronounce half the words correctly. It was tricky learning the song."

"Was that your guitar?"

Amanda shook her head. "When I signed up, I made arrangements to borrow it."

"How did you enter this competition? How did you even know about?"

"Let's just take a walk around the grounds, and I'll explain."

"Okay." Mitch wanted to put his arm around her waist and pull her close in the worst way, but he couldn't. As he fell into step beside her, he forced himself to be content just being with her. "Please explain."

"Charlotte's really responsible. She showed me the website for the games. Then I took the time to look at all the activities. I mentioned the singing competition to her, and she said I should enter and surprise you." Amanda shrugged as she gave him an impish smile. "Were you surprised?"

"Completely." Mitch chuckled. "When did you sign up?"

"I did that this morning when I went for that restroom break."

"You are a sneaky one."

Amanda grinned at him. "Just remember that."

"I'll have to." He wanted to learn how to sneak into her heart. Was that an impossible dream? He had to quit thinking about it, but her presence made the task difficult. "When did you learn the song?"

"Charlotte had some CDs, and I listened to them over and over again. Then I picked out the chords with my guitar, and I found some lyrics on the Internet. The language is so beautiful. I'd like to learn some more songs."

"I think you should sing that one at the fundraiser."

Smiling, Amanda nodded. "Yeah. That's a good idea since there are so many folks in Pineydale with Scottish ancestry."

"Do you want to stay for the Celtic Jam? It goes from six thirty till ten thirty?"

"Let's stay for part of it. We still have to drive back to Pineydale, and I don't want to be out that late, especially since Charlotte wasn't feeling well when we left."

"I think she's doing fine."

Amanda gave him an annoyed glance. "Don't be so sure. I think she very much wanted to come with us today."

"Okay. We'll stay for a little while." Mitch wasn't sure why Amanda didn't want to admit that people were trying to push them together. Maybe he just wanted it to be true.

They took in more of the festivities and joined the crowd as they listened to the different musicians and bands perform. Mitch loved watching Amanda enjoy the music. No doubt her musician's heart relished every beat and every note. They clapped and danced along with the audience as the moon rose over the meadow.

At the end of a jovial song, Mitch looked down at Amanda as he held up his phone. "It's past nine. Do you want to stay or go?"

Amanda sighed. "This has been so much fun, but I think we'd better head back."

"Okay. Let's go."

As Mitch and Amanda made their way down the mountain along with dozens of other folks, Mitch stopped himself from reaching out and taking her hand. He didn't want to ruin the day with an ill-advised move. "Did you have a good time?"

Amanda smiled up at him. "I had a wonderful time. I'm just sorry Charlotte had to miss this."

Mitch didn't know if he should remind Amanda that Charlotte had chosen not to go. He decided mentioning it would serve no purpose.

After they reached his pickup, Mitch took off his highland duds and put them in the bag in the backseat. Amanda hopped into the front seat and buckled her seat belt. Mitch opened the door, and the dome light illuminated Amanda's face. She made his heart sing like the fiddles, bagpipes, and harps all rolled into one. He didn't want to face the prospect of losing her.

He reached into the backseat. "I've got something for you."

Her eyebrows puckered above her green eyes. "What?"

Mitch held out a straw hat. "To keep the sun off your face. It has a Cunningham tartan band around the crown."

With awe on her face, she took it. "Thank you, but when did you get this? I never saw you carrying anything back. I'm not the only sneaky one around here."

Mitch laughed. "I got it when you went to the restroom and stuck it in my backpack. I've been carrying it around most of the day."

"Guess that restroom break served a lot of purposes." She put it on her head. "Thanks. Fits perfect."

Mitch gazed at her as moonlight lit her face. The hat was perfect. The night was perfect. She was perfect. A trifecta that had him wishing all the wrong things. Like how he'd like to make her a Cunningham. Wow! That was completely crazy. She was making him crazy, thinking things that went far, far beyond where his thoughts should be. Time to herd them back like the sheepdogs they'd seen today rounding up the sheep.

On the drive home, Mitch stuck a CD that he had bought into the player. Scottish music filled the cab of his pickup. Maybe the music would purge his mind of his troubling emotions.

With the music playing, Amanda barely said a word. Mitch wanted so much to know what she was thinking. He wished she was thinking about him. Maybe she was. She'd taken the time to learn a Gaelic song and sing in the competition. Could he hope he was making progress toward something more than friendship with him? Or was that only foolish thinking?

CHAPTER ELEVEN

Lights beamed from the living room windows of Charlotte's house. Worry stabbed Amanda's heart as Mitch stopped his pickup at the curb. She looked at him. "Do you think something's wrong with Charlotte? It's not like her to have the front room lights on at this time of night?"

"That is unusual. I'll go with you."

Amanda didn't wait for Mitch but grabbed her hat and backpack, then sprinted toward the house and up the steps. She turned the knob and found the door unlocked. That was unusual also. Her heart racing with anxiety, she flung the door open and looked toward the living room. She stopped in her tracks, her mouth hanging open.

"Don't just stand there. Come give me a hug."

Moving into the living room in a daze, Amanda couldn't believe her eyes. "Heather, what are you and Max doing here?"

Heather hugged Amanda, then stepped back. "I had an oncology conference in Asheville, and Max came with me. We couldn't be this close and not come to see how you're doing."

"It's so good to see you guys." Amanda hugged Max. "How did you know where to find me?"

"I talked to Kelsey, and she told us." Max turned to Charlotte. "And Charlotte has been entertaining us since we got here late this afternoon. She said you'd gone over to Grandfather Mountain for the day. I wish we'd known. We could've spent the day with you there."

"Yeah." Amanda could hardly contain her smiles. Then she remembered Mitch, who still stood in the dim light of the front hall. She looked his way, and her heart skipped a beat. She motioned to him as she tried to calm her racing heart. "Mitch, come meet my friends Heather and Max."

Mitch stepped into the living room and first shook Max's hand, then Heather's. "Glad to meet you. Amanda told me ya'll are riding in the PMC."

Heather nodded. "So you're the one from here who's participating in the PMC?"

Nodding, Mitch turned to Amanda. "Did you tell them?"

"I mentioned it in passing when I talked with Heather a few weeks ago." Amanda wondered what Mitch would make of that. Today's outing had only served to confuse her feelings more. She didn't want to care for Mitch in any way beyond friendship, but she feared she was fighting a losing battle. Maybe that battle had been lost the first time she'd seen him interacting with his beloved great-aunt.

"Well, why don't you two come on in and join the party?" Charlotte motioned for them to come into the living room, where she still sat on the floral print sofa.

Amanda went over to the sofa and sat next to

Charlotte. "Are you feeling better?"

"Much better. I took a nap, and that really helped." Charlotte patted the hand Amanda had in her lap. "How was your day?"

"Amazing. I'm so sorry you missed it." Amanda went on to tell the group about all the things she and Mitch had done, but she didn't mention the hat.

"That does sound amazing. I wish I'd known about it. My maiden name, Watson, has Scottish roots," Heather said.

Mitch sat forward in his chair. "You'll have to come for a visit next year and go to the games."

"Sounds like fun." Heather looked at Max. "What do you say?"

Max nodded. "We can make tentative plans."

"That would be wonderful. I would love for you guys to come down. We could make a weekend of it." Amanda didn't miss the look that passed between Heather and Max. Amanda realized her statement sounded as if she would still be in Pineydale a year from now. What did that say about her plans to make her mark on the Nashville music scene?

Were Heather and Max speculating that Mitch was someone special in Amanda's life? She had to keep reminding herself that he was just a friend, a special friend for sure. Today's outing had proved that. Right? Or was she trying to convince herself that she hadn't wanted to do exactly what Mitch had said he was waiting for her to do? Kiss him again.

Charlotte stood. "You young folks can visit as long

as you like, but I'm headed to bed. It's way past my bedtime."

Amanda stood alongside Charlotte and gave her a hug. "You take care of yourself."

"I am." Charlotte motioned to the other side of the room. "I showed Heather and Max where they're going to sleep tonight. I'll see you all in the morning. And that includes you, Mitchell."

"Yes, ma'am. I'll see you in church. Good night." With a salute, Mitch stood as Charlotte left the room.

A chorus of good nights followed Charlotte out the door. As soon as Amanda heard Charlotte's footsteps on the stairs, she turned to Heather. "How did Charlotte seem when you arrived? She said she wasn't feeling well this morning, and I worried about her all day."

Heather shrugged. "I think we awakened her from a nap, but she really seemed okay to me."

Amanda let out a harsh breath. "I hope you're right."

"She's probably right." Mitch gave Amanda a knowing look.

Amanda looked between Max and Heather and hoped the two didn't draw any wrong conclusions from the fact that Amanda had spent the whole day with Mitch. "So how long do you guys get to stay?"

"Our flight home is on Wednesday. We plan to do a little sightseeing in the Smoky Mountains."

"That's great!" Amanda still couldn't get the surprise of Max and Heather's visit out of her mind. Although Max was Amanda's stepcousin, they had never been that close. Amanda had bonded with Heather, and the bond had brought her closer to Max. His fight against cancer had served to bring them even closer. "Did you guys tour Biltmore while you were in Asheville?"

Heather nodded. "Yes, and I loved it. We did that this morning, then ate lunch there and drove here this afternoon."

"Heather is always trying to expand my horizons by dragging me on what I consider field trips." Max chuckled.

Heather frowned at Max. "You loved every minute of it. Don't deny it."

"Okay. I did learn some fascinating things," Max replied.

"Anyway, we came here on a mission," Heather said.

Amanda knit her eyebrows. "What mission?"

Heather reached into her purse and pulled out an envelope. "Tara and Caleb sent you this."

Amanda took it. "What's this?"

"Open it and see," Heather said.

Amanda fumbled with the envelope and finally pulled out a piece of paper. She looked it over, then gazed at Heather. "A voucher for an airline ticket?"

Heather nodded. "Yeah, so you can sing at their wedding."

Amanda didn't know what to say.

"And before you say anything, we've already cleared everything with Jimmy for you to get off work that Friday and Monday, if you need it."

Amanda shook her head. "How do you even know about Jimmy, and when did you talk to him?"

"It wasn't hard." Heather smiled. "After we got here today, we asked Charlotte about your boss, and she helped us get ahold of him. So you're set."

"I don't believe this." Amanda waved the paper in the air. "They didn't have to do this."

"Oh yes, they did. Hailey insisted, and that little girl is very persuasive." Heather chuckled.

"I hope they aren't expecting me to ride in the PMC, because I am not prepared for that."

"No. All you have to do is sing," Heather said.

Mitch wrinkled his brow. "What does a wedding have to do with the PMC?"

"The wedding is the weekend of the PMC," Max said.

Mitch raised his eyebrows. "That's an interesting choice of wedding dates, since you're all riding."

"They have a very personal interest in the PMC. Like me, Tara's little girl, Hailey, is a cancer survivor, so the wedding date is perfect for them." Max nodded in Mitch's direction.

"Then that makes sense." Mitch pushed himself up from his chair. "It's getting late, so I'll head home and let ya'll have a chance to visit. See you tomorrow at church."

Amanda hopped up as Mitch headed to the door. She caught him just as he stepped outside. "You didn't have to rush off."

"Yeah, I know, but you probably want to visit with your friends without me hanging around." Mitch shrugged. "Why didn't you tell me about the invite to sing? I would've helped you get there."

Amanda scuffed the toe of her shoe on the floorboards of the porch. "It wasn't your problem, and I didn't figure I could get off work."

"Seems that getting off work was an easy fix. You should've mentioned it to me, especially since you knew I was going to Boston." Mitch's expression showed his displeasure, but it morphed into a smile. "Charlotte probably had Jimmy begging for you to take off work."

"I can just hear that conversation." Amanda chuckled. "But you know, as far as being stuck here in Pineydale, I made my choices, and I figured I had to deal with the consequences of those choices."

"Yeah, but you've got friends here who are willing to help. Remember that friend thing you keep talking about? Don't push your friends away. Rely on them."

Amanda swallowed the lump in her throat. "I'll remember."

"You'd better." Mitch gave her a pointed look.

"Thanks for a wonderful, fabulous day. I enjoyed every minute." Amanda gave him an impish smile. "Especially the sight of you in your kilt."

"Maybe it will entice you to stay around Pineydale, since you told your friends to come visit next year." Mitch smiled wryly.

"Don't read anything into that." Amanda wasn't going to admit for a minute that her willpower was weakening where Mitch was concerned.

"Okay. I won't, but I'm still waiting for that kiss."

"You've got a long wait." Amanda had a feeling that

was not the complete truth. "I wouldn't want to ruin our friendship."

Mitch looked at her with a smirk. "But we could have so much more. I'd hate for you to miss out."

Amanda sighed. "Good night, Mitch. I'll see you in the morning."

Mitch shook his head. "I'm being dismissed like a naughty child, but I'm not discouraged."

Amanda let out a helpless laugh. "This is a very long good night."

"And I like it that way." He grinned. "But I don't want to overstay my welcome. Bye."

Before Amanda could reply, he sprinted down the walk to his pickup. He stopped after he opened the door and blew her a kiss. She wanted to yell out to him that he was cheating, but she forced herself not to react other than to wave goodbye. Was he right? Would she one day kiss him of her own volition?

Amanda pushed that question away as she hurried back to the living room, where only Heather remained. "Where's Max?"

"He decided to go up to bed. He's not much of a late-night person, and he is cautious about getting overtired."

Amanda sat down in the chair that Max had occupied earlier. "So is everything still good with Max?"

Heather nodded. "His last tests came back with good results, but I have to admit that the worry never goes away. I know we need to trust God with all of this, but sometimes that's hard to remember."

Amanda knew the feeling. "I'm glad to hear Max is

doing well. It seems like I've been gone for months rather than a few weeks."

Heather leaned toward Amanda. "How are you doing? I've been a little concerned about you."

"Oh, I'm good. It's not what I planned, but as you've learned, Charlotte is a jewel, and my job isn't horrible. I'm saving up for a car so I can get to Nashville."

"That's terrible what happened with Charlotte's car. She told us today that she's getting a new one."

Amanda nodded. "She has it all picked out. When Mitch took her to the car dealer, she was like a kid in a candy store."

"So what's going on with you and Mitch?"

Amanda's emotions were too mixed up to explain anything to Heather, but she expected some kind of response. "We're friends. That's it."

"Yeah. Sure." Heather chuckled. "Now tell me what's really going on."

Amanda sighed. "I'm not sure what to tell you."

"So you've never dated?" Heather narrowed her gaze. "What was today?"

"Mitch has gone to the games for years with his great-aunt and great-uncle. His uncle Wilbur died several years ago, but he still takes Charlotte. Today when we were ready to leave, she claimed a headache." Amanda let out a little giggle. "I just wanted to see Mitch in a kilt."

"And did you do that?"

Amanda nodded. "He looks really good."

A wry smile curving her mouth, Heather shook her

head. "And you want me to believe you're just friends?"

Amanda pressed her fingers to the bridge of her nose. "Remember when we were talking about you and Max at my open mic event that night in Concord?"

"Yeah. What about it?"

"I mentioned that I never had a relationship that lasted very long."

Heather nodded. "I remember you told me you had one that lasted six months and you were glad when it ended."

"That's the one."

"So what does this have to do with Mitch?"

"Mitch and I really, really don't have a romantic relationship other than one kiss."

A slow smile enveloped Heather's face. "And it was a kiss you can't forget?"

"How'd you know?"

"Good guess. Tell me about it."

Amanda hesitated. Did she want to kiss and tell? Is that what she'd be doing? She pressed her fingers to her temples, then looked at Heather. "The worst part is the kiss was mostly an accident. I tripped on the front steps. He grabbed me, and the next thing I knew, we were in each other's arms. He was kissing me, and I was kissing him back without a second thought."

"Sounds like the first time Max and I kissed."

"Really?"

"Yeah. It was the night of the open mic event. I took him home, and he tripped on the edge of the sidewalk. I steadied him. Then he was kissing me."

Amanda laughed. "Wow! That is almost exactly how it happened with Mitch and me."

"So then what did you do?"

"I panicked."

"And by that you mean what?"

Amanda went on to give Heather a brief accounting of the discussion she had with Mitch.

"Interesting." Heather raised her eyebrows. "Why are you so afraid of getting involved with him?"

Amanda took a deep breath and let it out slowly. Did it sound crazy to fear falling in love and losing yourself? "It's too much like that six-month relationship I mentioned before. The guy swept me off my feet, got my focus on him, and almost made me give up my music. Then he dumped me. Although my heart was broken, I realized he had saved me from making a grave mistake. I'm determined not to let anything get in the way of my goals again. I managed to resist my dad trying to dissuade me from pursuing a music career, but I almost let some guy do it. I won't let that happen again. Never."

Heather folded her hands in her lap and peered at Amanda. "And you think Mitch is going to keep you from your music?"

"Yeah. He's already told me he's going to persuade me to stay here in Pineydale with him."

Heather slowly nodded. "I see. So he's indicated a real interest in you, and you're afraid he's going to succeed in his quest to get you to stay?"

"I don't know. I'm afraid to let him get too close

because he might just do that." Amanda let out a deep sigh.

"But you spent the whole day with him."

"That was only because Charlotte backed out on us at the last minute. She was supposed to go along."

"Interesting. Do you suppose she's trying to do a little matchmaking?"

Amanda frowned. "That's what Mitch thinks."

"And he said that to you?"

"Yeah. Since that kiss, he's not shy about showing his interest in me."

"Maybe that's a good thing. Did you ever think that you got stuck here for a reason, and that reason is Mitch?"

Amanda sighed again. "Are you saying God has a different plan for my life than I do?"

"That often happens." Nodding, Heather chuckled. "I would never have dreamed that Max and I would wind up together."

"I understand your thinking there, but why would God give me this talent to sing and then not have me use it?"

"I can't answer that." Heather shrugged. "You just need to pray about it."

Amanda let out a harsh breath. "I hear that all the time. How do I know what God wants me to do? Do I just drift around waiting for something to happen, and if it happens, that must be what God wants?"

Heather reached over and touched Amanda's arm. "It's not easy to know what direction to take, but sometimes we do have to wait and let God work in our lives."

"At this point, I intend to choose my music over Mitchell Cunningham." Amanda straightened her shoulders as a sign of her resolve.

"Whatever happens, I'm excited that you get to be there for Tara and Caleb's wedding. Max and I insist that you stay with us."

"Thanks." Amanda smiled. "It'll be fun to come back for a visit. I'll have to see what kind of song Tara and Caleb want me to sing."

"If Hailey has her way, it'll probably be at least one of the songs you sang at our wedding."

"I'll have to give them a call." Amanda wondered whether she would cross paths with Mitch while she was back in Boston. She shook that thought away. Why did he have to invade her thoughts at every turn?

"Will you and Mitch travel together now that you're going to Boston at the same time?"

Amanda stifled a groan at her friend's question. Could Heather read minds? "I'm sure he already has his ticket, and I'm not going out of my way to be on the same flight."

"I'm not going to try to talk you out of that decision tonight. God will direct your path." Heather stood. "I'm going to call it a night."

Amanda joined Heather as they climbed the stairs together. As they stopped outside the door to the room where Max and Heather were staying, Amanda gave Heather a hug. "Thanks for coming. I appreciate your concern and your friendship."

"And I'm going to pray for you, my friend."

"Thanks for that, too." Amanda smiled. "Good night."

After Heather closed the door, Amanda tiptoed down the hallway to her own room. As she got ready for bed, she thought about her day spent with Mitch. They'd had a wonderful time. She had to be honest with herself. She was torn between her love of music and her growing affection for a guy who could derail her plans. Why did she have to meet him now? Would God really send her in the direction she ought to go? Did that direction include Mitch?

While those questions rolled through her mind, Amanda couldn't help thinking she had fallen into the same trap. Even though she wasn't dating Mitch, she had taken the easy way by staying in Pineydale. Her less-than-stellar results from her first venture into Nashville had left her with a feeling of failure, and she had retreated into the comfortable. If she really wanted a career in Nashville, she had to be there, not in Pineydale. She had to face the ups and downs. She couldn't be a coward.

Seeing Max again reminded her of the reason she had started this journey. She couldn't let a little discouragement or a handsome Scotsman dissuade her from her goal. She couldn't waste more time here. Nashville was her only choice.

***

The following Monday crawled by as Mitch waited for quitting time and a chance to see Amanda. He had an invitation to Charlotte's for supper, and he didn't plan to waste one more minute getting there. After closing up, he jogged to his pickup with a smile on his face and joy in his heart. He looked forward to discussing the trip to Boston. Since the trip to Grandfather Mountain and the visit from Heather and Max over the weekend, Mitch had the feeling he was making progress toward convincing Amanda to put down roots in Pineydale.

When he arrived at Charlotte's, he hurried to the front door and let himself in. "Charlotte, Amanda, I'm here."

Charlotte moseyed into the hallway from the kitchen. "You sound chipper."

"I'm looking forward to your good cooking." Mitch grinned. "Where's Amanda?"

Taking a deep breath, Charlotte shook her head. "She's gone."

"What do you mean, she's gone?" Mitch's stomach sank as a sick feeling hit his gut.

"Just what I said. She left for Nashville on the bus this afternoon."

"Without saying a word to me?"

"I'm afraid so." Charlotte shrugged. "She came down to breakfast all packed and ready to go. She talked to Jimmy early this morning and told him she wouldn't be coming in."

"You didn't give her your car again, did you?"

Charlotte shook her head. "I tried, but she insisted on taking the bus."

"And you just let her go?"

"I couldn't very well lock her in her room." Charlotte frowned at him. "She's got a good reason to go. She has an interview tomorrow for one of the jobs she applied for right after she arrived in town."

Mitch had no idea she had applied for jobs in Nashville. Why should that surprise him? Why couldn't he get it through his thick head that she was never going to stay? He'd held on to a false hope like a locked-up engine. The sympathy radiating from Charlotte's eyes did nothing to comfort him. Anger at the circumstances that took Amanda away bubbled up inside him. He rubbed the back of his neck, trying to push the anger aside.

"Did she say when she'd be back?"

"She bought a one-way ticket."

"So does that mean she's not coming back? What about her airline ticket to Boston out of the Tri-Cities airport?"

Charlotte held out her hands, palms up, as she shrugged. "She wasn't very forthcoming with her plans. She might take a bus from Nashville to the Tri-Cities. Your guess is as good as mine."

Mitch shouldn't be upset with Charlotte for not having all the answers, but he was frustrated that she didn't seem to know Amanda's plans. He wanted to hop in his pickup and take off for Nashville this very moment and tell Amanda that she had to come back to

Pineydale, but would that solve anything? "Do you at least know where she's staying?"

"I do."

When Charlotte didn't say anything else, Mitch wondered whether his aunt was keeping quiet on purpose. "Would you like to share that information with me?"

"I don't know." She gave him a no-nonsense look. "What do you plan to do with it?"

"Go after her."

"To what end?"

Mitch let out a harsh breath, then ran a hand across the top of his head. "I don't know. Why didn't she tell me?"

"Maybe because she knew she'd get this kind of reaction from you."

"So you think I'm out of line?"

"Why don't we eat and discuss this over our meal?" Charlotte motioned toward the kitchen. "Maybe a little comfort food will put you in a better frame of mind."

Eating would delay any plans he had to drive to Nashville tonight, and food wasn't going to give him any comfort. "I'm not sure my frame of mind is going to change."

"Well, let's give it a try." Charlotte strode toward the kitchen without waiting for Mitch.

He stared after her, not sure if he should follow. But he didn't know where Amanda was, and he wouldn't find out unless he talked to his aunt. So he didn't have a choice except to do as she said. He trudged toward the kitchen. He said nothing as he sat on one of the barstools at the island and leaned his head in his hands as he rested his elbows on the island's surface.

Charlotte came up beside him and put an arm around his shoulders. "You got over Whitney. You can get over Amanda, too."

Mitch looked up. "I'm not letting her go. I'm going after her."

"And just how do you expect to find her?"

"You're going to tell me where she's staying."

"Eat." Charlotte pointed to the casserole dish sitting in front of him. "Then we'll talk."

Mitch didn't feel much like eating, but if that was what it took to get information out of his great-aunt, then that was what he'd do. Eat. He dipped the serving spoon into the casserole and piled a steaming heap of the chicken dish onto his plate.

After he put the spoon back in the dish, Charlotte grabbed his hand. "Let's pray."

Mitch bowed his head, even though he didn't feel much like praying either. He tried to tamp down the anger and disappointment, but it rose in him like the steam rising from the casserole.

Charlotte squeezed his hand. "Lord, thank you for this day you've given us and for this food. Be with Mitch and please take away his hurt and give him guidance for the future. Amen."

Despite his negative attitude, Charlotte's prayer had softened his heart. He did need wisdom. He didn't want to lose again when it came to love. Yeah. He loved

Amanda, but she had left, taking his heart with her. Why did he always have to fall for the wrong kind of woman? He didn't have a thing to say to Charlotte. He was afraid he had only angry words. He ate just to keep from saying something he might regret.

Charlotte let him eat in silence for several minutes. Finally, she touched his arm. "If I tell you where Amanda is, do you promise not to leave tonight? I don't want you driving to Nashville this late. She'll still be there tomorrow."

Taking another big bite of the casserole, Mitch let his aunt's advice roll through his mind. As he swallowed, he turned to her. "What do you expect me to do?"

"Eat your supper."

Annoyed, Mitch eyed Charlotte. "I'm eating, but I want to know what to do about Amanda."

"Support her decision. If you care about her, you'll let her figure out what she wants."

"And if that doesn't include me, then what?"

"You'll have to accept that decision. You can't make her love you."

Mitch narrowed his gaze. "Who said anything about love?"

"Nobody had to. Your actions send out enough clues." Charlotte chuckled, then took a bite of her food.

Quiet filled the room as Mitch finished his meal. The hum of the refrigerator accompanied Mitch's troubled thoughts. He didn't know why he'd tried to deny that he loved Amanda. Maybe because he felt the fool all over again. Just like with Whitney. But he couldn't just let

Amanda go without a fight. Or had he already lost, and there was no point in pursuing her? What had made him think his charms would entice her to stay?

Charlotte tapped his arm. "I think a good night's sleep will do wonders for your decision to go after Amanda. Tomorrow morning, if you still think you have to go to Nashville, I'll tell you where she is."

"Tomorrow?" Mitch tried not to yell. "You keep moving the bar. First, it's eat. Now, it's sleep. What will it be tomorrow?"

"Calm down." Charlotte patted his arm again. "You're right. I did say I'd tell you after you ate. So I have to stick to that, but I don't want you going out of here with the thought in mind that you're going to drive to Nashville tonight."

Mitch understood his aunt's thinking because he was tempted to do just that, but she was right. He needed a plan. A good plan. But he felt so hapless, so hopeless, and so helpless.

He got up and rinsed his dish and put it in the dishwasher, then turned to Charlotte. "What should I do?"

Charlotte joined him at the sink. "You've got to let her go. If she's meant to be with you, she'll come back."

"So you're saying I shouldn't go to Nashville?"

Charlotte shook her head. "I didn't say that. Just not tonight. I think she'd like someone in her cheering section when she performs."

Mitch stared down at his great-aunt. "But you still haven't told me where she is."

Charlotte gave him an impish smile. "She's staying in the same hotel where she stayed the last time."

Putting an arm around Charlotte's shoulders, Mitch grinned. "Thanks, Aunt Charlotte. Amanda will have someone rooting for her in the crowd, because I'll be there."

"So who's going to be tending the garage while you're gone?"

"Johnny's got everything under control. He's been handling most of the work, while I've been working on Amanda's old car."

"Do you have plans for that car?"

"Not sure what I'm going to do with it. I'll know more after I get the parts I need." Mitch shrugged. "That's another reason to go to Nashville. I've got to check on some parts there."

"Then a trip to the big city makes more sense." Charlotte frowned at him. "You should've told me that in the first place."

"I was only thinking of Amanda, not auto parts."

"I can understand that." Charlotte chuckled as she wagged a finger at him. "You let me know what's going on when you get there."

"No worries." Mitch smiled and gave Charlotte a hug. "You'll be the first one I call. Now I've got to get going so I can get a hotel room and make my plan of attack."

Charlotte walked with Mitch to the front door. "The first thing on your list is prayer."

"Yes, ma'am." Nodding, Mitch opened the door.

"Wish me the best."

"I always do."

Mitch jogged to his pickup, his heart a little lighter than when he'd discovered Amanda had left again. He wasn't sure how she had taken such a hold on his life, but he couldn't deny that his heart was hers whether she felt the same way or not. She definitely liked him in the friendship category. Wasn't that a good start? Or was he fooling himself again? He couldn't sit around and wait—he'd do what he could to win her over. That plan would start tomorrow.

CHAPTER TWELVE

"Jo, I'm so glad you agreed to share a hotel room with me." Amanda flung herself on the bed closest to the window, then sat up as quickly.

Josie Adams sat on the side of the other bed in the hotel room. "Glad to be here. I'm blessed to work for my dad's trucking company, and he's always on board to give me time off when I want to come to Nashville for my music."

"Wish my dad felt the same way."

Josie frowned. "Why doesn't he?"

"I wish I knew. Maybe he's afraid I'll wind up without a penny to my name." Amanda sat cross-legged on the bed as she let out a halfhearted laugh. "I'm practically broke anyway, and I don't have much hope of landing a decent job after my less-than-stellar interview today."

"You probably didn't do as badly as you think."

"Oh yes, I did." Amanda let out a loud sigh. "It's been too long since I've gone for interviews. I should've practiced or at least thought through what kind of questions they'd ask and have a ready answer instead of fumbling around for one."

"You never know, just like with the open mic events."

Amanda shook her head. "I definitely know that I bombed out on the interview. It's one of my big faults—jumping into things without the proper preparation. That's what landed me in Pineydale."

"Did that lady who lent you her car ever get it back after it was stolen?"

"Nope, but she got a new one."

"You never did tell me how you got back to Pineydale."

Amanda wasn't sure she wanted to mention Mitch. She had never said a thing about him during the weekly phone call she had with Josie about their music. "Charlotte's nephew drove her to Nashville so she could talk to the police about her car. They took me back to Pineydale, and I've been staying with Charlotte, painting houses, and saving my money so I can buy a car."

"You are blessed that Charlotte lets you live with her."

"For sure. I'd be in a real mess if it weren't for her."

"Do I remember right that you met her through the nephew?"

Somehow Amanda knew the conversation would come around to Mitch. She couldn't avoid him, even when he was miles away. "Yeah. The nephew."

"And he's the mechanic who bought your car, right?"

"My dad's car. That's why I don't have any money or a car."

"Any more job prospects besides the one you had an interview for today?"

"I applied for several others, but I've never heard

back from those." Amanda blew out a puff of air. "I suppose I should follow up, but after painting all day, I just want to veg out when I get back to Charlotte's. I should probably make some phone calls while I'm in town, just to let them know I'm still out here."

"Yeah, and I could help you practice for interviews."

"Really? That would be super."

"My cousin's a job recruiter, and he has this website where he has all these interview questions." Josie grabbed her backpack and pulled a tablet out of a zipper pocket. "We can look at them right now."

Amanda glanced at the clock on the bedside stand. "I appreciate the help, but shouldn't we grab a bite to eat before we head out tonight?"

"We don't have to be there until nine o'clock. We've got plenty of time to go over them before we leave."

"Sure." Amanda couldn't argue with Josie. She had the transportation and way more experience with open mic events in Nashville.

"Let's make this as real as possible. Sit there, and I'll sit on the other side of the desk and barrage you with questions." Chuckling, Josie motioned to the small desk against the wall as she waved the tablet in the air.

"Okay, if that's the way you want it." Amanda hoped this would improve her interview skills.

For the next hour Josie quizzed, cajoled, and put Amanda through the paces as if she were having a real interview. When Josie finally zipped her tablet away in the backpack, Amanda felt as though she'd been through another round of interviews.

"Are you sure you don't have a sideline as a recruiter?"

Josie laughed. "My cousin lived with us for a few months while he was waiting for his house to be built. I listened to him do phone interviews. I was just copying his style."

"If that doesn't give me the practice I need, I don't know what will." Amanda jumped up from the chair. "Let's get ready to go. I'm hungry."

"Sure thing." Josie headed for the bathroom. "Just let me freshen up a bit."

"Guess I should do that, too." Amanda grabbed a brush from the small bag she had sitting on the desk. "You go first."

Amanda brushed her hair while she waited for her turn in the bathroom. Just as she put the brush back into the bag, a knock sounded on the door. "Jo, are you expecting someone?"

"No." Josie poked her head out of the bathroom. "Want me to see who it is?"

"Check the peephole to see if you recognize the person."

Josie stood on her tiptoes as she looked through the peephole, then she turned to Amanda. "It's a man, but I don't know him. Could it be someone you know?"

"I doubt it. I'm not expecting any visitors." Amanda wrinkled her nose. "But I'll take a look."

Amanda looked at the distorted image of a man on the other side of the door. With a sigh, she put her back to the door. "That viewer isn't much help. I have no clue who the man is. Do you think it's safe to open the door?"

"We've got the chain in the slot. We could open it just enough to ask who it is."

Amanda grimaced. "You want to do it, or should I?"

Josie pointed at Amanda. "You."

Amanda glanced around the room for something they could use as a weapon in case the unknown person had malicious intentions. Without saying a word, she motioned toward the iron in the closet. Josie grabbed it and held it over her head, equipped to attack.

Her heart pounding, Amanda pushed the lever down and prepared to open the door just a crack. She hoped she'd find a friendly person on the other side, but she was ready to slam the door closed in an instant. She held her breath and prayed.

***

Voices filtered through the door of Amanda's hotel room, but Mitch couldn't make out what they were saying. Was someone with Amanda? Charlotte hadn't said anything about Amanda meeting someone in Nashville. She had only given him the name of the hotel and her room number. Mitch swallowed hard. Who could be in the room with her?

He didn't want to think it was another man. He shook that foolish thought away. Amanda wasn't that kind of woman. He hoped he wasn't wrong. He strained to hear the conversation. Should he knock again or call out

Amanda's name? Maybe he had the wrong room. Maybe he should've called first.

A click sounded, and the door opened a crack. "Amanda? It's me. Mitch."

"Mitch?" Amanda's voice came out in a squeak, and the door slammed closed.

He stared at the door. What was he to make of that greeting? He might as well be banging his head against the door and not his knuckles. Just as he turned to leave, the door swung open.

Amanda bounded into the hallway. "What are you doing here?"

A gamut of emotions rolled over him as he looked at her. Relief, uncertainty, and the big one—love. What was he going to do with that one, when she didn't feel the same?

"I'm in town on business, and Charlotte told me where you were staying. So I thought I'd look you up. I hope I'm not intruding." Mitch tried to see who was in the room with Amanda.

She smiled. "We were just about to leave to get something to eat. You can join us if you want."

"We?" He hoped *we* didn't mean another man.

"Yeah." Amanda motioned for him to come into the room. "Come meet Jo."

Mitch's heart sank. A man. Someone she had met on the music scene? Mitch took a deep breath and prepared to meet the competition. He stepped into the room and came face to face with a petite young woman with shoulder-length light-brown hair, who stood there with

an iron in one hand. Relief washed over him, but regret chased it away. What had made him think the worst of the woman he loved?

Jealousy, insecurity, or stupidity? Probably all three. Whitney's betrayal colored his thoughts about women too many times. The image of her kissing Jimmy on her front porch haunted his thoughts more often than he would like. If he truly wanted to love Amanda, he had to put Whitney and all that baggage behind him.

The young woman stepped forward and held out her free hand. "Hi, I'm Josie. Amanda likes to call me Jo."

"She calls me Mitch." Feeling silly, he smiled.

Josie grinned. "You're the nephew, right?"

So that was how Amanda saw him. Charlotte's nephew. At least she had mentioned him to her friend. "Yeah. I'm Charlotte's great-nephew."

Amanda gave Josie's shoulders a squeeze. "Jo's the one who stayed with me the night Charlotte's car was stolen. She's a terrific songwriter and is helping me negotiate the Nashville music scene. We have an open mic event tonight, if you want to go with us."

The invitation filled Mitch's chest with a flutter of excitement, but he had to temper his emotions. Taking his pursuit of Amanda slow and easy would serve him better than an all-out assault. "I wouldn't miss it."

Amanda picked up her purse and guitar. "So if we're ready, let's get going."

"Gotta put this iron away." Josie hoisted it in the air, then placed it in the holder in the nearby closet.

Mitch knit his eyebrows. "Have you been ironing

without an ironing board?"

"Nope." Amanda gave him a sheepish grin. "That was our weapon of choice in case you tried to attack. We couldn't tell who you were through the viewer."

Mitch laughed out loud as he shook his head. "Glad you figured out I wasn't a bad guy before you used that on my head."

"Don't make fun of us." Amanda frowned at him.

"Not making fun, but I could just feel that thing against my skull." Mitch rubbed his head. "I commend your caution."

"Thanks. Amanda was the quick thinker when she pointed to the iron to use as a weapon." Josie grabbed her guitar case. "I'm ready."

"So where are we headed, and are we driving separate or together?" Mitch opened the door.

"That's up to Josie." Amanda slipped through the doorway.

"I'll drive since I know where we're going."

"Sure." Mitch hoped his disappointment didn't show. If he drove, Amanda could sit up front with him. With Josie driving, he would be relegated to the backseat.

As they rode down the elevator, Mitch gave himself a pep talk. He was here with Amanda, and she hadn't conked him on the head with an iron. She had invited him out to eat and to join them at the open mic event. What more could he have hoped for? This evening was filled with promise. That was all he had to remember.

***

The latest country tune played over the radio in Josie's car. Josie chattered on about what to expect at the open mic event. Amanda half listened. Her mind was focused on Mitch. She couldn't believe he had come to Nashville. He'd said he was here on business. She wanted to ask a dozen questions, but she didn't feel comfortable doing it in front of Josie.

Was he here only for business, or had he come to hear her perform or wish her luck? She wanted him to be good with her decision to come to here. She didn't know why it made any difference. They were just friends. But that was the problem. She wasn't thinking about Mitch in terms of just friendship these days. Her discussion with Heather had made that quite clear.

More than ever, the dreams of a music career and her feelings for Mitch battled it out in her heart. She feared which one would win. But this week was all about the music. She couldn't let his presence distract her from her main goal.

As Josie pulled into the parking lot at the restaurant, Amanda tried to figure out what kinds of things she should talk about while they ate. Maybe she'd just sit and listen, because Josie had enough to say for both of them.

Amanda's thoughts about Josie proved true during their meal. She laughed and talked and explained everything about what she expected the evening to bring. She had the poise and self-assurance about her music that Amanda wished she had. Ever since her first venture to Nashville, she had lost confidence in her music. That had never happened before.

The job interview had forced her to push herself out of her comfort zone and take a chance again. Amanda was grateful for Josie's encouragement, but right now Amanda was wondering whether her friend was flirting with Mitch. Amanda didn't have any right to be jealous of Josie's interest in him.

After they finished eating, Amanda excused herself to go to the ladies' room. Josie joined her. As soon as they reached the other side of the restaurant, Josie grabbed Amanda's arm and pulled her to a stop. "Why didn't you tell me that *the nephew* was such a good-looking man? Are you keeping him all to yourself?"

Amanda wanted to say yes, but she didn't want to give Josie the idea that Mitch and Amanda were anything except friends. "I have no claims on him."

"Too bad he doesn't live closer to me." Josie grinned. "I'd lay some claims on him."

Amanda shrugged as mixed feelings about Mitch rolled through her mind. "That's up to you."

"So you don't mind?" Josie raised her eyebrows.

Yeah, Amanda minded, but she wasn't going to say so. She either had to step out and make known her interest in Mitch, or she had to step away. "Do whatever you'd like."

Josie narrowed her gaze. "You seem a little reluctant to make that statement."

"I'm concentrating on my music right now. I don't need the distraction of a man in my life."

"Okay. If that's the way you feel, I'm not going to stand by and let a good-looking guy go unnoticed."

Amanda entered the ladies' room and hoped this would end the discussion about Mitch. She wasn't sure what to make of his appearance, and she didn't want to figure it out. Why did he have to be so nice, so handsome, and so available? Not to mention such a good kisser. She shoved that thought away before it could take hold in her mind. Why did he have to show up and throw her whole plan into indecision again?

When Amanda and Josie returned to the table, they found that Mitch had paid the bill.

"Thanks, but you didn't have to do that." Amanda didn't want to owe him anything, but she already owed him more than she could ever repay. She should be grateful and move on.

"Sure I did." Mitch grinned. "I need to do my part to support the up-and-coming musicians in my life."

"Yeah, thanks." Josie smiled up at Mitch, her interest obvious. "Let's head out. We've got some singing to do."

During the drive to the venue for the open mic event, Josie flirted with Mitch without apology. Amanda couldn't tell whether Mitch was just being polite or enjoying the whole thing. She tried to focus on the song she intended to perform. She and Josie had four nights of singing and networking opportunities lined up this week, and Amanda wanted to make the best use of every one of them. She wouldn't let Mitch's presence distract her from that goal.

They arrived at the venue about a half an hour before the sign-up for the open mic performances. They found seats, and Josie settled in beside Mitch and asked him about his car business. He appeared to lap up her interest, while Amanda sat by and tried not to be jealous.

After the sign-up time, the three of them settled in to listen to the other performers. By the time the open mic portion of the show rolled around, tension buzzed through every part of Amanda's body. She remembered her less-than-successful experience in the previous open mic nights. She tried to put those out of her mind and concentrate on the here and now. Tonight she had a new start. Could she win over this audience?

Josie sang first, and her tune had the audience clapping along, even Mitch. She had so much talent, and Amanda didn't know if she could compete. How would she stack up with one of the best performances of the night?

When Josie returned to her seat, Amanda leaned closer. "That was terrific. I hope I do half as well."

"Thanks." Smiling, Josie winked. "Now it's your turn to show them what you've got. You have a great song."

"I hope you're right." Amanda grabbed her guitar and headed to the stage as the MC announced her name. She could do this. She had to pretend this was family camp back in Pinecrest and she was singing for all those people back there. Or she could pretend she was back in Charlotte's music room, singing for her and Mitch. Either way, Amanda needed to forget herself and get lost in the music. That was when she performed the best.

Amanda took the stage and settled on a stool behind the microphone. "Hi, everyone. I'm going to sing a little tune I wrote called 'When to Let Go.' She glanced out at the audience as she strummed an opening on the guitar.

Mitch grinned at her and gave her a thumbs-up sign.

"How do I know

When to let go?

How do I know

When to love again?

Why do I try?

Why do I cry

when someone says your name?"

Her voice floated loud and strong into the audience. Unlike the last time she'd done an open mic event, the folks were listening to her song. Amanda's heart sang with the knowledge that her song had captured their attention. When she finished, the crowd showed their appreciation with resounding applause and cheers. Amanda bowed and gave a little wave to the audience as she left the stage. She couldn't quit smiling as she returned to her seat.

Mitch clapped her on the back. "You did a great job."

"Thanks." Amanda wanted to throw her arms around him, but she held her guitar tight instead, just as she was holding on tight to her music and resisting the temptation to throw it all away for this man.

Josie gave Amanda a hug. "That was one great performance. That should get you some notice in this town."

"Thanks. I appreciate your support and friendship."

Amanda let out a big sigh of relief. "Now I can relax and enjoy the other performances."

When the evening ended, Josie drove back to the hotel. "I think we got some notice tonight."

"Yeah, it was a good night for networking." Amanda glanced over at Josie. "Thanks for introducing me to all those people. I feel so much better about my music, so much better than the last time I was here. I went home pretty discouraged after that outing."

"You both should be happy about your performances tonight." Mitch laid a hand on the back of Amanda's seat as he leaned forward. "Thanks for letting me tag along. It was a fun time."

"You can tag along with us any time you want." Josie chuckled.

Amanda didn't say anything. What did Mitch think about Josie's obvious interest? She was an attractive woman, and he might share her interest. Amanda didn't want to think about that. Mitch was only a distraction, and she couldn't allow him to take her focus off her goals.

CHAPTER THIRTEEN

The next morning, Mitch awakened as the sun peeked around the edges of the blackout curtains in his hotel room. He put his hands behind his head as he lay there and stared at the ceiling in the dim light. His night had been filled with dreams of Amanda, who was just a few doors down the hotel hallway. Thoughts of her haunted him day and night.

He wished there was some way to make her love him, but that was not the way love worked.

Amanda had been surprised to see him, and he sensed her dismay at his appearance. At least she hadn't turned him away. Josie, on the other hand, made no secret of her interest in him. He was flattered because she was cute and fun, but she wasn't Amanda. Thankfully, tonight he would have Amanda all to himself, or that was his plan anyway.

Amanda planned to sing at the open mic event at the venue where Charlotte's car had been stolen. Josie had told them security had been beefed up there with a guard in the parking lot. Since Josie had already won the event there, she planned to sing at a different open mic event tonight. Mitch had to believe Amanda would be grateful that he was here to give her a ride rather than having to take a taxi.

As he slid out of bed and opened the curtains, he thought about her amazing performance last night. He didn't know why someone hadn't signed her to a contract right then and there, but he didn't know the ins and outs of the music business. He knew about cars, and that was his business here today. He had a breakfast meeting with a parts guy today and another meeting later in the day with someone who might have an interest in Amanda's car. He wasn't sure about selling that car, but he wanted to test the waters.

What would Amanda think? These days everything came back to her.

With her front and center in his thoughts, he got ready for the day. He made himself a cup of coffee and drank it while he gazed out the window at Nashville, the place where Amanda's dreams lay. How could he compete with that? How would Pineydale ever stack up to a bustling metropolis like this?

Draining the last of his coffee, he picked up his folder and headed for the door. As he stepped through the door, he glanced across the hallway toward Amanda's room, two doors down. Should he knock on her door?

Glancing at his phone, he shook his head. Too early. They might still be asleep. He would talk to her later today.

During his breakfast meeting, his mind was more on Amanda than on auto parts, especially while he discussed her car with a potential buyer. The man made arrangements to come and look at the car, but Mitch had the feeling he was more of a tire kicker than a potential buyer. And that thought made him remember seeing Amanda for the first time as she kicked the tire of her car in disgust.

He was certain her action that day had created a soft spot in his heart for her, and it had grown until that spot occupied his whole heart. As he drove back to the hotel, he prayed that somehow tonight's outing would bring both of them success. He didn't know how that was possible, but wasn't everything possible with God?

As soon as he returned to his room, he dumped his folders on the bed and called Amanda. When she answered, his heart did one of those crazy flip-flops.

"Hi, how was your day?"

Her question brightened his spirits. "I bought some auto parts. Not much excitement there."

"I thought auto parts made your heart go pitter-patter." She giggled.

You're the only thing that makes my heart do that. The words sat on the tip of his tongue, but she probably didn't want to hear them. "Not the auto parts, but the cars."

"Oh. I'll have to remember that."

Mitch wanted her to remember only one thing. Him. "Are you ready for tonight? What time do you want to leave?"

"I want to leave here around five. I want to make sure I'm there in plenty of time to sign up."

"When you're ready to go, just come and knock on my door."

"Okay. Thanks for being my chauffeur tonight."

"The pleasure's all mine." Mitch knew that for certain. He could hardly wait. "See you soon."

Mitch first tried to read, but his mind kept wandering to Amanda. He closed his book and turned on the TV, but the show did nothing to steer his mind in another direction. Finally, he gave up and hoped it wouldn't be a mistake to knock on Amanda's door.

He took a deep breath and let it out in a whoosh. His heart hammering, he waited for her to answer. He hoped Josie wasn't still there. What a time to think about that. He should've called to make sure Amanda was alone. If Josie was there, she would occupy all of his time, and Amanda would let it happen.

The door opened a crack, and Amanda peered through the slit between the door and the doorframe. "Oh, it's you. I thought you were waiting for me to come to your room."

"I was, but I got bored." Mitch hoped she'd undo the chain and let him in.

Amanda opened the door and stepped aside. "I'm not sure anything going on in here will solve your boredom problem."

Thinking just being with her would solve his boredom, he stepped inside and glanced around. No Josie. That was a relief. "Has Josie already left?"

"Yeah. She needed to get some new guitar strings, so she decided to head out a while ago." Amanda shrugged as she picked her guitar up from the bed. "Sorry you missed her."

Mitch wanted to set the record straight. He didn't

care about missing Josie. All he wanted was Amanda's company, but he feared telling her so would ruin the whole evening. "It's not like this was my last chance to see her. We've got two more nights of events."

Amanda raised her eyebrows. "You're going to be here that long?"

Mitch guessed she hadn't been paying attention when he'd mentioned not going home until Friday evening. "Yeah. I've got business here all week."

"I had no idea. When did this come about?"

When I found out you left. What would she say if she knew that? He didn't want to lie, but he didn't want to tell her his reason for the trip. "Monday."

"I wish I'd known. I wouldn't have had to take the bus."

"If you'd told me, I would've been glad to give you a ride." He waited for her reaction.

"That's me, going off half-cocked. I did it again." Amanda let out a loud sigh as her shoulders sagged. "Heather and Max's visit reminded me why I started this journey. My goal is to have a successful music career, and that wasn't going to happen if I was painting houses in Pineydale. Then that interview came up, and I felt that was a sign I should go."

"But why didn't you mention it to me?" He held his breath, wondering if he really wanted to know.

"The email about the interview popped up in my box Monday morning. I had to make arrangements with Jimmy to take time off work, pack, get all my gear, make hotel arrangements, and talk to Josie. Thankfully, she was able to come and share a room with me. That saved me a chunk of money."

"Do you want me to give you a ride back to Pineydale?"

"You'd stay that long?"

"Sure. I told you I have business here all week."

"What kind of business keeps you here until Saturday?"

Had she guessed that he had spread out his appointments on purpose? The business he could've wrapped up in a couple of days was taking him a lot longer this trip. "I come to Nashville a couple of times a year to visit vendors and check with people who might be interested in buying the cars I restore."

"Interesting. Are you trying to sell my dad's car?"

Mitch nodded. "I talked to a guy today about it."

"Is he going to buy it?"

Mitch wondered whether Amanda still wanted that car. "Does it make a difference to you?"

"It shouldn't. I've called it a hunk of junk, but I've had it ever since I went away to college. Guess I was more attached to it than I thought." She let out a little sigh. "But it's not mine anymore."

Listening to Amanda lament about that car made him rethink selling it. Could he win her heart with her former vehicle? He shook that thought away. Things didn't win hearts. What did make one person fall in love with another?

Why did he love Amanda? Sometimes he thought it was something beyond his control. He just loved her. It was as simple as that, but it wasn't simple at all, especially the fact that she didn't love him.

Maybe Charlotte was wrong about Amanda fearing his reaction to her leaving? He'd like to think so.

"So do you mind if I hang out here until it's time to go?"

"If you don't mind listening to me practice."

Did he dare say that would be a treat? "I don't mind."

"Okay, then." She motioned to the chair in the corner. "Have a seat, and I'll entertain you."

Mitch spent the next hour listening to Amanda and relishing every second with her. But the more he listened, the more he knew it would only be a matter of time before someone discovered her talent and she would be gone from his life. She was born to entertain. The thought made him sad, but he didn't want the sadness to ruin this time with her.

***

The cavernous room was filled with the buzz of conversation as Amanda led Mitch toward a table. "You can wait here while I sign up."

"Sure."

Despite the afternoon of practice and her successful performance the night before, Amanda's nerves still had her wired. Or maybe it was being with Mitch that made her feel that way. Or maybe it was trying so hard not to let him detour her from her goals.

The whole time he'd listened to her practice, she'd

kept thinking he was waiting for her to throw herself into his arms and kiss him. That thought didn't go away. No matter how hard she tried to push it out of her mind, it stuck there in a corner like an old piece of chewing gum stuck to the bottom of a chair.

When she returned to the table, he grinned at her, and her pulse took off like she'd just run around the block. "I'm all set."

"Do you want to order something to eat?"

Amanda grimaced. "You can order, and I'll just nibble. I'm too nervous to eat."

"I'm glad to share. You can eat as much or as little as you want."

"Thanks. I usually eat afterwards."

As Mitch ordered some food, Amanda surveyed the room. She recognized a couple of the folks who had been in the competition the last time she'd been here. While Mitch placed his order, she excused herself and went over to talk to them.

Mitch gave her a questioning look when she returned. "Someone you know?"

"Yeah. Folks I remember from the last time I was here."

"I suppose having me along is cramping your networking."

Amanda shook her head. "I like having you here. I know someone's in my corner."

"I'm glad to hear you say that. I wasn't so sure I was welcome."

Amanda straightened her shoulders and gave him a

little frown. Had she made him feel unwelcome? Or was it this whole friendship thing? He wanted more, and she couldn't let that happen. "It's always good to have a friend here to cheer me on."

Disappointment colored his expression even though he tried to hide it. "At least you never fail to let me know where I stand. I plan on being the best friend you've ever had."

His statement made Amanda feel guilty. Was she taking advantage of a friend? He was doing so much for her, but how was she being a friend to him? Maybe her push for friendship only made this an impossible situation, but she wouldn't change it. He had to understand that. "Thanks. I appreciate that."

Mitch's food came, and their conversation lulled as Mitch ate with gusto and Amanda nibbled. The upcoming competition and being with Mitch diminished her appetite.

After the first performances, Mitch leaned over. "You've got this won. Hands down. You're way better than any of those three who just sang."

"You've only listened to three songwriters."

"But your songs are so much better, and you sing better, too."

"I wish you were one of the judges."

"The audience does get to vote later, right?"

"Yeah, but you only get one vote."

He grinned. "Maybe I can find a way to stuff the ballot box."

Amanda laughed. "If I win, I want to do it fair and

square."

"I predict you'll win. I have no doubts."

"Remember. It's all about the song, not the performance."

"I still say you're going to win."

"I wish I had your confidence." Mitch always pumped her up. She should feel good about that, but it only made her sad.

They sat through three more rounds. After every round, Mitch wrote his scores for the singers on little pieces of paper like one of those judges on those TV talent shows and held it up for her to see. He leaned closer and whispered his critiques in her ear. She gave him an annoyed look, but his comedic comments took away her earlier nervousness. She wanted so badly to loop her arm through his and sit close, but that would be a mistake in so many ways.

Finally, her turn came, and Mitch gave her thumbs-up as she grabbed her guitar and headed for the stage. As she settled on the middle stool and plugged in her guitar, Mitch smiled at her. Her heart raced. She should be used to that by now, but his presence always made her insides a jumble of nerves and emotions. Emotions she didn't want to feel.

That had to be the subject of the next song she wrote. Maybe that would help get him out of her system. Here she was ready to sing, and all she was thinking about was Mitch.

Amanda tried to listen with interest to the woman who sang first, but in Amanda's opinion, the song was lackluster and so was the singing. She was sure she could do better, and Mitch thought so, too. Despite her worry about falling for him, his support gave her confidence.

When her turn came, she introduced herself and her song, her heart thundering in her ears. She glanced out at the audience. Mitch smiled at her and nodded his head. His confidence brought that same confidence to her heart. She would win this competition.

Her fingers played the chords with ease, and the song came from the depths of her heart as her voice filled the room. When the song ended, the applause was loud and long. She hoped the judges loved her song as much as the audience.

Mitch greeted Amanda with a high five when she got back to the table. "That was terrific, even better than last night. See. I told you you'd win."

"I like your confidence in me, but there's such a thing as too much confidence." She sat down and put away her guitar.

"Never too much confidence." He offered her what was left of the food. "Only six more contestants to go, and you're on your way to stardom."

Her stomach still churned with nerves, and she waved the food away. She had done her best, and now the waiting began. The other six songs were good, not great, in Mitch's opinion as he continued his little rating game. She was thankful for the dim lighting, because she didn't want the people around her to know what he was doing, even though it made her smile.

After all the contestants had sung, the MC explained the voting process and the time element involved with voting. Nervous tension created a whirling sensation in Amanda's chest as she waited.

Mitch gave her a little frown. "Why didn't you tell everyone back in Pineydale that they could vote for you on their computers? Sounds to me like a legal way to stuff the ballot box."

Amanda let out a helpless laugh. "The results will be what they'll be. I'm ready to accept whatever they are."

"You're too calm."

Amanda laughed again. "If you only knew."

He gave her a look that melted her heart. She closed her eyes against the feelings that swept over her. She did want to be more than his friend, but he probably didn't want to play second fiddle to her music. Or that was what she kept telling herself in order not to succumb to those feelings.

When the MC returned to the stage with the results, Mitch leaned closer. "This is it. You get to collect your prize."

Amanda held her breath as the MC named the audience winner, and that winner wasn't her.

Mitch frowned. "What was this audience thinking? Obviously they have no taste."

"Sh." Amanda flashed him an annoyed look.

"Okay. I'll behave myself."

After some photos of the audience winner, the MC stepped to the mic again to announce the judges' winner. Again Amanda held her breath. This time she closed her eyes. She wanted to hear her name so badly.

"And the winner is contestant number fourteen, Amanda Reynolds."

Amanda clapped her hands over her mouth to stifle the scream that sat on her lips. She jumped up and hugged Mitch without thinking. He held her close, and it felt so right. But this was her big moment.

"You'd better get up there," Mitch whispered.

Stepping out of his embrace, she nodded. "Thanks for believing in me."

"You're welcome. I'm always in your corner. Remember that."

She collected her prize and posed for photos, all the time thinking about what Mitch had said. He knew she'd win, and he was always in her corner. She wished she could be in his corner, be there for him, but her music called. She had to answer that call.

CHAPTER FOURTEEN

Mitch dragged his roller bag through the jet bridge as he tried to catch Amanda. She had sat a couple of rows ahead of him next to a window, while he had opted for an aisle seat. At least he'd managed to convince her to go on the same flight with him, thanks to a little help from Max and Heather.

During the whole flight, he sat thinking about the way she had thrown her arms around his neck when she won the competition. But he couldn't put any hope in her reaction. He was her friend, a friend who was there to cheer her on, nothing more.

Mitch had never been to Boston, and he was looking forward to it in more ways than one. Now that he and Amanda were here, they would go their separate ways until the wedding. Mitch wished it were different, but his plans had been made months ago, while hers had been made during Max and Heather's visit. At least the future bride and groom had insisted that Amanda bring Mitch to the wedding. He could tell she wasn't thrilled with the prospect, but to promote peace and harmony, she had agreed.

Sometimes he wondered whether he was just spinning his wheels with Amanda. She was polite and friendly but distant. He wasn't a quitter, but every time she reminded him that they were only friends, his heart hitched with disappointment. He couldn't help remembering the night of Max and Heather's visit how she'd told him she was stuck in Pineydale. He had to come to grips with knowing she felt that way.

Her recent visit to Nashville and her win at the competition should tell him all he needed to know about where her plans would lead. He needed to get that through his head, but his heart had put up a big blockade and told him not to give up.

Mitch caught up to Amanda just outside the jet bridge, only because she had been waylaid by the crowd. "Hey, I didn't know you went out for track."

She shook her head without looking at him. "I got a text from Max. He's already here. I don't want to keep him waiting."

"My friend won't be here for fifteen, twenty minutes, so I'll go with you and say hi to Max."

Amanda shrugged. "Whatever you'd like."

Downhearted that Amanda showed no interest in whether he came or not, Mitch tagged along beside her. Maybe this was a crazy pursuit. He kept thinking that might be the case, but his foolish heart wouldn't let go. What did it take to change the mind of a woman who was determined to blot him from her life? Persistence? Patience? Prayer?

He'd definitely been neglectful when it came to the last one.

After nearly sprinting through the airport, Mitch followed Amanda through the automatic doors that led outside. Hot, humid August air filled with vehicle exhaust greeted him. Buses, taxis, and passenger cars clogged the roadways outside the terminal as people found their rides. Mitch spied Max standing next to a car on the other side of the roadway nearest the terminal. Just as he was about to tell Amanda, she waved and rushed to cross the lane. Without saying a word, Mitch hurried behind her.

Amanda slowed down when she reached the other side. "Are you supposed to meet your ride here?"

"Yeah." Mitch guessed from her question that she hadn't been listening when he'd mentioned how long he'd have to wait for his friend. She was dismissing him again, but he wasn't going to let that get him down. "Hey, Max. Good to see you again."

Max stepped forward and shook Mitch's hand. "Yeah. Wish we could spend more time together, but I know you're eager to visit with your college buddy."

"Yeah. He said he's taking me to his favorite Italian restaurant in the North End." Mitch glanced at Amanda, who had already hopped into the passenger seat of Max's car. She certainly appeared ready to get away. Away from him? He had to quit being negative.

"We're headed that way ourselves. Heather and I have a favorite place over there, too. You don't happen to know where your friend is going, do you?" Max smiled as he took Amanda's suitcase and put it in the trunk.

Mitch shrugged. "He didn't say the name of the restaurant."

"Well, maybe we'll run into you, but that could be a long shot since there are dozens of restaurants in that area." Max opened his door and saluted before he got in. "We'll definitely see you at the wedding. Have a good visit with your friends."

Mitch waved as they drove off. He couldn't tell whether Amanda had waved. Why was he torturing himself over this woman? Somehow she had grabbed his heart, and he didn't know how to retrieve it. He had obviously learned nothing from his experience with Whitney.

While Mitch stood there trying to decipher his feelings, Brandon arrived in his gray sedan. Mitch wheeled his suitcase toward the curb as Brandon parked and got out to greet him.

"Hope you haven't been waiting too long." Brandon opened the door to the backseat. "You can throw your bag in there."

"Thanks." Mitch opened the passenger door. "I haven't been here long. Anyway, I was saying hi to a friend of my traveling companion."

"Traveling companion?"

"Yeah, Amanda Reynolds."

Brandon gave Mitch a speculative glance as he drove away from the terminal. "And just who is Amanda Reynolds?"

Mitch went on to explain how he'd met Amanda and how they had wound up together on the flight from Tennessee to Boston.

"So you're going to a wedding on Sunday?" Brandon

made his way into downtown Boston.

"Yeah. After Sunday's ride, the wedding's being held at some bed-and-breakfast west of Boston. The bride and groom are both doing the ride, the same route we're doing, Wellesley to Wellesley." Mitch took in the tall buildings, the traffic, and honking horns. He enjoyed seeing the city, but the chaos reminded him of why he preferred a quiet little town like Pineydale.

Brandon turned into a parking garage, and after taking a ticket, went up the ramps until he found an open space. "Got your bike ready. So we're all set for the ride."

"And I've been training. So I'm good to go."

"We're going to have a great time for a great cause." As Brandon shut off the engine, he looked over at Mitch with a nod. "I thought I'd show you some of the city before we meet Staci and her friend. I hope you don't mind that she invited her coworker to join us."

Mitch shook his head. "Fine with me. So have you and Staci set a date yet?"

Brandon headed toward the nearby elevator. "We're waiting to see what happens with her job. We were thinking in the late spring. We do have to decide soon because some of these wedding venues are booked over a year in advance."

"Maybe you should elope or do one of those destination weddings. Eloping would be much cheaper." Mitch chuckled.

"Staci would never agree to elope."

"Yeah. A lot of women have this fairy-tale image of

their wedding day." Mitch couldn't help thinking about Whitney and all the plans they had made. What kind of wedding would appeal to Amanda? Mitch shut down that question before it could take root in his mind.

"What's going on with you and this Amanda chick?" Brandon asked as the elevator descended.

Mitch wondered how truthful he should be. Did he want to say he was a complete loser in the realm of romance? "She's not interested in me. The only thing she wants is friendship and to find success with her music in Nashville. She's only in Pineydale because her car died there, and she doesn't have money for a new one."

As they stepped out to the sidewalk, Brandon pointed to his left. "I thought you might like to see Faneuil Hall."

Glad his friend didn't ask more questions about Amanda, Mitch nodded as he fell into step beside Brandon. "Thanks for doing all the touristy stuff for me."

"No need to thank me. I love showing off my city." Brandon gave Mitch a sideways glance as they stopped at a crosswalk to wait for the light. "So how bad do you have it for this girl?"

Mitch searched his mind, trying to figure out how Brandon knew Mitch had a more than average interest in Amanda. What had he said to give his friend that idea? "What makes you ask that?"

Brandon laughed. "You can't fool me. You sound just like you did when you were dating Whitney.

Besides, I wanted to make sure I wasn't getting you in trouble with Amanda because I let Staci set this thing up with her co-worker."

"I'm not dating Amanda."

"But you want to in the worst way. Don't try to deny it."

The light changed to green. Mitch hoofed it across the street as fast as he could, but he couldn't outrun the truth of Brandon's statement. "Okay. You want me to admit that I'm a failure when it comes to women."

"I didn't ask you to admit anything of the sort." Brandon waved a hand in the air. "I can tell by the way you talk about Amanda that she's important to you."

Mitch let out a long sigh. "Okay. She makes me crazy. Our paths cross all the time, but she insists there can be nothing between us but friendship. And lately it seems like she's trying to avoid me, and when she can't, she ignores me."

"You do have it bad." Brandon shook his head.

"I don't know what I've got, but let's talk about something else." Mitch wished he could purge thoughts of Amanda from his mind, but from the moment he'd seen her traipsing down the road in those red tennis shoes, she had been part of his thoughts. After he'd listened to her call him laddie as she'd laughed about seeing him in his kilt and heard her sing that Scottish lullaby, he was a goner. It was a sickness to care so much for someone when she didn't feel the same way. If lovesickness was a disease, he had it.

"If she's ignoring you, why is it that you're attending

that wedding with her?"

Mitch let out a halfhearted laugh. "That was arranged by her well-meaning friends. I think the whole world is trying to push us together, and she is resisting with everything she's got in her."

Brandon clapped Mitch on the back as they entered Faneuil Hall. "You'll win her over with the Cunningham charm."

"I wish I had your confidence. She has really deflated my ego."

"Well, at least you admit it."

"Let's forget her and take in all this history."

"Maybe Staci's friend will help you forget."

Mitch nodded his agreement, but he didn't have much confidence in that scenario. For the rest of the afternoon, he tried his best to concentrate on the history around him. But images of Amanda invaded his mind at every turn. Somehow he would get through this weekend.

***

The restaurant buzzed with conversation as Amanda followed Max and Heather into the small dining area with tables covered in red-and-white-checked tablecloths. The place seated thirty people at the most. Delicious aromas wafted through the air as the hostess led them to a table beside the window.

Max and Heather sat on one side while Amanda sat on the other by herself. She felt like a third wheel. That was good for a tricycle, but it only served to remind her of Mitch. She wondered where he was tonight. He'd told Max that his friend was taking him someplace here in the North End. Would they run into each other? No matter how many times she told him their association ended with friendship, she was having a hard time convincing herself of that with each passing day, especially after the way he'd come after her when she'd gone to Nashville.

Tonight she wasn't going to think about him. He would not ruin her evening from afar.

Max poked at the menu. "I recommend either the veal parm or the manicotti."

"I'm going to have the veal." Amanda put her menu back on the table. "Are you guys ready for your big ride tomorrow and Sunday?"

"That's what we've been training for." Heather leaned over and gave Max a kiss on the cheek. "What are you going to do with your time?"

"I'm spending the day with Hailey." Amanda played a little air guitar. "I'm going to teach her how to play."

"Won't the guitar be almost as big as she is?" Heather asked.

Amanda shook her head. "They have them for kids. Tara told me Hailey got one for her birthday, and she's been counting the days until I could teach her to play."

"And she's so excited about the wedding. She showed me just how she's going to toss the rose petals." Heather chuckled as she pretended to throw petals in the air. "Are you planning to watch any of the ride?"

"On Sunday, Hailey, Caleb's parents, and I are going to help man one of the water stations."

Heather nodded. "I remember now that Caleb told me his folks were in charge of a water station on Sunday."

"They're joining our team from church for the early-morning prayer service on Sunday before we start our ride." Max looked toward the door. "You'll never guess who just walked in."

Amanda didn't want to turn around. She could feel Mitch's presence without even looking. Should she pretend she didn't know who Max was talking about? That would be just plain silly. "Are you going to invite them to join us?"

"There are four of them. They'll need their own table." Max waved.

Four? Amanda wanted to turn around in the worst way, but she wouldn't. She would just sit here like a statue and pretend that his presence didn't affect her at all.

Max stood as Mitch stopped at the table. They shook hands. "I thought we might run into you tonight."

"Small world, this big city." Mitch looked her way as he stood next to the table. Although he smiled, he didn't look comfortable. "Hi, Amanda."

"Hi." She pasted a smile on her face but didn't say another thing.

"Introduce us to your friends." Max motioned toward the others who were with Mitch.

Mitch ushered the one man and two women over to the table.

Amanda's heart sank, and a big lump rose in her throat as she realized Mitch was with one of the women. She shouldn't be jealous. She'd told him over and over again that they were only friends, but in reality, she'd been lying to herself. She tried to hold her smile in place as Mitch introduced Brandon, his fiancée, Staci, and Lindsey, who was a tall, slender, and athletic blonde.

"We're all riding on the same team for the PMC." Mitch looked Amanda's way with a nod.

Amanda forced herself to smile again. She needed to say something, or she would appear unfriendly. "That's great. Maybe I'll see you on Sunday. I'm helping with one of the water stations."

"Nice to meet you guys. Have a good ride this weekend." Max resumed his seat as the hostess showed Mitch and his friends to their table on the other side of the small room.

Heather leaned across the table. "Looks like you've got some competition."

Amanda knew very well what Heather was talking about, but she wasn't going to acknowledge it. "I'm not riding, so I'm not competing with anyone."

Heather raised her eyebrows as she gave Amanda a pointed look. "This has nothing to do with bicycles and everything to do with the heart."

Sighing, Amanda looked over at Max. "Tell your wife not to jump to conclusions."

"She's not very good at following my instructions. Besides, more often than not, her conclusions are correct."

"I've been there. Fighting against my feelings." Heather reached over and took Max's hand. "This guy was the last person I wanted to have a relationship with, but I found out I was wrong. You should quit fighting your feelings and give Mitch a chance."

"Looks like he has other interests now." Amanda didn't want to discuss Mitch while he was sitting just feet away with another woman.

"Now, but not when you get back home, or even tomorrow at the wedding. What's-her-face won't be there, but you will, and you'll have Mitch all to yourself. Don't blow it."

"For the last time, it...won't...work." Amanda gave Heather an annoyed look. "You know what I said during your visit to Pineydale. I'm going to Nashville, and that's that."

Heather rubbed her fingers across her forehead. "You are stubborn."

"Yeah. I am." Amanda gritted her teeth before she said something she might regret. Max and Heather were her friends, but they were stepping into her business. They needed to leave her alone.

Amanda had a reprieve as the waitress came and took their orders. For a few moments after the waitress left, none of them said anything. Amanda hoped she could steer the conversation in another direction. Everything had been just fine until Mitch had shown up. He sat right in her line of vision. She could see every time he brushed shoulders with that blonde, every time he laughed at something she said, every time he leaned closer.

Amanda grabbed a piece of bread and slathered it with butter. She had to quit looking his way. He had every right to be with that woman, and Amanda had every right to ignore him.

"So what time do you guys start tomorrow?" Amanda took a bite of the crusty bread.

"We start around seven." Max looked over at Heather. "Gotta get this woman out of bed earlier than she likes."

Amanda laughed. "Should I get up to see you guys off?"

"That's up to you, but I think you should suffer, too." Heather shrugged. "Oh, I mean you should get up to wish us well."

Shaking her head, Amanda laughed again. "Heather, you're too funny, but I'm up plenty early with my job these days, so I won't suffer. I've kind of discovered I like being up with the sunrise."

"Well, sunrise here is very, very early." Heather frowned.

"I know. Have you forgotten already that I used to live here?"

Heather chuckled. "No, but I have a feeling you didn't see many sunrises when you lived here."

"You're right. I was never a morning person until I started to paint houses."

"And how do you like that?"

"Actually, I like it. I can see what I've accomplished as the day goes on. Jimmy has me doing a lot of trim work, both inside and outside." Amanda let out a happy sigh. "While I was in Nashville, I did go on a job interview and followed up on some other jobs I had applied for."

"How did that go?" Max asked.

Amanda grimaced. "Not as well as I had hoped, but I'm not giving up."

Heather opened her mouth to say something, but before she could, the servers appeared with their meals.

Amanda waved a hand over the plate in front of her. "Wow! This is a lot of food. There goes my diet."

Heather knit her eyebrows. "You're not on a diet."

"Yeah, you're right, but if I don't watch it, Charlotte's good cooking is going to show up on my hips."

Max held out his hands. "Let's pray and not worry about food going to the hips."

Heather took Max's hand. "Easy for you to say. Men burn more calories than women."

"I'll love you no matter what your hips look like." Max gave her a peck on the cheek.

Heather looked at her husband with adoration. "Remember that a few months from now."

"You'll look beautiful."

Amanda wrinkled her brow. "Is there something you guys are trying to tell me in a roundabout way? Like you're expecting?"

Joy radiating from every inch of her face, Heather nodded. "You're the first one we've told besides our parents."

"When is the baby due? Do you know what you're having? Is it okay for pregnant women to ride so far on a bike?"

Heather held up a hand. "Hold on. I'll answer all your questions after we give thanks for the food."

Amanda bowed her head and listened as Max prayed. Their news brought joy to Amanda's heart. Max had been through so much, and now something wonderful would brighten their days. She thanked God for their friendship and their good news.

When the prayer ended, Amanda looked over at her friends. "I'm so happy for you guys."

"Thanks. Now I'll answer your questions." Heather grinned. "Due date is February 4."

"Maybe it'll be a Valentine baby."

Heather shook her head. "Don't wish extra days on me."

"Sorry. Wasn't thinking about that." Amanda grimaced. "Girl, boy?"

"We just found out." Max grinned. "A girl, and yes, doctor okayed Heather's ride."

Amanda couldn't quit grinning. "This is such wonderful news! Any names picked out?"

"Not yet." Heather took a bite of her manicotti.

"But we're thinking about using a combination of the grandmothers' names." Max shrugged. "We've got plenty of time to figure that out."

Amanda devoured her salad and veal parmesan, realizing she'd forgotten about Mitch while she'd been rejoicing in Max and Heather's good news. But as soon as thoughts of Mitch invaded, sadness filled her heart. She had kept him at arm's length, and now he was enjoying the company of another woman. Amanda steeled herself against the temptation to let another woman make her jealous, just as she'd done when Josie had flirted with Mitch.

Only heartache would come from letting Mitch get too close, but that might be a moot point if he found a new interest in the pretty blonde. Amanda forced herself not to look in Mitch's direction again. Hopefully, out of sight meant out of mind.

"You're awfully quiet all of a sudden." Heather cocked her head in the direction of Mitch's table. "Thinking about Mitch?"

Amanda didn't want to lie, but she didn't want to admit the truth either. "I've got a lot of stuff on my mind. Work, Charlotte, the wedding, Nashville. You name it. It's rolling through my mind."

"You do have a lot to think about." Heather nodded. "Do you have plans for another trip to Nashville for some open mic events?"

"Yeah, I have to go back for the semifinal round of the contest I won the last time I went. I'm saving my money so I can go." Amanda set her fork on her plate. "I have two funds. My car fund and my Nashville trip fund. I put part of my pay in each fund every week. I've almost got enough for another trip to Nashville. I don't dare think of using Charlotte's car again, even though she said I could."

"But someone stealing Charlotte's car wasn't your

fault." Heather knit her eyebrows.

"True, but I wouldn't take her car again, especially now that she has a brand-new one."

"I suppose that makes sense. You'd be worried the whole time that someone would take her car again." Heather gave Amanda a questioning look. "So it seems like your job is working out. Right?"

"It is, but if you'd asked me two months ago if I'd like to paint houses for a living, I would have shuddered at the thought. It's temporary and still a means to an end, but it isn't altogether terrible."

Heather smiled. "I'm hopeful everything will work out for your dreams, but I still think you shouldn't dismiss Mitch from your life."

Amanda took a deep breath. She didn't want to argue with Heather. Amanda didn't want Mitch or his companions to hear what Heather was saying. Amanda glanced in Mitch's direction, then back at Heather. "This isn't the place or time to discuss that."

"Okay." Heather looked contrite. "But it will be discussed."

Max laughed as he looked at Heather. "She's like a dog with a bone. She's not going to let it go. Believe me. I know all about that."

Heather gave Max a playful punch in the arm. "And where would you be without me?"

"Sad and lonely."

As they continued eating, they all laughed. But Amanda couldn't help thinking she could be really lonely in Nashville. In the short time she'd been in

Pineydale, she'd made friends, friends she would be sad to leave behind. Charlotte and her book-club ladies, the gang at work, even Mitch's mom. They were all people who had touched her life and made it better. Why did everything in life come with choices, decisions, and sometimes disappointments because she had picked the wrong option?

Amanda didn't want to make more mistakes. If she continued to push Mitch away, was that one more wrong decision to add to her growing list of blunders? She couldn't keep second-guessing herself. She had to have confidence in what she decided, but shouldn't that confidence come from her reliance on God?

***

The highway leading to the bed-and-breakfast wound its way through small towns filled with town squares, clapboard houses, and white churches with tall steeples. Mitch took in the scenery as he sat in the back of Max and Heather's car. He was a little sore from the long bike ride, but if Heather, who was pregnant, didn't complain, he certainly shouldn't.

He glanced sideways at Amanda, who shared the backseat with him. Her auburn hair hung in loose curls around her shoulders. Her green lace dress brought out the green in her eyes and made him wish he could make her see him as someone she needed in her life.

During the ride so far, she had barely said two words to him but instead spent her time talking to Heather about Hailey and her guitar lessons and the practice for the songs Amanda would sing at the wedding. Amanda gave of her time to help others, just one more thing that drew her to him. He realized more than ever how much music meant to her, and she was willing to share it anytime, anywhere. He could still hear her sweet voice as she sang that Scottish lullaby. It haunted his thinking and put an ache in his heart that he couldn't somehow convince her that they belonged together.

He feared going to a wedding would make his heartache even worse. But if he could ride a bike over one hundred and fifty miles, he could get through this wedding. And that was what he intended to do tonight.

"Hey, Mitch. You're awfully quiet back there. Did the bike ride take all the wind out of your sails?" Heather gazed at him in the rearview mirror.

"Can't get a word in edgewise with you two women gabbing all the way." Mitch grinned, trying to hide his discomfort.

"So how was your ride?" Max asked.

"Great. Brandon put together a great group. We had a good time, and I plan to ride again next year." Mitch glanced at Amanda. Did she care about his ride? When she wasn't talking with Heather, Amanda seemed lost in another world.

"Hey, that's wonderful." Heather turned to the backseat. "You should get Amanda to ride with you next year either on our team or with your friend's team."

Mitch motioned toward Amanda. "What do you say?"

She shook her head. "I'm not making any commitments that far in advance. I don't have a clue what I'll be doing a year from now, but I hope to be living in Nashville by then."

"You can still come from Nashville, unless you'll be too famous to associate with us by then." Heather grinned.

Amanda didn't look amused. "Sorry. I'm not in a joking mood. I know you guys are just kidding around, but it's my dream, my goal to make a success of my music career. I know it's a longshot, but I have to give it a try. And if I make it, I won't forget my friends here or in Pineydale."

Mitch wanted to reach over and comfort Amanda. He was sorry he'd had negative thoughts about her dreams, even though those dreams didn't have room for him. "And we won't forget you. You can count on our support."

"Thanks. I appreciate that. I need someone to believe in me."

She smiled at him, and his heart raced like he was riding his bike uphill.

Heather reached over the backseat and touched Amanda's arm. "Hey, I didn't mean to make fun of your music. You know we love you and want you to succeed."

Amanda's eyes sparkled with tears. "Yeah, but sometimes it seems like an impossible dream, and I want it so much."

It took all of Mitch's willpower not to gather Amanda

in his arms and hold her tight. He wished there was a way he could make all of her dreams come true. He knew more than ever after spending two days with Lindsey, who did nothing to hide her interest in him, that Amanda was the only woman for him. Why did he have to care about a woman whose heart was set on a music career in Nashville?

But Mitch vowed to be there for Amanda. Would she consider taking money from him so she could go to Nashville?

When they arrived at the Hawthorne Inn, Mitch took in the beauty of the surroundings. The blue-and-white Victorian house stood nestled among tall evergreens and large shade trees of several varieties. The gazebo at the back of the house was festooned with flowers and some kind of gauzy material that rustled in the breeze. Rows of white chairs sat in front of the gazebo. Obviously the ceremony would take place there.

Folks were already gathering on the lawn near the gazebo. The outdoor evening wedding was somewhat informal, the men were dressed in shirtsleeves and pants and the women in casual dresses or slacks. A string quartet was warming up on a small platform just right of the gazebo.

Mitch looked over at Amanda as Max parked the car along the edge of the long drive. "Do you need help with your guitar?"

She shook her head. "I can manage, but thanks for asking."

"Do you have to set something up?"

Amanda shrugged. "I think I know where I'm supposed to go, but I'll check for sure. I'll see you later."

Mitch stood there and watched her hurry away, the dark-green dress catching the rays of the sun as it hovered just above the tree line. She looked gorgeous in that dress, but she looked good in the old paint clothes she had borrowed from Charlotte. He had promised himself that he'd not try to keep her from her dreams, that he'd support her dreams, but how was he going to survive not having her around?

"You look lost in thought," Heather came up beside him.

"Just thinking about Amanda and her music. I wish I could make things happen for her." Mitch smiled wryly. "She's got too much talent to let it go to waste."

"I know," Heather said.

Max joined them and looked over at Mitch. "You know Amanda has a lot of conflicting feelings about you."

"She does?" Mitch's heart took a leap.

"Max." Heather frowned. "You can't go sharing Amanda's thoughts."

"Why not? I know when two people are dancing around their feelings for each other." Max put an arm around Heather's shoulders. "I believe I remember another couple who took a while to get things right because they were trying not to show their feelings."

Heather's laugh was punctuated with a sigh. "I know, but we figured that out on our own. Someone didn't step in and try to interfere."

"But wouldn't it have been easier if someone had?"

"I'm not sure we would've listened." Heather shook her head, an annoyed expression radiating from her eyes.

Mitch listened to Max and Heather and wondered what Amanda had said about him. Were they going to tell him, or would he have to guess? "Are you guys just going to argue about it or tell me something?"

Heather and Max stopped and looked at each other. Then Max turned Mitch's way. "Maybe Heather's got a point. I don't have any business sharing what Amanda told us. But I have to say one thing. You shouldn't give up on her."

Hope sprang up in Mitch's heart, but he wasn't going to get too excited or admit how discouraged he'd been about Amanda. "Thanks for the advice."

Heather nodded. "Sometimes a relationship looks hopeless, but you can work through it."

"I'll keep that in mind." Mitch let the information filter through his thoughts. What had Amanda said that should give him encouragement? He felt like he was walking a tightrope trying not to push too hard while still pursuing her.

As they neared the gazebo, a man and a woman, accompanied by a boy and girl who looked to be about the same age, came toward them. Heather gave each of them a hug. A lively conversation ensued.

Max motioned for Mitch to join the group. "Mitch, come meet the owners of the inn, Kurt and Molly Jansen."

As they all walked toward the chairs, the string quartet finished warming up and started playing peaceful classical music. Mitch learned that Kurt and Molly had restored the Victorian house and made it into a bed-and-breakfast several years earlier. They were just beginning to do weddings, and all the employees of the bed-and-breakfast were women who lived in the women's shelter nestled away on the back of the property.

Mitch glanced around, looking for Amanda. Would she remain up front with the wedding party, or would she sit with the other guests after she finished singing? He should find out in case she wanted him to save her a seat. Max and Heather's talk had given him the courage to seek her out.

While Mitch went in search of Amanda, he thought about these people who were Amanda's friends. They all had one thing in common. They worked together to help people in need. He thought about his own life. This PMC ride was the first time he'd actually done anything for those less fortunate. He'd been buried in his own little world in Pineydale, feeling sorry for himself because of what happened with Whitney. His life was good, more than good. He had to think more about doing things for others.

"You look lost."

Mitch turned at the sound of Amanda's voice. "Not lost. Just looking for you."

"Why would you be looking for me?"

Mitch could think of a dozen reasons, but he better stick to the one that had started his search. "Do you need a place to sit after you sing? If you do, I can save a place for you."

"Thanks. That would be nice. Can you sit near where the string quartet is playing? I'm using the microphone there." Amanda smiled.

Mitch's heart tripped. She made him feel alive. "I can do that. When do you sing?"

"I sing one song while they are seating the family and another while Tara and Caleb do their unity ceremony." Amanda pointed toward a small table set on the gazebo. "See the glass block?"

"Yeah." Mitch squinted in that direction. "What is it?"

"They're pouring the sand into that for the ceremony. If you look at it closely, you can see the bicycle on it." Amanda let out a sweet little sigh. "It's lovely."

Mitch wondered whether they made those with guitars printed on the front. Would Amanda want something like that? He'd been through all that with Whitney. She'd planned everything down to the last detail. Her plans for a unity ceremony involved candles. She just forgot to stay faithful, a sure sign of disunity.

He shook the thoughts away. He shouldn't let old heartaches intrude on this day, but disunity stood like a fortress separating Amanda and him. She wanted a career in Nashville, and he had a garage to run in Pineydale. And yet Max and Heather said not to give up. Mitch didn't see any way around their differences.

None.

But he wouldn't give up hope.

"Hey, are you still here?"

Mitch looked down at Amanda, who stood there giving him a curious look. What was he going to say? That he was thinking about his fiancée's betrayal? He was one messed-up guy. He had to get himself in the right frame of mind. "Yeah. What are you singing?"

"'You Raise Me Up' and 'Bless the Broken Road.'"

"I know you'll do a great job."

"Thanks." Amanda hugged the guitar case as she stood there looking at him. "The second song is so perfect because both Caleb and Tara have been through a lot, but their broken road led them to each other."

"You'd know about perfect songs." Mitch knew how perfect the song sounded for him. Had the trouble with Whitney brought him to Amanda? He'd like to think so.

She motioned toward the string quartet. "Got to take my place."

"Sure." He had dozens of things he'd like to say to her, but most of them she didn't want to hear. Someday, sometime, he would say them and prayed she would be willing to listen. "I'll be waiting for you when you're finished."

She nodded as she hurried away, and Mitch thought about what he'd just said to her. Maybe that was the key. He'd be waiting for her.

With a feeling of uncertainty dogging Mitch, he found a seat nearby and saved the one next to him for Amanda. He noticed Max and Heather sitting on the bride's side as more and more people filled the chairs.

When Mitch looked back toward the gazebo, Amanda walked to the microphone with her guitar. She adjusted the microphone as the quartet played a prelude. Then Amanda's voice rang out strong over the audience. The words of the song resonated with Mitch. He wanted to be the man to raise her up, and she would definitely make him a better man, more than he had ever expected to be.

By the time she had finished singing the song, all the relatives of the bride and groom had been seated. Amanda slipped into the row beside him just as Hailey started down the aisle and tossed rose petals along the white runner. The maid of honor followed, then everyone stood for the bride's entrance. Amanda's presence beside him made his heart zing. He had a feeling he would spend the rest of this ceremony trying to figure out how to get past her defenses.

CHAPTER FIFTEEN

The ceremony ended with applause as Caleb kissed Tara, then turned to face their guests. The happiness radiating from their faces made Amanda glad she had come, even if it meant having to fight her interest in Mitch.

Seeing him with that other woman had crystalized her feelings for him. He was everything she had ever wanted in a man. He loved God. He loved his family. He loved his work. He was respected in his community—a community he didn't want to leave.

Would her attachment to him put her music career on a sidetrack? The conflict didn't go away just because she knew how much she cared for him. She wanted both. Mitch and her music. Could she have that? It would be simple if they both lived in Nashville, but she didn't see him leaving Pineydale or the garage.

"You did fantastic, but I knew you would."

Mitch's statement shook Amanda from her thoughts, and she turned his way, her stomach doing little flip-flops. "Thanks."

"Do you need to put your guitar in the car? I can do that, if you'd like."

"We can walk together to find Max so we can get the keys."

"Yeah, that would be a good idea." Mitch chuckled, a flash of surprise in his eyes as he fell into step beside her. "I don't often lock my pickup in Pineydale, so I forget about that kind of thing."

Mitch's statement, one more reminder of why he loved his little town, emphasized their differences. She had to think about something else. "That was a wonderful wedding. Everything was perfect."

"Especially the singer."

Amanda chuckled. "You don't have to keep complimenting me."

"Sure I do. I came to the wedding to be with you just so I could tell you how great you are."

Ever since the night of that kiss, he had let it be known he intended to pursue her. But he had backed off in the last couple of weeks and left her wondering whether she had finally pushed him away one too many times. Guess he didn't give up easily. Was that a good thing?

"You're making me blush."

He looked down at her with a wry smile. "I can see that, and I think you're cute when your cheeks turn pink."

Thankfully, Amanda spied Max and Heather and didn't have to respond. "Hey, Max. I need the keys so I can put my guitar away."

"Hey, loved your songs. They were great." Max fumbled in his pocket and brought out the key fob to his car. "Here you go. Just bring it back when you're done."

"Thanks." Amanda held out her hand, and Max

dropped the fob into it. "See you in a little bit."

Heather sidled up to Amanda and whispered, "Looks like you two are finding something to share."

"Don't read anything into this. You know we're friends."

Heather didn't say a word, just gave Amanda a knowing look, then turned back to Max.

"What was that all about?" Mitch raised his eyebrows as they walked toward the parking lot.

"Heather just noticed that we're together."

Shaking his head, Mitch knit his eyebrows. "Well, of course we're together. Why wouldn't we be? We came together."

Everything inside Amanda begged her to throw caution to the wind and let her feelings for Mitch show. Yet caution circled her like a buzzard circling roadkill. Would her love life wind up like roadkill if she let Mitch and his southern charm sweep her away? Would she be sorry when she got back to Pineydale and had to face reality there?

The questions joined caution and jumbled her brain. She wasn't going to let questions or caution ruin today. Today would take care of itself. She would worry about tomorrow, tomorrow.

Amanda smiled up at him as she unlocked the car. "I hope you're prepared to dance."

"Don't you remember my moves up at Grandfather Mountain?"

"It was dark." She grinned.

"That's when I make my best moves, because no one

can actually see them clearly."

Amanda laughed as she laid the guitar on the backseat. "I plan to test your dancing skills tonight."

Mitch nodded. "And I am prepared to be tested. Just try me."

"You're on." Amanda hurried ahead.

Mitch caught up to her. "I still can't figure out how you walk so fast in those shoes. Are you sure you can dance in them?"

"If they cause a problem, I can always dance without them."

"You don't want anyone stepping on your toes."

"Does that mean you?"

Mitch laughed out loud. "I don't step on toes. You just wait and see how light I am on my feet."

"I'll hold you to that." Amanda stopped at the steps leading up to the wraparound porch.

"Not to worry."

Amanda made her way onto the porch with plenty of worry in her mind. She wasn't worried about Mitch stepping on her toes but about him stepping on her dreams. She didn't want to choose.

Amanda tried to put her worries aside as they ate the scrumptious buffet provided by the inn. She and Mitch shared a table with Max, Heather, Heather's uncle Parker, and his wife, Brittany, who had come from Montana to share in Tara's special day and ride in the PMC.

Amanda wondered what Mitch would think if he knew Brittany and Max had dated all through high school and college before they broke up. They'd both found someone else to love. Love didn't always work out like people planned. Was that what Amanda should expect?

As folks ended their meals, the best man and the maid of honor gave their toasts to the happy couple. Hailey sat at the head table as she beamed from ear to ear.

After everyone had finished eating, the party moved indoors. The inn's usual dining room had been transformed into a dance floor surrounded by a few small tables and numerous chairs. Amanda followed Mitch, who found a couple of chairs in the far corner. A disc jockey had his equipment set up in the adjoining living room. He announced the happy couple, and Tara and Caleb took the dance floor.

While the bride and groom had their first dance together, Mitch leaned closer. "I don't mean to brag, but I can dance as well as the groom."

"I'm withholding judgment until I see for myself."

Mitch held up a finger. "You don't have long to wait."

Amanda's heart skittered at the thought of dancing in Mitch's arms. The memory of their kiss skipped across her mind, lingering like the taste of sweets on her tongue. How could one kiss be so unforgettable?

The other family dances followed the bride and groom's dance. When Caleb danced with Hailey standing on his shoes, the place erupted with applause. Hailey hammed it up for the crowd, and laughter filled the room.

Amanda thought about all the things Tara and Caleb had come through to find love. Tara had lost her husband when Hailey was just a toddler, and then Hailey had been diagnosed with a rare cancer that had brought them to the Boston area for treatment. Tara met Caleb because of those terrible circumstances. Amanda wondered whether she had met Mitch because of a broken-down car. She couldn't help remembering what Charlotte had said about the reason why Amanda had wound up in Pineydale.

Amanda wished the answers were easy, but they weren't.

"The dance floor is calling us." Mitch stood and held out his hand as other couples began dancing.

"Unforgettable" played over the speakers as Mitch pulled Amanda closer and moved her around the floor with ease. Funny that she'd been thinking of his unforgettable kiss. Was this going to be an unforgettable night? Did she have a chance at protecting her heart, or had Mitch already captured it?

"Do I pass?"

Amanda looked up at him and smiled. "You do."

"Good, because I intend to dance with you all night long, and I wouldn't want you wishing you had a different partner."

Amanda's breath caught in her throat. Did she dare admit to him that she didn't want another partner even if Mitch stepped on her toes? She had to make the move she'd been fighting almost from the first day she'd met him. "I'm not looking for another partner. I like the one I've got."

Mitch pulled her a little closer. "Good to know I don't have to search for another one."

Being in Mitch's arms meant contentment. She wouldn't think about the future tonight. Tonight she would only think about how right the world felt when she and Mitch were together.

***

"Mitch, I need your help. Everything has gone wrong with the fundraiser while you and Amanda were away."

"Calm down, Mom. I'm sure it's not as bad as you think." Mitch had been back home less than twenty-four hours, and now he had to face his mother's problem.

"Oh, yes it is." Panic sounded in his mother's voice. "Our main headliner for the fundraiser concert has developed a severe case of laryngitis, and his doctor has ordered that he rest his voice for several weeks. He can't do the concert. Who am I going to get at the last minute to take that spot? I'm talking about the headliner, not some secondary act."

Mitch's blood pressure rose a few notches. "Like I said. Calm. Down. We'll deal with it."

"I don't know how. I don't know where to start." His mother's voice came out in a high-pitched whine.

Mitch gritted his teeth. "Have you talked with Amanda? She could probably fill in."

"But she's just an amateur. Who's going to pay good

money to hear her sing?"

Anyone who has listened to her. The words sat on the tip of Mitch's tongue, but they were better left unsaid. His mother didn't realize what talent Amanda had. So he'd talk to her and see if she had any suggestions. "I'll ask Amanda if she has any ideas. She might know someone from the days she spent in Nashville."

"My hopes aren't very high there," his mother replied.

Mitch restrained himself from telling his mother what he thought. Her low opinion of Amanda's value didn't make Mitch happy. After all, Amanda had helped his mother for weeks with this fundraising thing. He wanted to give her an earful about how well Amanda sang and played, but that would be a fruitless endeavor. He didn't need to make his mother more upset than she already was. "Let's just wait and see what she says."

His mother sighed. "I hope someone can come up with something good."

"I'm sure it'll all work out. Talk to you later, Mom." Mitch ended the call, glad not to be listening to his mother whine.

Mitch stared at his phone. What would Amanda have to say about the situation? He certainly couldn't relay to her his mother's thoughts on Amanda's musical talent. The time he had spent with Amanda in Massachusetts had given him hope that her attitude toward him was thawing. She hadn't kissed him as he had hoped, but they had spent almost the whole evening at the wedding reception dancing, laughing, and talking. He loved her interaction with her friends there.

Her love for all things music had shone through. The wedding had showcased her remarkable singing talent again and made Mitch realize what she had undertaken when she'd left her friends, fellow musicians, and the comfort of the familiar to head to Nashville. She'd been willing to leave it all behind to pursue her dream. Did he have the right to dissuade her from it? How could he win her love when she wanted something that didn't include him?

Love. The word sat in his mind. He had to face reality. He loved Amanda. He'd known that, but loving her brought with it the fear of losing her. But if he loved her, could he keep her from her dream? Maybe that was where he'd gone wrong with Whitney. He hadn't thought enough about her dreams, only his own of running Wilbur's Garage. How did he fix this?

He didn't have time to figure that all out now. He had to help fix his mother's dilemma before he moved on to his love life.

He punched in Amanda's number. When she answered his heart raced. "Hi, got time to talk?"

"Yeah, I'm just finishing up. What's on your mind?"

Mitch sighed. "I've got bad news from my mom, and I'd like to get your input."

"What kind of bad news?" Amanda asked.

"The headliner for the fundraiser concert has laryngitis and can't perform."

"But the fundraiser is almost three weeks away. Won't he be better by then?" Concern sounded in

Amanda's voice

"Nope. He can't perform for several weeks. Doctor's orders." Mitch gripped his phone tighter and wished Amanda could be the headliner, but his mother would be appalled at the idea.

"Wow! That is a problem. What does she plan to do?"

"That's just it. She has no plan, so I thought I'd see what you thought." Mitch held his breath as he waited for Amanda's response.

"Let's talk after I get off work. I think I have a possible solution. I'll be done in about half an hour."

Mitch could only pray that Amanda had a worthwhile answer. "I'll pick you up."

"I'll be waiting for you."

"See you in a few. Bye." Mitch wished she was waiting for him because she loved him.

Thirty minutes later Mitch pulled to a stop in front of the house where Amanda was working. He got out of his air-conditioned pickup, and the hot, steamy air hit him like a wet blanket. Jimmy, who greeted Mitch first, did nothing to brighten his mood as he walked to the house.

"Here to see Amanda?" Jimmy grinned.

"Yeah. She said she'd be done about now." Tamping down any ill feelings toward Jimmy, Mitch glanced at the screen on his phone. "Is she finished?"

"Come with me, and we'll see." Jimmy waved him onto the porch that extended across the entire front of the white clapboard house. "I gotta tell ya. She's a great little worker. She's the best trim painter I've had in years."

"Glad she's working out." Mitch wondered what Jimmy was getting at while he was bragging on Amanda.

"Too bad she's hung up on you and not me."

Jimmy's comment didn't deserve a response, but Mitch figured he shouldn't let it go. Jimmy was probably trying to rile Mitch by saying something that wasn't entirely true, or maybe Jimmy was fishing to find out what was going on with Amanda. "Those are the breaks."

As Mitch followed Jimmy into the empty house, Amanda was hunkered down as she pounded the lid back on a paint can. She had her hair pulled back in a ponytail and a streak of white paint on one cheek. Mitch couldn't explain the feeling he had every time he looked at her. A jumble of emotions coiled through him like a tangle of vines growing on the trellis outside this house.

"Hey, Amanda, your beau's here." Jimmy smirked at Mitch.

Amanda looked up and smiled at Mitch but raised her eyebrows as she looked in Jimmy's direction. "I'm ready to call it a day."

Mitch gritted his teeth as he squinted at his cousin. Just like Amanda, Mitch refused to take the bait. "Great. Let's head out."

Without a backward glance, Mitch headed for the door. When he reached the porch, he turned to Amanda. "I hope you don't let Jimmy's comments bother you."

"I just ignore them most of the time. I let him know

from the first day that I wouldn't put up with any funny business."

"Good for you." Mitch decided not to say that his cousin needed to be put in his place. "Does that apply to me, too, or do I get beau privileges?"

Amanda laughed. "Don't press your luck."

Disappointed, Mitch gave her a salute as he opened the door to his pickup for her. "Got it. Where do you want to go to talk?"

"Charlotte's."

"Sure." Mitch chastised himself for thinking he might turn this conversation into some time alone with Amanda. Charlotte would surely be there. Not that he didn't want to see his aunt, but he wanted Amanda all to himself.

As he pulled away from the curb, he turned on the radio for an excuse not to talk. He was afraid his disappointment would show through if he had a discussion with this woman who had his heart in a twisted knot. Amanda didn't seem to mind the lack of conversation as she fiddled with her phone. Why had he let the seemingly wonderful weekend in Boston with her make him think anything had changed?

After Mitch stopped his pickup in front of Charlotte's house, Amanda hopped out and loped up the front walk. Mitch sauntered behind her, not bothering to catch up.

When she reached the door, she turned to him with a smile. "Tough day at work?"

"No. Why?"

Her look had curiosity written all over it. "You're

moving a little slow."

"I'm not that eager to discuss my mom's problem, but it has to be done." Mitch joined Amanda on the porch as she opened the door. "You know you've got paint on your cheek."

"Where?" She put a hand to her face.

"Right here." He put his index finger on her right cheekbone. His heart thundered as he touched her, and he swallowed hard. She gazed up at him, her mouth parted slightly. He wanted to kiss her in the worst way right here in broad daylight on his aunt's front porch.

She rubbed her cheek. "Did I get it off?"

"Nope. Still there." Taking a step back, Mitch took a deep breath and let his racing heart slow to a gallop. "But a little soap and water will take care of it."

Amanda's laughter trilled around the front porch. "I don't know how I manage to get paint on myself every day without knowing it."

"Hazards of the job. Like I'm always getting grease on myself." Mitch took a deep breath, knowing he'd sidestepped a land mine of emotion. He'd almost kissed her, and that would have been a big mistake.

"I guess." Amanda looked back at him as she stepped into the front hall. "You're going to be happy you called me."

Mitch was always happy to call Amanda. He just wished she was happy to call him. "And why is that?"

"Come inside, and I'll tell you all about it." Amanda strode toward the kitchen. "Hi, Charlotte. How was your day?"

Mitch stopped as Charlotte gave Amanda a hug. Amanda had not only captured his heart but Charlotte's as well. "Hey, Aunt Charlotte."

"Mitchell, what are you doing here?"

"Came over to talk to Amanda about Mom's dilemma." Mitch proceeded to give Charlotte the scoop on the latest disaster in his mom's life.

"Oh dear. That is terrible."

"I think it's going to be all right. At least, I hope I have a solution," Amanda said.

"You know somebody who can be a headliner for the fundraiser?" Mitch didn't want to hope too much.

Amanda put her purse on the kitchen snack bar, then grabbed a paper towel and wet it under the faucet. She took a few seconds to scrub at her cheek, then turned to him. "All gone?"

"Yeah." For sure. His resistance to this woman was all gone.

She turned away from the sink and pulled out one of the stools at the snack bar. She patted the stool beside her. "Sit down, and I'll tell you the most amazing thing."

Mitch hopped onto the stool and looked at her, his heart roaring again. "So what is this amazing thing?"

Amanda sat up tall, a smile on her face. "Kelsey, my little sister, called me last night after we got back from Boston."

"What does she have to do with this?" Mitch frowned.

Amanda patted his shoulder. "Just hang on and I'll explain."

"All right." Mitch let out a loud sigh, trying not to react to her touch.

"Anyway. Every year in August the church we attended back in Pinecrest has this work day out at this boys' ranch run by the youth pastor. It's kind of like a family camp. I actually hated it when I was a kid. I was a real brat."

Mitch chuckled. "Nice of you to admit it."

"Yeah, well, I've grown up a little since then. Just ask Max."

"He had a lot of good things to say about you." Mitch loved so many things about her. Too bad he couldn't say so.

"Good to know. Now let me finish my story."

"Okay." Mitch gestured for her to continue.

Amanda pulled her hair out of the band that held it back in a ponytail. "Kelsey told me Sam, the youth pastor, asked about me. She told him what happened with me and my plans to go to Nashville. When he found out, he told her that he knows Willow Childs."

"You mean Willow Childs the country and gospel singer?" Mitch couldn't keep the incredulity out of his voice.

Amanda nodded. "Anyway, he talked to her, and she said I should come to Nashville and meet her."

"Wow! Now that is some good news." Mitch nodded. "I can drive you."

"You'll take off work instead of letting me drive your pickup?" Amanda gave him a silly grin.

"Yeah. It might be safer." Mitch leaned an elbow on

the counter, wishing she wanted more than a ride from him.

"You mean you wouldn't trust me with your vehicle?" Amanda put on a fake sad face.

"It's not you I don't trust. It's those car thieves in Nashville." Mitch wished he could trust his heart where Amanda was concerned, but he had to keep his mind on solving his mother's problem. "How come you waited until now to tell me?"

"I just talked to Kelsey this morning, and then I had to work."

"So when are you supposed to meet with Willow Childs?" Mitch asked.

"She's supposed to call."

Mitch didn't have a good feeling about that, but he wasn't going to say so to Amanda. "So you think you can talk to her about doing this fundraiser?"

"Maybe. I'm hopeful." Amanda shrugged. "Kelsey tells me that Sam knows Willow Childs very well."

"Thanks for some encouraging news."

"But you can't tell your mom until I know something for sure."

"So how do I stall her?" Mitch raised his eyebrows.

"Just tell her I have a promising lead."

"Let's hope you hear from her before it's too late to ask."

"And we have to hope she's free. From what I was told, she'll do just about anything for Sam."

"How does he know Willow Childs?"

"Not sure, but I'm glad he does." Amanda shrugged

again. "Believe it or not, I think they used to teach together at Pinecrest High School."

"That is interesting."

Charlotte stepped up to the counter. "I was fixin' to make something for supper. You two want to eat?"

Mitch stood. "I don't want to put you out. I eat over here enough. Let me treat the two of you and hope it's a bit of a celebration for future good news."

Charlotte nodded. "That suits me fine. The steak house?"

"Works for me." Mitch held out his arm for Charlotte. "What's better than taking out my two best girls?"

"Getting Willow Childs to do the fundraiser." Amanda grabbed her purse from the counter and took Mitch's other arm.

When they got out to Mitch's pickup, Amanda hopped into the backseat and let Charlotte sit in front, despite her protests. Amanda was so kind to his aunt, and he wished he could make all of Amanda's dreams come true, but those dreams probably didn't include him. He had to prepare himself to deal with another heartache.

CHAPTER SIXTEEN

··

The sound of a Willow Childs's song filled the cab of Mitch's pickup. Amanda listened with a growing sense of excitement as Mitch maneuvered his vehicle onto I-40, going out of Nashville. The singer had given them the CD along with her promise to do the fundraiser. Amanda kept thinking she should pinch herself to make sure the meeting with Willow Childs wasn't a dream.

Mitch hadn't said much during the whirlwind trip from Pineydale to Nashville. Now on the way back, he should be pleased for his mom, but he seemed troubled for some reason. Amanda wished she knew what was going on in his head.

"So I expect your mom will be thrilled when she gets the news."

"I already talked to her, and yes, she's excited. She says thanks."

"When did you talk with her?"

"While you were getting that autographed CD." Mitch motioned toward his pickup's built-in CD player.

"That was really sweet of Willow to give us that. She seems like a super-nice person. I wasn't sure what to expect when I went to talk with her." Amanda let out a low whistle. "Boy was I nervous walking into that room, but she made me feel like I'd known her forever. We talked a little about Sam, and I was right. They did teach together in Pinecrest, but I got the feeling there may have been more between them."

"Did you get a chance to talk to her about your music?"

Amanda shrugged. "I mentioned it, but I didn't think it was appropriate to be pitching myself when I was there to talk about the fundraiser. I figured I'd get my chance to share the stage with her eventually. That would be enough."

"Well, I've got to say you saved the day. My mom's happier than a bee in a patch of clover."

"You don't seem to share your mother's excitement. Is there a reason for that?"

Mitch didn't say anything immediately, but Amanda noticed how his hands gripped the steering wheel tighter.

Finally, he glanced her way before looking back at the highway. "I'm going to lose out."

Amanda knit her eyebrows. "What's that supposed to mean?"

"It means Willow Childs is going to hear you sing, and you'll be on your way to Nashville for good." Mitch sighed. "I know I should be happy for you, but I was still hoping I'd have time to convince you that we should be more than friends."

Amanda rubbed fingers across her forehead. Was Mitch right about this being her chance? The fundraiser was a built-in audition for her in front of one of

Nashville's current stars. She didn't want to think of the implications. Leaving Pineydale. Leaving Charlotte. Leaving Mitch.

On the day Amanda's car had broken down, she had bemoaned the circumstances that had brought her to the little town. Now she wasn't sure she wanted to leave. Or at least, she didn't want to leave the people who had made her feel at home. How had this happened?

"I know I shouldn't have said that." Mitch shook his head. "You've made it perfectly clear from the beginning that I didn't have a chance for anything more than friendship, but I just keep on trying."

Amanda punched the button on the CD player, and the music stopped. "Mitch…it's not that simple."

"Seems pretty simple to me." Mitch looked straight ahead, a muscle working in his jaw. "You want a music career, and I don't fit into that plan."

Amanda's heart ached. Was that how he saw things? So cut and dried? Had she made him think that way? How could she explain to him when she didn't understand her own feelings? "You're making a lot of assumptions about what will happen with Willow Childs."

Mitch shook his head. "I'm not. When she hears you sing, there's no question in my mind she'll recognize your talent."

"Thanks. I think. But what you're saying makes me sad." Amanda swallowed the lump in her throat.

He looked her way again, a little smile tilting the corner of his mouth. "So you're saying I still might have a chance to win your heart?"

Amanda captured her head in her hands. "I don't know. You make my head and my heart hurt."

"Maybe you need to see a doctor."

A love doctor. Did she dare tell Mitch how much she cared about him? She didn't want to give him false hope. She'd been down that road before where she thought she could have a relationship with a guy and still pursue her music. But Mitch wasn't like that other guy. Mitch didn't want to stand in her way.

"So it's back to that same old thing? You can't get beyond friendship?" Mitch gave her another sideways glance.

Amanda laid her head back against the headrest and closed her eyes. Fear of doing the wrong thing, making the wrong choice, ate at her heart. Opening her eyes, she sat forward. "I wish I knew that answer. I do care for you, Mitch."

"Care for me how? Like a brother?"

Way more than a brother, but she was scared silly to say so. Amanda's shoulders sagged. "More than a brother—"

"But not enough for a real relationship."

Amanda shook her head. "Please. Let's not talk about this and ruin a good day."

"So talking about our feelings is going to ruin a good day?"

Amanda sighed. "I didn't mean it like that. See what you're doing? You're…you're…"

"I'm what? Trying to pin down how you feel about

me?"

Amanda pressed her lips together. She didn't want to cry in front of Mitch. Why couldn't she make up her mind? Why wasn't there an easy solution? Was she a selfish person? The questions bombarded her mind like the bugs splattered on the windshield of Mitch's pickup. They were a mess. A mess she didn't know how to fix.

"Okay, you win. We won't talk about it, but I've just got one thing to say. This isn't about collecting a kiss. It's about how I feel, and whether you like it or not or want to hear it, I love you. Plain and simple."

Amanda's heart sang and cried at the same time. There was nothing plain or simple about having Mitch's love. She wanted in the worst way to say those three words back to him, but she couldn't. Something held her back.

Apprehension. Selfishness. Ambition. Maybe all three.

Mitch deserved someone who could love him with everything she had to offer. Amanda wasn't sure she could be that person. What would it take to let go and love someone with abandon?

Amanda tried to think of something to say. Everything sounded lame, trite, or downright stupid. "Mitch, I…"

He shook his head. "You don't have to say a thing. Your silence says it all. I know where I stand. I've known all along. You haven't been trying to lead me on. I've led myself down that trail all by myself. I want the best for you, and that isn't me, much to my regret.

You'll go to Nashville for good, and some cowboy with a guitar will sweep you off your feet, and the two of you will ride off into the sunset singing your song."

Amanda wanted to cover her ears but resisted the childish gesture. Poised to say something, she caught Mitch's frowning glance and decided any kind of rebuttal would only cause more strife. This day that had started on such a high note with Willow Childs was ending with a resounding thud of misery. Amanda turned the music back on and said nothing for the rest of the ride home.

When Mitch finally stopped in front of Charlotte's house, it was the welcome end to a silent, tension-filled ride. Mitch politely thanked Amanda for rescuing the fundraiser and nodded his goodbye without getting out. On any other day, he would have walked her to the door and probably stayed awhile as he laughed and joked with Charlotte. Not tonight. Was tonight the end of even a friendship with Mitch? She didn't dare ask.

"Good night. Thanks for the ride."

Mitch gave her a salute without another word. As he drove off, Amanda stood on the walk and watched his headlights punctuate the darkness. Eventually, his taillights disappeared from view, and a sob erupted from deep down in Amanda's chest. Could she convince herself this parting was for the best?

As Amanda trudged up the steps and into the house, she hoped Charlotte had already retired for the night. Amanda closed and locked the front door. Silence greeted her. She breathed a sigh of relief that she wouldn't have to talk to Charlotte. She would surely know that Amanda was troubled. Maybe by morning she could perfect her game face and give a positive report on her trip to Nashville.

In the big scheme of things, the trip was a resounding success. They had a new headliner. Amanda had the chance to perform with one of Nashville's stars. Everyone was a winner. Everyone except Mitch. Without him in her life, she didn't feel like much of a winner either.

***

The Pineydale High School gymnasium was filled with as many people as the fire marshal would allow. Hoots and hollers punctuated the resounding applause that rang out from every corner of the space as Amanda joined Willow Childs on stage along with all the other performers who had been a part of the concert to raise money to benefit cancer research. Everyone in Pineydale had loved Wilbur Cunningham, and this benefit was always in his honor.

As the crowd called for an encore, Willow invited all the performers to sing one last song with her. While the group joined her, she asked the crowd to sing along. A lively tune from one of her latest albums filled the air as people clapped and sang. When the last note died, more applause and shouts echoed through the room.

Donna Cunningham hurried onto the stage and thanked Willow as the audience continued to applaud.

Donna took the microphone and thanked all those who had come out to support a good cause and all those who had a part in the success of the event.

While Donna continued her praise, Amanda looked over the crowd. During her portion of the concert, she had barely seen the audience because of the lighting. Now that the lights were up all over the gym, she saw Mitch sitting in the second row with Charlotte.

In the weeks since their meeting with Willow in Nashville, Amanda had only seen him in passing at church. Charlotte had invited Mitch over for supper a couple of times, but each time he had an excuse as to why he couldn't come. Charlotte hadn't said anything, but Amanda was sure the older woman had plenty of thoughts on what was going on or not going on between Amanda and Mitch.

As Amanda stood on the stage, she looked straight at Mitch. He didn't smile, but he didn't look away. The crushing sensation in Amanda's chest didn't go away when she looked toward the rest of the crowd. She had pushed him away one too many times, and now she was reaping the consequences. She didn't know if he would listen if she tried to talk with him. Besides, she didn't know what she would say to him anyway. Nothing had changed.

While Amanda stood there linking arms with the others and pasting a smile on her face, she watched Mitch say something to Charlotte, then leave. What was he doing? He was invited over to his parents' house to join the celebration for a successful fundraiser. Did he plan to skip out on that?

Finally, the crowd began to disperse, and Amanda retrieved her guitar and put it in the case. The sound of the locks clicking shut on the case reminded her that she had locked up her heart as well.

"Amanda." Willow walked across the stage. "Great job tonight."

"Thanks." Amanda could hardly believe a famous singer was saying *great job*. "We really appreciate all you've done to make this night a success."

"I couldn't have done much without the rest of you." Willow waved a hand toward the others who were still gathering their things. "This has been a great evening for me because I got to listen to you perform. As soon as you finished your set, I called my husband, and we talked it over, and we'd like to offer you the opportunity to be part of the tour I'm doing."

Amanda wanted to throw her arms around Willow but managed to restrain herself. She placed her hands over her heart. "Really? You want me to tour with you?"

Willow smiled. "Yeah. It's a twelve-city tour that goes through the South. This has been set for over six months, but one of my warm-up acts has had to cancel. We had decided to go with the acts we had, but after hearing you sing and play, I'd like you to join us. Do you have an agent?"

Agent? Amanda hadn't even thought far enough ahead to consider an agent. "No. Do I need one?"

"Not necessarily, but I'd have a lawyer look over the contract our company plans to offer you."

Amanda knew about some of the pitfalls of the music business, but she didn't know much about Willow and her company. But surely a friend of Sam's wouldn't be unscrupulous. The fact that she'd suggested Amanda contact a lawyer said something good about the future of the arrangement. "Oh, okay. I can do that. When and where is the tour?"

"It starts in three weeks. It's our 'Fall into Love' tour. In the spring we're doing another one—'Spring into Love' tour." Willow chuckled. "Not very original, but it suits our purpose."

Amanda wanted to ask if she'd be included in the spring tour, but this tour was probably a test of her talents. Just this fall gig was a dream of a lifetime. "What cities?"

"This is our southeast tour." Willow motioned in the air as if she had an imaginary map in front of her. "We're starting in Orlando, then Jacksonville, Florida. Atlanta. Next Charlotte, then Raleigh in North Carolina. Then we head over to Knoxville and Memphis in Tennessee. We'll have stops in Jackson, Mississippi, and Shreveport, Louisiana, then on to Mobile and Birmingham, Alabama. We finish in Nashville at the Ryman."

"Wow! The Ryman. That's amazing."

Willow gave Amanda a hug. "I'm glad you're excited. My husband and I run the company, and once we have our lawyers draw up the contract, you and I can discuss it. I'll be giving you a call in the next few days so we can get everything settled."

Amanda nodded, still stunned. "Thanks. I'll be waiting to hear from you."

"I'm headed over to the Cunninghams' for the celebration party." Willow motioned toward the door. "Are you?"

"I wouldn't miss it." Amanda nodded, thinking she would have to face Mitch, who would probably be there.

What would she say to him? How would he take her news? He'd probably say he'd told her so. Everything he'd predicted had come true so far. But one thing he said wouldn't come true. No cowboy with a guitar was going to sweep her off her feet.

She couldn't tell Mitch her heart belonged to him. Not now. She had to see where this music thing led her, but she wasn't ever going to forget Mitchell Cunningham and his ready smile, his kind heart, and his unforgettable kiss.

As Amanda walked to the parking lot to meet Charlotte, who was waiting to give Amanda a ride, she thought about everything involved with this music gig. What was she going to do for a car or a place to live in Nashville? She had to talk to Jimmy. What would he say about her leaving?

Charlotte would be thrilled for Amanda, but the thought of leaving this lovely lady behind left Amanda's heart melancholy. Then there was Mitch. Would he give her time to figure this out? Or had he already given up on her? The trip back from Nashville had pretty much spelled the end of Mitch's patience with her. She had to live with the choice she'd made. Her music instead of

Mitch.

***

Lights beamed through the windows of his parents' house as Mitch found a space to park in the circular driveway. He sat in his pickup for a few minutes just staring into the night. Darkness painted his mood. He would have to go to this party and feign happiness. He should be thrilled the fundraiser that bore his beloved uncle's name was an overwhelming success, but all he could think of was Amanda. Tonight surely meant she would be headed to Nashville. He had no doubt.

Somehow he had to find his happy face and put it on, or maybe he shouldn't pretend. He honestly didn't want to go to this party at all, but he trudged up the pavers to the front door and let himself in. Laughter and conversation buzzed from the back of the house, where people were gathered by the pool in the backyard.

Smiles lit up faces like the party lights in the tree and surrounding fence twinkling in the darkness. The water from the fountain in the spa bobbed and weaved and created little rainbows in the lights. Mitch closed his eyes to the scene. None of the lights, smiles, or rainbows could push the darkness out of his heart.

"Mitch." His mother approached and slipped her arm through his. "I was afraid for a minute that you wouldn't make it."

Mitch gave her a halfhearted grin. "You don't think I'd chance upsetting you by not being here."

His mother sighed. "I never know about you these days. Did you hear Amanda's news?"

Stopping in the kitchen, Mitch shook his head, but he was pretty sure he had an idea about her news. "What's that?"

"She's going to tour with Willow." His mother looked up at him.

Speechless, Mitch stood there and stared. He had guessed that Amanda's performance tonight would mean good things for her career, but he never figured something this good would materialize. "Wow! That's all I can say."

"She's such a talented young woman. She deserves this."

Mitch wasn't about to remind his mother that only weeks ago she was downplaying Amanda's talent as something no one would pay to listen to. "She is."

"Come out here and congratulate her."

Mitch followed his mom to the screened-in pool area. She grabbed his arm and propelled him toward Amanda, who was talking with Charlotte, both of them all smiles.

"Amanda, look who I found lurking in the front hall." Donna shoved Mitch forward like he had no will of his own.

"Hi, Amanda. I understand congratulations are in order." Mitch tried to smile. "I knew something big would happen for you."

Amanda looked his way. Her smile mirrored his. All for show and nothing genuine behind it. The happiness she'd shared with Charlotte drained from Amanda's eyes. Seeing her down, when joy should be the cornerstone of her countenance, made Mitch want to punch something. The last time he'd done that, Jimmy had wound up with a black eye. Now Mitch wore a figurative black eye. His presence here was as good as punching Amanda in the gut.

Had he pushed her away too soon? He'd let impatience ruin their chances, or was he kidding himself again? How could he get out of this conversation without appearing rude?

"Well, cuz. Looks like we're both losers today, but Amanda's the big winner."

Mitch turned to find Jimmy standing there grinning. Mitch balled his hand into a fist. He wanted to wipe that grin off Jimmy's face in the worst way, but nothing good had come from the last time Mitch had used his fist on his cousin. Tension grabbed every muscle in Mitch's body, but he didn't succumb to the temptation. "Yeah. Looks that way."

Jimmy put an arm around Amanda's shoulders and gave them a squeeze. "Congratulations, gal. You're going places, and I'm happy to see it."

Mitch took a deep breath. He suspected Jimmy's actions were meant to rile, but Mitch wouldn't let his cousin win. Punching Jimmy wouldn't make Amanda happy, and that was what Mitch wanted, even if that meant not being in her life.

Charlotte rescued him. "Mitch, isn't this just the best news?"

"It is." Mitch looked at Amanda, who had extracted

herself from Jimmy's embrace. Mitch wanted to say something else, but his thoughts jumbled around in his head, making a coherent thought hard to come by. Finally the tangle in his head and heart unraveled. "You deserve this chance. Now I'm going to help myself to some of this food."

Mitch walked away, feeling as though someone had taken a knife and sliced out his heart. As much as he wanted her to stay, he couldn't stand in her way.

Mitch piled his plate with appetizers. Just as he popped a piece of cheese into his mouth, Willow Childs approached him.

"Hi, Mitch. It's good to see you again." She held out her hand. "I understand you're Donna's son. I didn't get the connection when we first met. I just thought you were a friend of Amanda's when you were with her in Nashville."

Mitch nodded, wiping his hand on the napkins before he shook her hand. Mitch didn't want to reveal too much about Amanda's circumstances, because he had no idea what Amanda and Willow had talked about other than the fundraiser. How ironic was the friendship angle. "We are friends, but she was on a mission to help my mom, and I said I'd drive her to Nashville because she's been without a car since hers broke down."

Willow smiled. "If all goes right with this deal, Amanda can get a new one."

"She sure will." And drive away, taking his heart with her. "I hope everything works out for her."

"I have a good feeling about Amanda."

Mitch nodded. He just wanted to get out of here. Did he dare ditch the party? He didn't feel much like celebrating. Going home to sulk was more his speed tonight. All this joy gave him a headache. "Thanks for recognizing her talent and giving her this chance to realize her dream."

"It's my pleasure. She's not only talented but a kind person, too."

Although everything Willow said was true, Mitch didn't want to hear it because he knew what he was losing. He wished he could fix this, but there didn't seem to be a solution to their divergent paths. "She is."

"Willow." Donna approached. "There's someone I'd like you to meet."

"Certainly." Willow turned to Mitch. "I enjoyed talking to you."

"Likewise." Mitch nodded, seeing his chance to escape. With his mother occupied, he wouldn't even have to make his excuses to her.

Stepping out onto the front porch, Mitch took a deep breath and exhaled slowly. A wispy cloud floated across the moon kind of like Amanda had floated across his life. As he descended the steps, he heard his name. The familiar female voice made his heart skip a beat. He turned. Amanda stood in the doorway, silhouetted against the light inside. "Did you need something?"

She stood there, her lips parted like she wanted to say something, but she remained silent. Finally, she took a step toward him. "Do you have a minute to talk?"

The jumble that had been in his brain earlier moved

into his stomach as a crushing pressure filled his chest. How could one little woman twist his insides and make him forget everything except her? What could they possibly have to say to each other that hadn't already been said? "Sure."

"Willow told me I should get a lawyer to look over the contract her company is offering me. Can you recommend one?"

Mitch wasn't sure why Amanda was asking him. Was she trying to make it perfectly clear that she was moving on, leaving Pineydale and him in the rearview mirror of that new car? "You should talk to my dad. He'll know someone."

"I knew you'd give me some direction. Thanks." Amanda smiled. "I'd like to ask a favor of you."

"Go ahead." He hoped he wouldn't regret this.

"The last stop on the tour is the Ryman in Nashville. Willow told me that they'll have tickets for family and friends. Could you make sure Charlotte gets to come?"

"What's the date?"

"I'm not sure of the exact date, but I think it'll be sometime toward the end of October." Amanda held up a hand. "I know it's hard for you to say when I can't give you an exact date, but I just wanted to tell you ahead of time so you'd have that in mind."

Mitch wondered if this was Amanda's backhanded way of making sure he was at the concert as well as Charlotte. Lots of folks could give her a ride. It didn't have to be him. Here he was again assigning motives to Amanda that probably didn't exist. This was about

Charlotte, not him. "Just let me know, and I'll be sure to get her there."

Amanda gazed up at him, her green eyes filled with an emotion he couldn't quite decipher. "Mitch, I want you to be there, too. Please."

So he'd been right about her motives. Did he want to be there? Yeah. But could his heart take the disappointment of knowing she couldn't be his? Now or then? The silly hope that things could work out between them resurrected itself every time she made one of these requests. He couldn't keep torturing himself with the idea. "No promises."

Her breath hitched as she stared at him. "Okay. I understand, but I hope to see you in the audience."

Don't hope too much. The words begged to spring off his tongue, but he gritted his teeth to keep them contained. "Charlotte will be there. I'll just say goodbye and best wishes. Your talent will take you as far as you want to go."

"Thanks." She blinked rapidly as a forced smile curved her mouth.

"Goodbye, Amanda." Mitch turned and walked away. He used every ounce of his willpower not to turn back and pull her into his arms. Somehow he managed to get to his truck before he succumbed to the temptation.

Mitch drove through the quiet streets of Pineydale, his heart full of misery. He'd never even gone on an official date with Amanda, but his anguish over losing her far exceeded any he'd felt after the breakup with Whitney.

The headlights of his pickup pierced the blackness, but nothing could pierce the darkness in his heart. He turned onto the street leading to the garage. He parked in the lot. A security light shining down from the pole at the edge of the lot cast long shadows. Could he give this up? He shook his head as he got out of the pickup and headed for the door.

Why did this false hope keep begging him to follow? Amanda had never said she loved him even after he had declared his love for her. So what kept him tethered to a hopeless cause?

He let himself into the building and walked into the area where he restored cars. Amanda's little sports car sat there, looking brand new. It was ready for the next car show. He could take it there and probably sell it for a sizeable profit, but he had hoped to give it to Amanda as a gift, a wedding gift. He let out a halfhearted chuckle that echoed off the walls. What had ever given him that idea? The worst kind of false hope, the kind that made a person deceive himself.

His feelings for Amanda had gone from zero to sixty, like the sports car. Hers had not kept pace, and he had left her back at the first mile marker. If he'd slowed down, would that have made a difference, or was any future with her always nonexistent? He didn't have an answer, and he needed to quit thinking about it. He'd tortured himself enough for one night.

A car show was in his future, not a marriage proposal.

CHAPTER SEVENTEEN

The hum of the bus's engine did nothing to soothe Amanda's thoughts. The bus zipped along the highway toward Nashville and home, but Nashville wasn't home. She didn't have one, not since she'd left Pineydale. With one concert left on the tour, she had some decisions to make.

Willow had said nothing about the future after this tour. Was this it? One and done? If Amanda was honest with herself, she wouldn't be all that sad for that scenario. But she had to make plans for the future. She just wished Mitch was a part of that future. Would he be at the concert tomorrow night?

"Hey, why the long face?"

Amanda looked up to find Willow standing next to the table where Amanda sat. "I didn't know I had a long face. Just thinking about the concert tomorrow."

"Is all of your family going to make it?"

"My dad, stepmom, and little sister, Kelsey, are coming. I could hardly believe it when I talked to Kels and she told me. My good friends from Boston are coming, too. I'm so excited to see them." Even if Mitch wasn't there, Amanda had a lot to be thankful for.

"That's great. So glad to hear it. Since this is the last stop on the tour, I'd like to talk to you." Willow glanced toward the back of the bus. "The kids are down for a quiet time, so this is a good time to discuss the future. May I sit here with you?"

"Sure." Amanda's stomach took a flip-flop as she scooted along the seat. This was it. Was she ready to plan the rest of her career?

Willow sat down and leaned her elbows on the table. "I just want to tell you how pleased Zach and I are about having you on this tour. You've done a fabulous job, and we'd like to have you as a part of the spring tour. Terms would be the same. What do you say?"

Amanda stared down at her hands. She couldn't look Willow in the eye.

"Is something wrong?" Willow asked, as Amanda remained silent.

Amanda wished she'd prepared herself better for this conversation. She rubbed her fingers across her forehead. "First, I want to thank you again for this opportunity. It's taught me a lot."

"You're welcome." Willow raised her eyebrows. "I sense a 'but' coming."

Amanda steepled her hands in front of her mouth and tried to come up with the right words. "Can we just talk?"

Willow tilted her head as she gazed back at Amanda. "What's on your mind?"

Mitch. His image crowded her mind day and night in every dream and with every song she sang. "You've given me an opportunity of a lifetime, and I don't want to sound ungrateful. But I realized on this tour that this isn't the life I want."

"The touring life?"

Amanda nodded. "I know that's part of promoting an album. It's part of the business."

"Yeah, it is."

Licking her lips, Amanda hoped she wasn't demolishing her whole career. She gestured around the interior of the bus. "You travel in style. The hotels are luxurious. The audiences are fun and receptive. There's so much to like, but I hate living out of a suitcase."

Willow nodded. "I understand. You're right. This life isn't for everyone. For Zach and me, it's something we both enjoy. We can bring the kids with us because we homeschool, and it's a fabulous opportunity for them to see and experience the country. We've worked it out so it suits us. We love living in Nashville, but we love to tour, too."

"That's just it. I don't feel like I have a place to belong, and I don't love the touring."

"Does any of your doubt have to do with a certain guy back in Pineydale?"

"Maybe. I'm not sure." Amanda frowned as she pressed her lips together. "I could never figure out how to deal with Mitch or my feelings for him. I didn't want to lead him on because I knew I wanted this music career. I was in Pineydale temporarily until I could save up enough money to move to Nashville. I told him from the beginning that all we could be is friends."

"And was he good with that?"

"For a while, but he told me he loved me the day we

came to see you." Amanda could still hear the words, and they turned her heart inside out because she loved him, too, but she hadn't told him. She feared it was too late to do it now.

"He looked like he was trying very hard to be happy for you, but I read the sadness in his eyes when we talked at his parents' place after the fundraiser." Sympathy filled Willow's eyes.

Amanda put a hand over her mouth and tried to hold in the misery. Finally she looked up at Willow. "I'm afraid I hurt him and he won't forgive me. I just didn't know where this would lead. He wants to stay in Pineydale. His life is there, and I thought mine was going to be in Nashville. I didn't see how we could overcome that."

Willow nodded slowly. "I'm going to tell you about Sam and me. Not many people know the details of our relationship, but I think it might help you."

"My sister, Kelsey, said she thought there was more between you and Sam than just being fellow teachers."

"Yeah, we dated for a good while." Willow nodded. "I was traveling with my band during the summers off from school. When I got my big break, Sam wanted to marry me, and I just wanted him to move to Nashville with me."

"Wow! I had no idea." Amanda sat there wide-eyed.

"Despite his proposal, I always felt like Sam's heart still belonged to Jillian. I was his rebound love." Willow shook her head. "Besides that, I wasn't a Christian at the time, and Sam was determined to follow the Lord. So we parted ways. I went to Nashville, and he stayed in Pinecrest."

Amanda frowned. "And how is this supposed to help me with Mitch? Are you telling me I should forget Mitch and move to Nashville?"

"Not necessarily." Willow shook her head. "When I came to Nashville, the band and I had signed a recording contract. So I knew where I was headed, at least where my career was concerned. I had no clue about the change God had in store for me."

"But I thought you said you weren't a Christian at the time."

"True." Willow gave Amanda a little smile. "But I soon met Zach, and his witness to me about God's love and the seed that Sam planted in my heart led me to give my life to the Lord. I'll always be grateful to Sam for that tiny little spark he left in my life. And I'm grateful to him for suggesting I talk to you."

"Mitch and I are both Christians." Amanda sighed. "So I'm still not getting the connection."

"What I had with Sam wasn't strong enough to keep me from leaving with or without him. And I get the feeling that isn't the case for how you feel about Mitch. Am I right?"

"I want both Mitch and my music." Amanda's voice came out in a muffled cry. "I've been struggling with this for weeks, and I just don't see a solution."

"I do." Willow smiled.

"Tell me. I'd sure like to know."

Willow laughed and took one of Amanda's hands.

"I've enjoyed touring with you so much. You've inspired me. Our little jam sessions have been fantastic. If you're interested, we can work together on songs. We can sign you to a contract for your songs. You can be a songwriter anywhere, if you don't want to cut your own albums or tour. What do you think?"

Amanda blew out a puff of air. "Something to think about. I never thought about separating the two because I do love to perform, but I've learned I hate the traveling."

"You can have a great career as a songwriter, and maybe we can even coax you out for a concert or two."

"Your offer is very generous." Amanda folded her hands on top of the table. "But I'm afraid Mitch has already washed his hands of me."

"Do you think he'll be at the concert tomorrow night?"

Amanda shrugged. "Maybe. Maybe not. When I asked him to make sure Charlotte was there, he said he'd make sure she got there. He made it sound as if he would make sure she had a ride, not that he'd be taking her."

"If he doesn't come, that doesn't mean you can't go back to Pineydale and talk to him."

"What if I've used up all my chances with him?" Amanda closed her eyes against the thought. When she opened them again, Willow was staring at her with a sympathetic smile.

"There's only one way to find out. Go after him."

"Funny that you should say that." Amanda picked up

her guitar from the seat on the other side of the table. "I've been working on this song. It's for Mitch."

"I'd like to hear it."

Amanda strummed a few chords, then sang the first verse. She looked up at Willow.

"I like it. Is it finished, and does it have a significance?" Willow raised her eyebrows.

"It is, and it does." Amanda smiled. "Mitch kissed me not long after we met, and I told him it shouldn't happen again and we could only be friends. He told me he intended to kiss me again, but I would be the one doing the asking, not him."

"Now I understand the song." Smiling, Willow nodded. "I think you should sing it tomorrow night. If he's there, he'll know it's meant for him. If not, you can serenade him in Pineydale. I don't know how he could resist that song or you."

"I hope you're right."

Willow held out both hands to Amanda. "Let's pray about this. Sometimes God has plans for us that we can't imagine. I had no idea when God led me to Nashville that he was leading me to Zach. I want to pray for you and Mitch."

Nodding, Amanda bowed her head. What plan did God have for her life? Did it include Mitch? She let the words of Willow's prayer soothe her heart.

When Willow finished praying, she squeezed Amanda's hands. "Now it's in God's hands."

Amanda nodded. She wanted to believe Mitch would be a part of her life, but she was willing to accept whatever God had in store for her. He knew what was best for her life. He had given her this tour to show her where her music fit in to her life. Now He just had to show her whether Mitch was a part, too.

***

"Mitchell Cunningham, you'd better get yourself into that concert hall." Charlotte waved a gnarled finger at him. "You don't fool me. You love Amanda. Hiding out and pretending you don't will get you nowhere. After you park the car, I'd better see you sitting right beside me."

Mitch wanted to argue with his aunt, but she knew him inside and out. Even if he didn't argue, he couldn't change the fact that Amanda had moved on. Whatever she felt for him, and he knew she had some feelings for him, wasn't enough to keep her from taking her talent to Nashville.

Could he find a job in Nashville so he could be with her? Would she want that, or was he still chasing after something he could never catch? Her love. Conflicting thoughts raced through his mind like the lights chasing each other on marquees all over this town.

If he left Pineydale, who would keep Wilbur's Garage running? One day Bobby could take over, but that was a long way off, and Johnny was nearing retirement age. Mitch just couldn't see letting Wilbur's legacy die. If he closed the garage, folks in town would have no repair place close by.

While he parked the car and walked to the entrance, the solution to his dilemma still evaded him. He clutched the ticket in his hand as he stared at the famous building.

"Mitchell, what are you doing out here? I thought you'd already be inside."

Mitch turned at the sound of his mother's voice. He forced a smile as his mother looped her arm through his. Guess there was no backing out now. "Waiting to escort you inside. Did you and Dad have a good drive over?"

"We did, but you and Charlotte should've ridden with us."

"I know, but there was no talking her out of driving her new car, and I certainly didn't want her driving all by herself."

"You're so good to her." Donna patted his arm. "So many people from Pineydale have come for this concert. I'm so excited to see Amanda perform on this stage."

"Me, too." Mitch smiled down at his mom and realized, despite his angst about the situation, he couldn't deny his own excitement. This was a big deal for the woman he loved. He wanted the best for her whether that included him or not.

"Did you get checked into your hotel room?" Donna asked. "We checked in as soon as we arrived in Nashville."

Mitch nodded. "We did the same. Charlotte leaves nothing to chance."

When they walked into the lobby, a group of folks from Pineydale greeted them. Jimmy emerged from the crowd, a pretty brunette in tow. How had Jimmy managed to pick up a woman in the lobby of the Ryman? Mitch gave himself a mental shake. He didn't need to be concerned about his cousin's penchant for going after the first pretty woman he laid eyes on.

"Hey, Mitch." Jimmy waved as he approached. "You gotta meet Amanda's sister, Kelsey."

Stunned, Mitch remembered to smile as he finally saw the resemblance between Amanda and her sister. "Hi, Kelsey. Glad to meet you. I had no idea you were going to be here."

"Mitch!" Kelsey grinned. "You're the car guy. Thanks for helping out my big sister."

The car guy. Nodding, Mitch wondered if that was how Amanda had described him to her sister. "She pretty much helps herself."

"Yeah, but you introduced her to Charlotte. That was a godsend." Kelsey turned to Jimmy. "And Jimmy here gave her a job. You guys are the best."

Mitch nodded. "I do believe God did have something to do with that. Amanda has been a blessing to my great-aunt. Charlotte sure missed Amanda while she was on tour, but only wishes the best for her."

"Is Charlotte here? My parents and I would love to meet her."

"Your parents are here?" Mitch wondered whether he wanted to meet the man who never believed in his daughter's music.

"Yeah. We all came. We couldn't miss Amanda playing at the Ryman. That's a big deal."

"It is." But her music had always been a big deal to

Amanda. It was too bad it took this to make people realize it. He kind of had to include himself in that category, at least, in the beginning. So he shouldn't judge.

"I'm so excited to hear her sing." Kelsey's blue eyes twinkled with joy. "I can hardly believe my sister is playing here!"

"Let me find Charlotte so I can introduce you."

"I'll get my parents and meet you right here, okay?"

"I'll stay and mark the spot," Jimmy said.

"Good thinking." Kelsey smiled at Jimmy as if he'd given her the moon.

Shaking his head, Mitch went in search of Charlotte and wondered how Jimmy managed to charm every woman he met except Amanda. Mitch was thankful that Amanda hadn't been attracted to his cousin. Minutes later, Mitch escorted Charlotte to the spot where Jimmy stood.

"So Kelsey hasn't returned yet?" Mitch raised his eyebrows. Did that mean Kelsey was speaking out of turn when she said her parents wanted to meet Charlotte?

"Her parents were probably talking to someone and couldn't break away immediately." Jimmy craned his neck to look over the crowd. "There they are."

Mitch gazed toward the tall man who walked next to Kelsey. With his light-brown hair not showing a speck of gray, he looked almost too young to have grown daughters. What would Grady Reynolds have to say when they met face to face?

Kelsey outpaced her father as they approached. "People are already starting to go into the auditorium, so we have to make some quick introductions. Dad, this is Mitch Cunningham and his great-aunt Charlotte. They're the ones who were so kind to Amanda."

Grady extended his hand to Mitch. "We've spoken on the phone. It's nice meeting you in person. How's that car?"

Smiling, Mitch prayed he could be generous in his thinking about this man. After all, this was Amanda's dad. Loving her meant loving her family. Not that it made any difference at this point. But Mitch wondered if the man was more concerned about the car he'd sold than about his daughter. "Nice to meet you, too. And I just finished restoring the car. Looks brand new."

Grady eyed Mitch. "You didn't happen to drive it here? I'd love to see it."

Mitch shook his head. "No. That baby is headed to a car show next month."

Charlotte offered her hand to Grady. "You have a lovely daughter. She has brightened my life more than you know."

Grady nodded. "I'm glad she could repay your kindness."

"She has a thousand times over." Charlotte glanced toward the pregnant woman standing next to Grady. "And this must be your wife, Maria. Amanda has told me so many wonderful things about you. I'm so glad to get to meet you in person."

Maria smiled and enveloped Charlotte's hand with

both of hers. "Thank you. And she has sung your praises. I almost feel like I know you."

Charlotte motioned toward the doors. "We'd better head to our seats. I hope we'll see you later at Willow's house. Amanda told me we're all invited there after the concert."

"And you never miss a party." Mitch patted his aunt's hand.

"Of course not, especially when one of my favorite people is celebrating." Charlotte looked up at Mitch and winked.

As they found their seats, Mitch had second thoughts about his second thoughts. Why did he always zig when he should zag when it came to women? He would have to sit through the entire concert with the after-party on his mind. How could he wish Amanda well when he knew this was the end? He'd gone through this same thing at the fundraiser celebration. Now he would have an encore. His thoughts were already a tangle. So what was one more strand in the big jumble clogging his brain?

Mitch sat back and tried to relax, but he wasn't having much success. Tension claimed every nerve. He might as well be the one performing.

As the lights went down and the first act introduced their first song, Charlotte leaned closer. "When does Amanda play?"

"She comes on right before Willow." Mitch read the anticipation on Charlotte's face. "She'll be worth the wait."

"That's a given." Charlotte settled back in her seat.

Mitch glanced around looking for Kelsey but didn't see her. He didn't know why he was concerned about Amanda's parents. Maybe he was just concerned about the whole evening. He took a deep breath and let it out slowly. He would enjoy the concert. He would attend the party and smile. He would survive this.

When the PA announcer finally introduced Amanda, the crowd from Pineydale erupted with applause. Mitch clapped loudest, his heart swelling with pride and something much more as she took the stage. Red cowboy boots replaced her red tennis shoes and complimented the red-and-black dress with the multilevel hem, which came just to the top of the boots.

Amanda smiled and waved to the audience. "Thanks, everyone. It's a pleasure to be here. It's been one of my dreams to perform here at the Ryman, and I want to thank Willow Childs for giving me this opportunity to share some of my songs with you. I've written a lot of songs, some good and some not so good."

"Let's hear the good ones," a voice called from the audience.

Amanda shaded her eyes as she surveyed the auditorium. "Is that you, Max?"

More laughter ensued.

"Yeah, it's me," Max yelled back, laughter in his voice.

"Glad you're here, and just because you asked I won't sing any of the bad ones." Amanda strummed her guitar as she talked. "I have a lot of family and friends here in the audience tonight, who have come out to cheer for me. And I appreciate that more than you know. This first song is dedicated to one of those people, one of the sweetest ladies I know, Charlotte Cunningham. The tune is mine, but the words are hers."

Applause filled the auditorium as Amanda started to sing. Mitch loved the way she interacted with the crowd. Not only could she sing, but she had a rapport with her audience, a stage presence that went a long way in making a good entertainer. She was a natural.

Charlotte grasped Mitch's arm as if she were hanging on to him for dear life. "Oh my! She's singing one of my poems."

Mitch nodded as he noticed the tears welling in Charlotte's eyes. He leaned over and whispered, "She sang this to you before she went on tour."

Charlotte nodded, dabbing at her eyes with a tissue. "But I didn't know she was going to sing it tonight."

Mitch put an arm around Charlotte's shoulders and gave them a squeeze as they listened to Amanda's voice filling the auditorium with a song about God's love. Amanda sang several more songs. Each one warmed Mitch's heart.

After she finished a song that had the audience singing and clapping, she raced toward the side of the stage. Someone handed her something, and she walked back to the center of the stage. Mitch peered at the straw hat in her hand. Was that the hat he'd given her at the Highland Games?

With a smile, she placed the hat with the

Cunningham tartan band on her head as she motioned toward the audience. "This next song is in honor of the wonderful folks who are here to support me from Pineydale, Tennessee. Many have Scottish roots, and my hat sports the Cunningham tartan because there are a lot of Cunninghams in Pineydale. I sang this earlier this year at the Scottish Highland Games at Grandfather Mountain. I'd like to share this lovely Scottish lullaby in Scottish Gaelic."

As the soothing melody and Scottish Gaelic words grabbed hold of Mitch's heart, he decried the success that took her away from him. But he didn't have to let that happen. He would find a way to still keep the garage open when he moved to Nashville. He might be pursuing an impossible dream, but he wasn't going to give up trying to win Amanda's love.

Mitch glanced over at Charlotte as Amanda sang. Again tears welled in Charlotte's eyes. His aunt was going to miss Amanda, too. She had found her way into the hearts of so many people in Pineydale. The town would seem empty without her.

When Amanda finished the song, she took a bow as the Pineydale contingent went wild with applause, hoots, and hollers. With a huge smile lighting her face, Amanda took another bow. Mitch was prepared for this song to be the end, but she grabbed a stool and sat on it, her guitar in her lap.

"This last song is dedicated to one special person. He knows who he is."

As the words of the love song floated through the air,

Mitch wanted to believe that special someone was him, but he wasn't sure. Amanda had been gone for six weeks, and during that time, he hadn't heard from her. The only time he knew anything about what was happening with her came from conversations he'd had with Charlotte.

Then Amanda came to the song's chorus.

"Please kiss me once.

Kiss me twice.

Kiss me for the rest of my life."

Mitch wished Amanda would look his way, so he'd know if this was meant for him. Maybe she didn't have a clue where he was sitting. Or maybe she didn't even know if he was there after the way he had dismissed her request to bring Charlotte to the concert. He'd given her a negative response, so maybe this wasn't meant for him at all but some other guy. The thought made him sick.

Trying not to let negativity dominate his thoughts, Mitch listened to the chorus again. Did the song harken back to the challenge he'd given her after the kiss they'd shared? He wanted that to be true. Could he talk to her backstage after the concert, or would he have to wait until the party at Willow's place? Either way he would let Amanda know that if moving to Nashville to win her heart was his only option, he was ready to make that move.

***

Amanda stood in the circle of musicians and bowed

her head as Willow said a prayer thanking God for a successful tour. Before and after every concert, she had prayed. Sharing that time with these people was something about the tour Amanda would miss. The constant travel not so much.

After Willow said the last amen, she looked over the group. "Are you guys ready to celebrate? Zach told me everything's ready, and we have guests, lots of them from Pineydale. So let's head over there."

Amanda's stomach churned at the thought of facing Mitch. What had he thought of the song she'd written especially for him? She'd been worried that he wouldn't even show, but she'd caught a glimpse of him sitting next to Charlotte. But the darkened audience and the bright spotlights streaming onto the stage made seeing the audience difficult.

On the drive to Willow's home, Amanda tried to calm her nerves, but her anticipated conversation with Mitch scrambled every nerve and filled her chest with a fluttering sensation. The bright lights pouring from the windows should add some cheer to her thoughts, but instead they served as caution lights. What if he had only been there because of Charlotte? What if he refused to talk to her?

As Amanda walked through the door, she took a deep breath and determined to make the best of this evening.

The jovial gathering spilled out into the back yard and the pool deck. Conversation and laughter greeted the performers as well as hugs and congratulations. Glancing around the room, Amanda looked for Mitch but didn't see him. Her parents and Mitch's parents were gathered in a tight circle as they conversed.

Her dad looked up. When he saw her, he broke from the circle, a broad smile covering his face. He enveloped her in a hug. "Amanda, I'm so proud of you. You were fabulous tonight."

"Thanks, Dad."

When the hug ended, he held her at arm's length. "I'm sorry I didn't support your music before. I was stubborn and totally didn't get what a talent you have."

Tears welled in Amanda's eyes, her heart soaring over her dad's words. She hugged him tight. "Thanks again."

Grady continued to hold her. "You made it on your own despite my resistance."

"I had help. Sam contacted Willow. That made all the difference." Amanda extracted herself from his embrace. "And you did support me as long as I was in school."

Her dad smiled wryly. "Yeah, but I could've made it a lot easier on you, and I apologize again for standing in your way."

Amanda gave her dad another quick hug, then smiled up at him. "It's okay. We're all good."

"I get to have a hug, too." Maria put her arms around Amanda. "Congratulations on a wonderful performance. I especially enjoyed the lullaby."

Grinning, Amanda patted Maria's protruding abdomen. "I can't believe you guys are having a baby. That's so exciting."

"Congratulations!" Mitch's dad squeezed Amanda's

shoulders. "You were terrific."

"Thanks." Amanda smiled, wondering where Mitch was hiding out.

Donna gave Amanda a hug. "I knew you'd go places after your performance at the fundraiser. I'm so happy for you."

"Thanks." Amanda held her smile in place, but she was dying to know where Mitch was. She was grateful for all the well-wishes, but she longed for Mitch's congratulations.

As Amanda continued her search, Kelsey ran up with her arms open wide and enveloped Amanda in another hug. "Congrats, big sister. You were awesome!"

Amanda held onto Kelsey. "And I owe this to you. You were the one who got me connected with Willow through Sam. Thanks so much!"

As Kelsey stepped back, Jimmy appeared at her side and held up his hand to Amanda for a high five. "Hey, Amanda, your performance was amazing. Not only can you paint houses, but you can sing."

"Thanks." Amanda laughed. More congratulations, but none from Mitch. She wanted to ask Jimmy about Mitch in the worst way, but the bad blood between them kept her silent.

"Can I get you two ladies something to drink?" Jimmy motioned to the bar by the pool.

"I'll have a cola with lots of ice." Kelsey smiled up at Jimmy.

"You can get me the same." Amanda wondered what was up with her little sister and Jimmy. Her smile gave

Amanda the impression that his charm had worked on Kelsey. As he walked away, Amanda eyed Kelsey. "What's with you and Jimmy?"

Kelsey shrugged. "Can't I enjoy the attention of a good-looking guy?"

"Sure." Amanda looked at her sister. "I thought you had a guy at home."

"Not anymore." Kelsey grimaced. "He broke up with me a couple of weeks ago. So Jimmy's attention is helping to soothe the wounds."

"Jimmy's a charmer all right." Amanda glanced around again but still didn't see Mitch. No one had mentioned Amanda's last song. Didn't anyone know she'd been singing to Mitch? Maybe everyone was just ignoring it because they knew he had moved on after she'd left town. That thought curdled Amanda's stomach.

"So what about the car guy, Mitch?" Kelsey eyed Amanda. "Was that song for him?"

Finally, someone got it. "You met Mitch?"

"Yeah. Jimmy introduced us before the show." Kelsey raised her eyebrows. "So spill. Was the song for him?"

Amanda nodded. "But I haven't seen him, and now I'm afraid it was a mistake to sing it."

Kelsey shrugged. "I don't know, but I haven't seen him either. Are you sure he came to the party?"

"I don't know anything, except I'm tied in knots over him." Amanda maneuvered Kelsey toward a corner of the room, away from the other guests. "I love him, and

I'm afraid I've lost him."

Kelsey grabbed Amanda's hand. "What are you doing in this corner? Let's go find him."

"I can't just accost him here at the party," Amanda hissed.

"You're not going to accost anyone. You're just going to say hi." Kelsey shoved Amanda toward the backyard. "You haven't even gone outside. I'm sure he's out here."

"You saw him?"

"No, but let's have a look." Kelsey propelled Amanda into the dim light outside.

The pool light illuminated the water and sent shadows into the surrounding landscape. Laughter cascaded through the crowd like the sound of splashing water in the fountain feature of the pool spa. Little clusters of people talked as they stood around the pool.

Peering into the dimness, Amanda surveyed the area. Mitch wasn't anywhere to be seen. "He's just not here."

"Here comes Jimmy with our drinks. Let's ask him if he's seen Mitch." Kelsey motioned toward the other side of the pool.

Amanda touched Kelsey's arm. "Please don't. I can't really explain, but it's better that you don't."

"Okay." Kelsey gave Amanda a curious frown, then turned to Jimmy as he held out a drink to her. "Thanks."

Jimmy handed Amanda her drink. "Do you mind if I take Kelsey and introduce her to some folks from Pineydale?"

Amanda shook her head. "Be my guest."

Backing into the shadows near the edge of the house, Amanda tried to console herself, but it didn't work. This was what it meant to be alone in a crowd and feeling sorry for herself. She took a sip of her drink as she watched Jimmy plying his charms on Kelsey. He really was a good guy underneath all that bluster. So if Kelsey needed a little ego boost, Jimmy would definitely give her one.

"Hey, pretty lady, you looking for some company?"

Amanda's heart skipped a beat as Mitch's voice came out of the darkness. She turned. "Mitch, I've been wondering where you've been."

"Sorry I wasn't here earlier, but Charlotte was extra tired from the trip and the late hour. I took her back to the hotel before I came here. She sends her congratulations. She's so sorry she didn't get to say so in person." He stood there grinning at her. "And I heard that you might want to kiss me, or was that song meant for some other guy?"

Amanda's breath caught in her throat, and her response stuck there. She stared up at him, her only thought to throw her arms around his neck and kiss him. So she did. He pulled her close, and she melted into his arms. For a moment only the two of them existed as she kissed him with abandon until a smattering of applause made her remember where she was.

"That was worth all the waiting." Mitch relinquished his hold on her as they turned to the bystanders. He waved to the crowd. "Ya'll can go on about your business. I was just collecting my kiss."

Some laughter and shouts of encouragement came from the folks nearby. Mitch put a hand to her back as he maneuvered her toward a quiet corner near the fence at the back of the property. "Did you mean what you said in that song?"

Amanda nodded, still overcome with emotion.

"Here's twice." Mitch pulled her close and kissed her again. When he ended the kiss, he just held her close. "Now about that for-the-rest-of-your-life part. I'm willing to move to Nashville, find a job here, and be here for whatever your career brings, if that's what you want."

Amanda took a shaky breath as she stepped out of his embrace. "Mitch, I love you, and I'm sorry I didn't say so before I left on tour. I was so worried that I'd pushed you away one too many times."

"I still love you, and I wasn't going anywhere. I just had to figure out that I couldn't let you go. No matter what."

Her heart soaring, Amanda gazed up at him. "And I had to figure out that I don't like touring. I just want to write songs. You don't have to move to Nashville. I'll be happy in Pineydale."

A slow grin spread across his face. "Are you sure? Really sure?"

Amanda nodded. "Yes, I can write songs anywhere."

"And you won't miss performing? You have a fabulous talent."

"Willow plans to offer me a contract for the songs I write. I might occasionally do a concert with her. She has been such a wonderful mentor and will continue that."

"So a trip to Nashville now and then will be on your agenda?"

Amanda nodded again. "That's the plan. I hated being on the road and living out of a suitcase. I want a permanent place to be, and that place is Pineydale."

"With me?"

Happy tears welling in her eyes, Amanda nodded. "Is this a proposal?"

Mitch gave her a wry smile. "I had actually planned something a little more romantic, but this will do. Amanda Reynolds, I love you. Will you marry me and spend the rest of your life with me?"

"Yes." Amanda put her arms around his neck and pulled him close for another kiss. "I love you. This is just the beginning of so many wonderful things in the rest of my life."

Dear Readers,

Thank you for reading *A Song to Call Ours*. I hope Amanda and Mitch's story touched your heart and brought you a lesson about not being afraid to follow your dreams. Both Amanda and Mitch learn how to trust in God's plans for their lives.

I would love for you to let other readers know what you think about *A Song to Call Ours*. You can do so by posting an honest review wherever you purchased this book and also on Goodreads or Book Bub.

Please consider mentioning *A Song to Call Ours* on your social media sites, especially where you talk about reading! Word of mouth is the number one reason people pick up unfamiliar books. Every review and mention helps.

I've had so much fun writing these stories. If you haven't read the other books in the series, I hope you'll look for them. Although each book can be read without having read the others, I enjoy connecting the books through characters and settings. Please check out the other books in the Front Porch Promises series, *A Place to Call Home*, *A Love to Call Mine*, *A Family to Call Ours*, *A Song to Call Ours*, *A Baby to Call Ours*, and *A Place to Find Love*.

If you would like to get information on my upcoming books, please sign up for my newsletter on my website.

Blessings,

Merrillee Whren

ABOUT THE AUTHOR

Merrillee Whren is an award-winning and a *USA Today* bestselling author who writes inspirational romance. She is the winner of the 2003 Golden Heart Award for best inspirational romance manuscript presented by Romance Writers of America. She has also been the recipient of the RT Reviewers' Choice Award and the Inspirational Reader's Choice Award. She is married to her own personal hero, her husband of forty plus years, and has two grown daughters. She has lived in Atlanta, Boston, Dallas, Chicago and Florida but now makes her home in the Arizona desert. She spends her free time playing tennis or walking while she does the plotting for her novels. Please visit her website, www.merrilleewhren.com or connect with her on social media sites.

https://twitter.com/MerrilleeWhren

https://www.facebook.com/MerrilleeWhren.Author/

OTHER BOOKS by
MERRILLEE WHREN

Dalton Brothers Series
Four Little Blessings
Country Blessings
Homecoming Blessings

Kellersburg Series
Hometown Promise
Hometown Proposal
Hometown Dad
Hometown Cowboy

Front Porch Promises Series
A Match to Call Ours
A Place to Call Home
A Love to Call Mine
A Family to Call Ours
A Song to Call Ours
A Baby to Call Ours
A Place to Find Love

Pinecrest
Second Chance Love
Second Chance Gift
Second Chance Forgiveness

Novellas
Puppy Love and Mistletoe
Puppy Love and Jingle Bells

Puppy Love and Christmas Cookies

Other Books
Miracle Baby
Second Chance Christmas

Village of Hope
Annie's Hope
Kirsten's Mission
Melanie's Resolve

www.ingramcontent.com/pod-product-compliance
Lightning Source LLC
Chambersburg PA
CBHW021530250626
47154CB00006BA/2057